W9-CAE-478
3 5674 05296944 2

RADIANT
SHADOWS

Also by Melissa Marr

Wicked Lovely

Ink Exchange

Fragile Eternity

HARPER
An Imprint of HarperCollins*Publishers*

Radiant Shadows

 For information address HarperCollins Children's Books, a division of HarperCollins Publishers, 10 East 53rd Street, New York, NY 10022.
www.harperteen.com

Library of Congress Cataloging-in-Publication Data
is available.
ISBN 978-0-06-165922-5 (trade bdg.)
ISBN 978-0-06-165923-2 (lib. bdg.)
ISBN 978-0-06-199484-5 (international edition)

10 11 12 13 14 LP/RRDB 10 9 8 7 6 5 4 3 2 1

First Edition

*To Asia and Dylan, my amazing beasties. It's a privilege to be your mother. (And, really? I do so love you more, most, and always. *grin* How's that for getting the last word?)*

Acknowledgments

Anne Hoppe continues to be my champion and my nemesis. For both things, I am grateful. Without having Anne battling for us and with me, these books would be lesser things.

Creating a book is not done alone. So many wonderful folks at Harper take care of my books (and me), and although I don't get to know all of you, I am grateful for your work. That said, special gratitude must go to those of you who have the task of putting up with me: publicist extraordinaire Melissa Bruno, subrights angel Jean McGinley, marketing wisewoman Suzanne Daghlian, art goddess Alison Donalty, and the all-seeing Susan Katz.

Thanks to my readers, especially those of you (Meggie, Maria, Phe, Tiger, Meg, Tegan, Aine, Karen, Ashley, and all the rest) who joined me not only at events but also for evening walks, aquarium outings, or meals while I was on tour. It means a lot to me that you all are willing to share your time with me in person, online, and in letters.

Many thanks to: Mark Tucker for finding the model who is Ani; Jen Barnes, Rachel Vincent, Jeaniene Frost, and Asia for reading; Merrilee Heifetz for exceeding my expectations so often; Jeaniene for the title; Susan for insights, especially the very valuable mantra "protect the work"; and Neil for sensory tours and wisdom.

A very special thank-you goes to Fazi Editore for bringing me to meet my Italian readers. Elido Fazi, Pamela Ruffo, Maria Galeano, and Cristina Marino not only took care of my family and of me, but also they enabled me to fall hopelessly in love with Rome. Thank you.

My oddest thank-you, perhaps, goes to a few people who will never see these words, but without whom I couldn't have written any of the *Wicked Lovely* books. I can't write without music, so each book has a set of songs I listen to over and over. For this book, thanks go to Ani DiFranco (yes, my Ani is named for her), She Wants Revenge, and The Kills. However, for *all* of the books I've written, gratitude goes to Marilyn Manson, Maynard James Keenan, Damien Rice, and Tori Amos. Their art inspires me.

As always, thanks to my parents, my children, and my spouse. My world would crumble without you.

PROLOGUE

LATE 1800S

Devlin stood immobile as the spectral girl approached. The plume of her hat and the dark ringlets that framed her face were motionless, despite the breeze that swept over the field. The air did not touch her; consequently, he was unsure if he could.

"I seem to be dreaming or, mayhaps, *lost*," she murmured.

"Indeed."

"I was resting over"—she gestured behind her, frowned, and gave him a shaky smile—"in the cave that seems to have vanished. Am I still resting?"

The girl presented Devlin with a dilemma. All those uninvited to Faerie were to be brought before the High Queen—or dispatched if he deemed them threats. His function was to assure order, to do what best served the good of Faerie.

"In a cave?" he prompted.

"My guardian and I had a quarrel." She shivered and folded her arms over her chest. The dress she wore was not this season's fashionable attire, but it wasn't horribly outdated.

When he didn't reply, she added, "You look like a gentleman. I don't suppose your manor is near here? Your mother or sisters? Not that my aunt expects me to make much of a match, but she *would* be . . . displeased if I were to be found unchaperoned in the company of a gentleman."

"I am not a gentleman."

She blanched.

"And meeting my mother-sisters is not something I'd wish on the innocent," he added. "You should turn back. Call this a bad dream. Go away from here."

The girl looked around at the field; her gaze took in the landscape of Faerie—the spider-silk hammocks that hung in the trees, the pink-and-gold-tinted sky that the queen had fashioned for the day—and then settled on him.

Devlin did not move as she observed him. She did not falter at the sight of his opalescent hair or inhuman eyes; she did not flinch at his angular features or otherworldly stillness. He wasn't sure what reaction he expected: he'd never been viewed as he truly was by a mortal. Over in their world, he wore a glamour to appear like them. Here, he was known for *what* he was, the Queen's Bloodied Hands. The girl's assessment was a singular event.

Her cheeks became pink as she boldly stared at him. "You certainly look like a kind man."

"I am not." He stepped toward her. "I exist to keep order for the queen of Faerie. I am neither kind nor a man."

The girl fainted.

Devlin leaped forward to catch her and knelt on the ground, arms empty—as her form settled inside of his skin. He couldn't hold the insubstantial, but she apparently could take residence in his body as if it were her own.

Her voice was in his head. *Sir?*

He couldn't move: his body wasn't his to control. He was still inside of himself, but he was not animating his body. The girl's spectral form had filled his skin as if it were her own body.

Can you move? he asked.

Of course! She sat up and, in doing so, left his body.

He swallowed against the burst of peculiar emotions coursing through him. He felt free and excited and a number of the things that were unlike the restraint of the High Court—and he liked it.

She lifted a hand as if to touch him, but it passed through him. "I'm not dreaming, am I?"

"No." He felt unexpectedly protective of her, this foundling mortal. "What is your name?"

"Katherine Rae O'Flaherty," she whispered. "If I am awake now, that means you are an *ethereal creature*."

"An ethere—"

"I have three wishes!" She clapped her hands and widened her eyes. "Oh, what do I wish for? True love? Eternal life? Certainly, nothing frivolous like gowns! Oh, perhaps I just want to save my wishes!"

"Wishes?"

"You cannot force me to make my wishes now." She squared her shoulders and looked at him. "I've read texts. I know there is dispute over the *goodness* of your kind, but I do not believe for a moment that *you* could be other than kind. Why, just look at you!"

Devlin frowned. He did not idle away his time with foolishness; he did only that which his queen required. *Except for those stolen moments of pleasure in the mortal world.* His queen knew of his indulgences, looked the other way even. *What harm an indulgence here?* She was a specter of a mortal girl, no threat to the queen of Faerie. *Sheltering her violates no order.* He tried to smile at the girl. "Katherine Rae O'Flaherty, if you're going to stay in our world, the term you will want is *sidhe*, *faery*, or *fey*."

"I will use those . . . since I *am* staying." She scrambled to her feet. "I have read Reverend Kirk, in fact. My uncle's library has quite a few books of your people. I have read Mr. Lang's fairy tales as well. The sweet—"

"Books are not the same as reality." Devlin stared at her. "My world is not always kind to mortals."

The look in her eyes was no longer guileless. "Nor is the mortal world."

"Indeed." He looked at her with a pleasant burst of curiosity.

She stepped closer. "If I return to my body, would I still be alive? If I return there, how long will have passed?"

"Time passes differently, and I've no idea how long

you've wandered. If you stay, you might die as well. The High Queen does not allow uninvited guests in Faerie." Devlin tried his gentlest smile, one he'd not had much use for in his life. "If she learns of your presence—"

"Do I get my three wishes?" Katherine Rae interrupted.

"You may." It wasn't traditional to grant wishes, but he found himself wanting to please her.

She tilted her chin. "Then, my first wish is that you keep me safe from harm . . . what is your name?"

Devlin bowed. "I am Devlin, brother and advisor to the High Queen, assassin, and keeper of order."

"Oh." She swayed as if she might faint again.

"And now, protector of Katherine Rae O'Flaherty," he quickly added.

He'd never had anyone in his life who was truly his, never had a friend or confidante, never had a lover or partner. He wasn't entirely sure he *could* have any of those. His first duty was to his queen, his court, to Faerie itself. He had been created to serve, and it was his honor to do so.

It was also very lonely.

He glanced at Katherine Rae. She had no body, no power, no allegiances.

What harm can taking in a spectral girl do?

LATE 1900S

When Devlin entered the banquet hall, the room was empty—save for the queen herself. In the center of the hall, out of place among the stone pillars and woven tapestries, a waterfall splashed down. The spray formed misty shapes in the air, and then the water washed away and vanished into one of the far walls. The High Queen stared at the falling water, at the threads of possibility she saw there. The filament-fine images of what *could be* weren't certainties, but Sorcha kept order by monitoring potential futures. She'd realign them if the disorder was within the boundaries of Faerie, but if the aberration was in the mortal world, she'd dispatch him to correct it.

He approached the dais upon which her throne sat. For all of eternity, he had served as her Bloodied Hands. He was made for violence, but he served the court of order.

Without taking her gaze from the water, she stood and extended a hand, knowing he would be where she reached.

None other has been in her trust for all of eternity.

That didn't mean she should trust him, though.

Devlin released her hand, and she crossed the room.

He followed.

"Look at them." Sorcha gestured toward the air, bringing a woman's image into focus. The mortal was pretty: a heart-shaped face, light brown hair, and olive-green eyes. In the room with her were two small children, one of whom tackled the other. They giggled as they rolled around on the floor together.

"The youngest whelp is a problem." The High Queen paused, her features softening into what looked like longing. Then her expression stilled as the image dissolved into mist, and the temperature plummeted. "It needs to be remedied."

"Shall I retrieve it?" Devlin washed his hands in the now-frigid water that ran through his mother-sister-queen's hall. He'd collected squalling infants and silent artists; he'd brought musicians and madmen to his queen at her command. Retrieving mortals or halflings was common—but not as pleasurable as some tasks.

"No." She glanced at him for a long moment. "This one should not enter Faerie. Ever."

Sorcha stepped forward so the edge of her skirts touched the water. Her ever-bare feet were exposed in the icy water, and for a brief second, he saw her as she was: a candle with a dim flame surrounded by the darkness of chaos. Her flame-toned hair shifted in a breeze that only existed because she willed it. Around her, the room changed from a chilly hall to a fecund jungle to a desert and back again to the hall, reflecting her briefest thought—as all things in Faerie did. She was their source, his creator. She was order and life. Without Sorcha's will, only she and her antithesis, her twin Bananach, would exist.

"What would you have of me?" he asked.

Sorcha didn't look at him. "Sometimes death is required to keep order."

"The child?"

"Yes." Her voice was emotionless even as she ordered the death of a child. She was reason personified, sure of her place, certain of her righteousness. "It is born of the Dark Court, daughter of the Wild Hunt, of Gabriel himself. It will cause unacceptable complications if it lives."

She stepped farther into the water. The waterfall paused mid-flow, so her words were the only sound in the suddenly silent room. "Correct this, Brother."

He bowed, but she didn't turn her gaze from the suspended flow of water, didn't turn her attention to him as he left. She knew, though, where he was. The water crashed down louder than before as he exited the hall.

She knows even when she does not look. Devlin wondered sometimes just how much of his life Sorcha did see. He lived for her, at her will, and by her side. *But I am not solely hers.* She never forgot that truth. Out of earth and magic, will and need, the twins—Sorcha and Bananach—had made him, the first male faery. They'd needed both male and female to exist within their world, a balance in that, as in all things, was required.

Not son, but brother, she had told him. *Like me, you are parentless.*

Order and Discord made him as if carved of stone, a sculpture crafted by two who would never work together again. They gave him too many angular features and too many softened spots: his lips were too-full and his eyes too-cold. He was their best traits compromised. Where Bananach had hair of the purest black and Sorcha had multitoned hair of living flame, his was opalescent white: all colors shifting in and out of existence. They gave him purest-black eyes and strength not unlike Bananach's, but none of her madness. They gave him tall stature and Sorcha's love of art, but none of her physical restraint. Together, they'd made him a thing of extreme cruelty and extreme beauty.

And then they'd fought over his loyalty.

Chapter 1

Present day

Ani pulled open a side door to the stable. It was as much a garage as a true stable, and as she walked through the cavernous building she drew in the mingled scents of diesel and straw, exhaust and sweat. Most of the creatures kept the illusion of vehicles when they were outside the building, but here, in their safe haven, the beasts roamed in whatever form they chose. One of the steeds crouched on a ledge under the skylight. It was something between an eagle and a lion; both feathers and fur covered a massive body. Several other steeds were lined up in a row of various motorcycles, cars, and trucks. One anomalous steed was a camel.

A Hound looked up from polishing a matte black Harley with plenty of chrome. The cloth in his hand was one of the many swaths of fabric imported from Faerie specifically for their steeds. "You looking for Chela?"

"No." She stayed in the walkway, not invading his space or the steed's yet. "Not Chela."

Her father's semiregular mate was a source of comfort, but Chela wanted to be more maternal than Ani could accept from her. Similarly, her father's attempts at fatherhood veered toward something akin to mortal pretenses. She didn't want a facsimile of a mortal family. She had a family, with Rabbit and Tish, her half-mortal siblings. During the past year when she had been brought to live in the Dark Court, she had hoped for something else: she wanted to be a true part of the Wild Hunt, a full member of her father's pack. That hadn't happened.

The Hound paused his steady motions only long enough to glance at her. "Gabriel's not here either."

"I know. I'm not looking for anyone in particular." Ani came to the stall. "I just like it here."

The Hound looked up and down the open aisle. This early no other Hound was in sight, but there were more than a score of steeds close enough to see them. "Do you need something?"

"Sure." Ani leaned against the wall. It would be an insult not to flirt, even though they both knew action wasn't possible. "A little fun. A little trouble. A ride . . ."

"Get the boss to agree"—the Hound's eyes flashed a vibrant green—"and I'll gladly take you."

She knew her own eyes were shimmering with the same energy that she saw in his. They were both born of the Wild Hunt. They were the creatures that rode the earth, drawing out terror, exacting vengeance, unrestrained by order. They were the teeth and claws of Faerie, living now in the mortal world, bound to the Dark Court by their Gabriel.

A Gabriel who would chew up anyone who touched his daughter.

"You know he won't give permission," she admitted.

Her father was in charge. His rules meant that only one who could stand against him in a fight was allowed to date her.

Or anything else.

"Hey?"

She looked at the Hound.

"If you weren't *his* daughter, I'd risk it, but crossing Gabe isn't something I'm going to do."

Ani sighed, not in disappointment, but at the futility of ever getting a different answer. "I know."

"Convince him that you're not going to get broken by a little fun, and I'll be in front of the line. Promise." The Hound leaned forward to drop a quick kiss on her lips.

It was no more than a second of affection, but he was ripped away and hurled across the aisle toward the opposite stall. The thud of his body hitting the wooden slats covered most of the curses he was yelling.

"Don't touch my pup." Gabriel stood in the middle of the aisle. He was grinning, but his posture was one of menace. Of course, he was the Hound that controlled the Wild Hunt, so menace was as natural as breathing for him.

The Hound on the floor felt the back of his head as he leaned on one partition of the wooden stall. "Damn, Gabriel. I didn't touch her."

"Your lips were on hers. That's *touching*," Gabriel growled.

Ani stepped in front of her father and poked him in the chest. "Don't act like it's wrong for them to respond to me."

He glared at her but didn't lift a hand. "I am the Gabriel. I run this pack, and if any of them"—he looked past her to the Hound on the floor—"want to challenge me over you, all they need to do is say the word."

The Hound on the floor spoke up. "I turned her down."

"Not because she lacks anything," Gabriel growled.

"No, no." The Hound held up his hands. "She's perfect, Gabe . . . but you said she was off-limits."

Gabriel held a hand out to the Hound on the floor without looking at him.

The Hound glanced at her. "Sorry . . . I, umm, touched you."

Ani rolled her eyes. "You're a peach."

"Sorry, Gabriel. It won't happen again." The Hound straddled his bike and left with a roar that was more growl than a real Harley's engine could mimic.

For a heartbeat, it was perfectly quiet in the stable. The steeds stayed silent and motionless.

"My perfect pup." Gabriel stepped up and ruffled her hair. "He doesn't deserve you. None of them do."

She shoved him away. "So, you'd rather I'm skin starved?"

Gabriel snorted. "You're not starved."

"I would be if I followed all of your rules," she muttered.

"And I wouldn't have so many rules if I thought you'd follow them all." He threw a punch, which she dodged. It was nice, but not backed by the full force of his strength or weight. He always held back. *That* was insulting. If she were truly a part of the Hunt, he'd fight with her the way he fought with all the rest. He'd train her. *He'd accept me in the pack.*

"You suck at fatherhood, Gabe." She turned away and started down the aisle.

He couldn't taste her feelings, not like most of the Dark Court. Hounds weren't nourished on the same things, so her emotions were hidden to them. The peculiarity of the Hunt's inability to taste emotions while everyone around them could made them very blunt in their own expressions. It worked out well: Dark Court faeries were nourished by swallowing dark emotions; Hounds required physical touch for sustenance. So the Hunt caused the fear and terror that fed the court, and the court provided the touch the Hounds required. Ani was abnormal in that she needed both.

Which sucks.

"Ani?"

She didn't stop walking. There was no way she was going to let him see the tears building in her eyes. *Just another proof of my weakness.* She gestured over her shoulder. "I get it, *Daddy*. I'm not welcome."

"Ani."

Tears leaked onto her cheeks as she stopped in the doorway, but she didn't turn back.

"Promise to follow the rules while we're out, and you could probably borrow Che's steed again tonight." His voice held the hope he wouldn't say aloud. "*If* she agrees."

Ani turned then and smiled at him. "Yeah?"

"Yeah." He didn't move, didn't comment on the tears on her cheeks, but his voice softened and he added, "And I'm *not* an awful father."

"Maybe."

"I just don't want to think about you wanting . . . things . . . or getting hurt." Gabriel folded the cloth that the Hound had dropped, looking at it rather than at her. "Irial says you're okay though. I ask. I do try."

"I know." She shook her hair back and struggled to be reasonable. That was the worst part sometimes; she *did* know that Gabriel tried. She knew he trusted Irial's judgment, trusted Chela, trusted his pack. He'd never raised a daughter—these past few months that he'd had her around were the sum total of his father-daughter parenting experience. But, she'd never had pack hungers before either. It was a new experience all around.

Later, after she'd secured Chela's consent, gone over the regular stay-close-to-Gabriel rules, and promised to stick with the pack, Ani was back in the stable with her father.

"If Che's steed has anything to say, it'll tell me, and I'll tell you." Gabriel's reminder that she couldn't hear Chela's steed—*that I'll never hear one*—was delivered with an ominous rumble in his voice. He was already feeling the heightened connection to the Hounds who were filling the aisles.

Somewhere in the distance, a howl rose like the scream of wind. Ani knew that only the Hunt heard it, but both mortal and faery *felt* it in the shivers that raced over suddenly chilled skin. To some, it was as if sirens came toward them, as if ambulances and police sped to them carrying words of sudden deaths or horrific accidents.

The Wild Hunt rides.

As Ani looked over the assembling Hounds, the green of their eyes and the clouds of their breath were clear. Wolves filled the room where the steeds were not. They would run between the hooves of the steeds, a roil of fur and teeth. Steed and wolf all waited for their Gabriel's word to begin, to run, to chase those foolish enough to attract their attention. Terror built and filled the air with a prestorm charge. Those not belonging to the Hunt would have to struggle to breathe. Mortals on the nearby streets would cringe, scurry into their dens, or turn into other alleys. If they stayed, they'd not see the true face of the Hunt, but explain it away—*earthquake? trains? storms? street fights?*—with the willful ignorance mortals clung to so fiercely. They didn't often stay; they ran. It was the order of things: prey runs, and predators pursue.

Her father, her Gabriel, strode through the room assessing them.

Ani felt the stroke of icy fingers on her skin as they prepared to ride. She bit down on her lip to keep from urging her father to sound the call. Her knuckles whitened as she clenched the edge of the wooden wall beside her. She looked at their horrible beauty and shivered.

If they were mine . . . I'd belong.

Then Gabriel was beside her.

"You are my pup, Ani." Gabriel cupped her cheek in his massive hand. "To be worthy of you, any Hound would have to be willing to face me. He'd need to be strong enough to lead them."

"*I* want to lead them," she whispered. "I want to be their Gabrielle."

"You're too mortal to hold control of them." Gabriel's eyes were monstrous. His skin was the touch of terror, of death, of nightmares that were Un-Named. "And too much mine to not be with the Hunt. I'm sorry."

She held his gaze. Something feral inside of her understood that this was why she couldn't live with Rabbit: her brother wasn't as fierce as her father was. Tish wasn't. Ani desperately wanted to be. Like the rest of the Hounds mounting their steeds, Ani knew that Gabriel could kill her if she disobeyed. It was a restraint she needed: it kept her closer to following rules.

"I can't take the Hunt from you"—she flashed her teeth at her father—"yet. Maybe I'll surprise you."

"Makes me proud that you want to," he said.

For a moment, the pride in her father's eyes was the sum of her world. She belonged. For tonight, she was included in the pack. He made it so.

If only I always was.

But there were no unclaimed steeds, and her mortal blood meant she'd never be strong enough to become Gabriel's successor, never be truly Pack.

A taste of belonging . . .

It wasn't enough, not truly, but it was something.

Then a howl unlike anything else in this world or the next came to his lips, and the rest of the pack echoed it. *She* echoed it.

Gabriel tossed her atop Chela's steed and growled, "We ride."

Chapter 2

Devlin stepped into the High Queen's private gardens. The ground under his sandals hummed when his foot touched it. Sometimes, he considered telling Sorcha that he noticed the barely perceptible alarms she'd set. With rare exceptions, he'd devoted eternity to Sorcha, but she was a creature of logic and order. She knew—and Bananach did—that he made the choice to serve Faerie every day, every hour, every moment. The only thing that kept him from choosing to align himself with Sorcha's antithesis was his own willpower.

And affection.

For all of her adherence to logic, the Unchanging Queen cared for him. Of that, he was certain.

"My Queen?" He walked toward her, waiting a heartbeat between steps to see if she'd let vines tangle his path or if she'd remake a passageway for him.

She glanced his way, and the undergrowth vanished in a narrow corridor. Briars reached from plants that were typically without thorns, tracing dozens of thin scratches on his arms and feet. It wasn't necessarily a conscious strike at him: the world around them bent to her will, but Sorcha had long since stopped noticing. It was like noticing that her heart beat. It simply *did*, and if her will injured others, so be it.

It's not personal.

"I can't see him," Sorcha whispered. "He's out there in the world. What if he's hurt? What if he's in danger?"

"You'd know," Devlin assured, as he had every day since Seth left. "You'd know if he was hurt."

"How? How would I know? I'm *blind*." The Queen of Order looked far from reasonable. Her skirt had tears in the hem. Her hair, usually as vibrant as liquid fire, was pale and snarled at the ends. Since Seth, the newly made faery, had gone back to the mortal world, Sorcha was increasingly not herself.

"I need to know that Seth is safe." She folded her arms over her chest. Her voice steadied. "I see *her*, the Summer Queen, and he is not with her. That's why he went back. Her. She should treat him better."

Misty figures formed in front of Sorcha. Somewhere in the mortal world, faeries were unaware that she was watching them. In the haze of the garden, Devlin stood near his queen and watched the faeries who were the focus of

Sorcha's attention. Unless the faeries' or mortals' threads twined too closely with her own thread, Sorcha could see into their lives.

The Summer Queen, Aislinn, stood in front of a fountain, talking to one of the water fey, Aobheall. In the background, the land flourished even though fall had come. In the patch of earth the Summer regents had claimed, Winter wouldn't ever reign again. Shrubs bloomed out of season, and faeries danced over green earth. Aislinn laughed and sat down on the edge of the fountain. One hand idly traced patterns on the surface of the water, and in its wake, water lilies blossomed.

Aobheall lazed in the fountain like a half-bared Grecian statue come to life. The water streamed around her in a small waterfall. "I think that dress is the one you wore just a few moons ago. We could shop, or"—Aobheall leaned forward—"get a dress *made* for you."

"I don't know." The Summer Queen glanced behind her to where several members of her Summer Court were weaving flowers into garlands. "Does it really matter what I wear?"

Aobheall frowned. "It *should* matter, Aislinn."

"I know . . . and . . . choose happiness, right?" A too-bright smile lit the Summer Queen's face. The Summer Queen had reigned for barely more than a mortal year, but during that time she'd had to deal with intercourt conflicts, being stabbed, losing a friend to the Dark Court, and trying to make sense of centuries of rivalry, allegiances, and old angers. An illogical urge to send her good advisors flared to life in Devlin, but he quashed it: the Summer Queen was not his priority.

Sorcha jabbed a finger toward the misty tableau, sending ripples through the image. "How can she be happy if he's not?"

"She *chooses* to pursue happiness for the good of her court," he pointed out. "It's not the same as true happiness. You can't fault her for trying to keep her court strong."

Sorcha obviously disagreed: thorns continued to grow, weaving together like threads on a loom until they formed a daunting barrier between Sorcha and Devlin.

"Tell me, Brother." She sounded fragile, not at all like the confident queen she'd been since the moment Devlin had first drawn breath.

"Summer is happy by nature," he reminded, but even as he said it, he watched the Summer Queen. Her eyes were shadowed as if she wasn't sleeping, and her mannerisms were out of synch with the frolicking around her. Aislinn was doing what Sorcha *should* be doing: making the best of whatever sorrows plagued her. Of course, the difference was that the High Queen shouldn't be lost in sorrows at all. Emotional flux was not a High Court trait: it was out of order.

"I want him home," Sorcha whispered. "Their world is unsafe. Bananach grows stronger. The courts are in discord.

If there is true war there, the mortal world will suffer. Do you remember the times she has been strong, Brother? The mortals die so easily. He will not stay out of her path. . . . He is too recently mortal. He needs to be here where he is safe."

"Soon." Devlin didn't try to reach through the thorns that now twisted around his queen like a cloak. He wanted to comfort her, to tell her that he was there, but such displays of untoward emotion had always offended her. He'd made a life of hiding the emotions that proved that he was not truly High Court, not truly hers, not worthy to advise the Queen of Reason. The rest of the court might not realize that he was filled with illogical emotions, but she knew. She'd always known—and found it abhorrent.

Sorcha watched the translucent figures silently. In the hazy images, the Summer Queen startled and looked up. She smiled, looking hopeful. Whatever or whomever she saw was invisible to them, and in a blink, Aislinn vanished as well.

"He's there," Sorcha murmured, "with her."

"Perhaps." Devlin suspected that it *was* Seth, but there
e others whose presence was invisible to Sorcha—some
hom Devlin had hidden from her.

o you think he is well?" Sorcha caught and held
gaze. "What if he needs to talk or . . . art sup-
or . . . to come home? Maybe he wants to come
be he is unhappy. How am I to know?"

"I will visit him again." Devlin would rather bring Seth back to Faerie, but Sorcha had given Seth a choice, and he had chosen to return to the mortal world where his beloved Summer Queen lived. Devlin had objected. Killing Seth or keeping him in Faerie would be better for Sorcha—and therefore for all of them.

"Perhaps you should stay there." The High Queen's voice didn't sound noticeably different as she said this, but Devlin felt increasingly uneasy. In all of eternity, Sorcha had never sent him away for more than a quick trip.

"Stay there?" Devlin had traveled back and forth to the mortal world too often of late, and, as a day in Faerie was almost a full week in the mortal world, the disconnect of such travel was beginning to wear on him. His own emotions, more easily contained when he stayed in Faerie with his queen, were becoming increasingly present. His sleep was restless, leaving him tired—and prone to emotions.

"You would have me *stay* in the *mortal* world?" He spoke the words slowly.

"Yes. In case he needs you. I'm . . . I need you more there than here." She stared at him, as if daring him to question her.

He wanted to: there was more to this than Seth's protection, but Devlin didn't know what his queen was hiding. "He's with Irial and Niall, my queen. Cloistered safely in the Dark Court but for when he's with the Summer Queen. Surely—"

"Do you refuse my orders? Have you finally decided to disobey me?"

He knelt. "Have I ever refused your orders?"

"You have acted without direct orders; but refused? I don't know, Devlin." She sighed softly, a whisper of air that made the garden seem to hold its breath. "You could, though. I know that."

"I am not refusing your order," he said. It was not a real answer. Truth would lead them into a discussion he had avoided for fourteen mortal years: it would mean admitting that he had disobeyed her direct order to kill one half-mortal child.

An offense for which I could be executed, abandoned, cast out of Faerie . . . and rightly so. A feeling that he recognized as guilt twisted inside him. *I am High Court. I am Sorcha's to command. I will not fail my queen ever again*, he repeated his daily reminders silently to himself. Aloud, he added, "I am not refusing, but I am your advisor, my Queen, and I do not recommend leaving you alone when you seem . . ."

"Seem what?"

Devlin's position was one of obeisance, but he caught and held her gaze with a boldness none other in Faerie would dare. "When you seem to be developing *emotions*."

She ignored the reality he'd spoken and said only, "Tell him I wish he would come home. You will stay there . . . for as long as he needs you."

"I am yours to command, my Queen."

"Are you?" Sorcha leaned into the veil of thorns that had grown around her, and just as the jagged edges would pierce her, they vanished. Then, thorns sprouted from the earth at his knees, around her feet. The vines climbed her body, and crept over her arm to her fingers. She raised her hand and pressed it to his cheek, so that the sharp edges pierced them both. "Are you truly mine, Brother?"

"I am." He did not move away.

"You will see her." Sorcha's blood dripped onto his skin, mingling with his own.

His body absorbed the blood she offered. As with the twins who'd created him, Devlin needed the nourishment of blood. Unlike them, he needed the blood of both Order and Discord.

"I will see Bananach," Devlin admitted, "but she does not command me. Only you. I serve the Unchanging Queen, the High Court, *Faerie*."

The vine crawled from her flesh onto his, where the nourishment she'd filled it with was his to take.

"For now." Sorcha brushed her hand across his cheek. "But nothing lasts forever. Things change. *We* change."

Devlin couldn't speak. This was the closet to open affection his mother-sister had ever shown him. He wasn't sure whether to be happy or alarmed. Reason wasn't to act thusly, but in some hidden part of his mind, he'd wondered if she felt tempestuous emotions, if she merely hid them away better, if she'd chosen to let logic reign over her.

"Everything changes in time, Brother," Sorcha whispered. "Go to Seth, and . . . be wary of War. I would rather you were not injured."

He opened his mouth to question her, but she turned away, leaving him silent in her gardens.

Chapter 3

Ani had gone to the Dark Kings' home knowing it would be another painful experience—*and not the fun kind of pain*.

Irial held one of her hands in his. It was a comfort of sorts. "Are you ready?"

"Take it." Ani extended her other arm toward the former Dark King. She stared at the fleur-de-lis wallpaper, at the flickering candles, at anything other than the faery sitting beside her. "Take *all* of it if that's what you need."

"Not all, Ani." He squeezed her hand once more before releasing it. "If there was another way—"

"You're my king. I will give whatever you ask of me. Do it." She watched as he jabbed a thin tube into her skin. Bruises from the last several tubes decorated her skin like love bites.

"Not your king now. Niall's the Dark King."

"Whatever." Ani didn't resume the argument she'd

lost too often: Irial might be king-no-more, but he had her loyalty. Truth be told, he had the loyalty of many of the denizens of the Dark Court. He might not rule them, but he still looked after them. He still handled those matters too disquieting for the new Dark King. Irial cosseted Niall.

Ani, however, wasn't sheltered. *Not anymore.* When Irial learned that Ani could—*that I need to*—feed from both touch and emotion, he'd begun trying to find out how to use that for the Dark Court. According to Irial, as a halfling, she shouldn't have either appetite. She certainly shouldn't have both; and she definitely shouldn't be able to find nourishment from mortals. Irial believed that Ani's blood might hold the key to strengthening their court, so she'd become the subject of his experimentation.

Which is fine. For my court. For Irial.

"More?" she asked.

"Just a bit." Irial bit the cork that sealed the next vial and tugged it out. He spoke around the cork held between his teeth and added, "Tilt down."

She lowered her arm, clenching and unclenching her fist to pump the blood faster. She wasn't sure if it actually helped the flow of blood, but it did give her the illusion that she was doing *something*. Bloodletting hadn't become easier despite the number of times she'd done it.

With her free hand, she took the cork from his mouth. "I have it. Grab the next one."

As the vial filled, Irial took another empty one from the rack and lifted it to his lips. Once it was uncorked, he switched the empty vial with the now full one. "Take this?"

Silently, she accepted the glass container with the same hand that held the cork. She sat it beside the other vials, all recorked, all filled with her blood. Then, she pushed the cork into the top of it.

"Last one," Irial murmured. "You're doing great."

Ani stared at the empty space in the sixth rack; the others were all filled with vials of her blood. "Good."

Irial handed her the last tube of blood and pressed a kiss to the inflamed extraction site. Neither of them spoke as he took the final container, settled it with the others, and carried all of it to the doorway and handed it off to a faery she didn't see.

Their experimentation was a secret that neither Niall nor Gabriel knew of, but it was one of the myriad things Ani would do if Irial so much as hinted that he wished it of her. *Not as painful as what I have done.* At Irial's request, she had let a trusted thistle-fey embrace her on one particularly unpleasant evening. Her hair and skin were collected by his touch. Should the court at large know of Irial's experiments on her blood and flesh, should they learn why he sent samples to be tested and hopefully copied, she'd be at risk.

As would Iri.

Few faeries knew of her abnormalities—and she was

grateful for that—and while Niall *did* know that she was unlike other faeries, he did not know of the experiments. He thought her ability to feed on the emotions of both faery and mortal was hidden from those who would kill, use, or champion her. Niall was a humane king. He allowed their faeries to do as they must, but he kept the court on a leash.

In a time when Bananach—the carrion crow, the bringer of war—grew stronger, leashes were dangerous. The faery courts, at least those on the mortal side of the veil, were on the verge of violence. The growing conflict nourished the Dark Court, who fed on the chaotic emotions, but it was also a threat to those Ani held dear. Upheavals between courts, whispers of deaths to come, these were all well and good—up to the point at which her own court was in jeopardy.

And Bananach will not spare the Dark Court. Or the mortal world my family lives in.

Irial did as he had done when he was king: moving pieces behind the scenes, making bargains, bending rules. This time, though, Ani's safety was one of the rules he bent.

With my consent.

When Irial came back into the room, she watched him warily. For all of her adoration of him, she knew that he was rarely influenced by weakness or tenderness. He hadn't held the throne of the court of nightmares for centuries by being easily swayed.

"You know I wouldn't do this if there were better options." His words weren't a lie; they weren't fully true either. Unless there was one clear option that would assure his court's safety, he would do this—*and much worse.*

Yet, the former Dark King still thought of her as a child, as one foolish enough to accept the misdirection in his words. She wasn't a child.

Perhaps foolish, but not naive, not innocent, not easily misled.

She leaned on the wall. The room was out of focus. "You've kept me safe my whole life. Kept Tish safe . . . and Rab . . . and . . . we're good. It's fine."

The world around her spun. Tonight's experiment had begun with her being as hungry as she could stand before the bloodletting. It wasn't the least pleasant of the experiments, but it wasn't pleasurable either.

Irial walked over to feed the fire—away from her so she could have the privacy to pull herself together—and asked, "You okay?"

"Sure." She sat down, not feeling exactly *well.* Most days, she was only barely above starved. During the first few months of her hunger, she'd had humans and a few halflings. Since she'd moved to Gabriel's care, she'd been restricted to the point that her hunger was hurting her physically. She'd been barely nourished by the emotion Irial shared and the scant contact that Gabriel grudgingly allowed her to pursue in court. Hugs and feather touches weren't anywhere near enough.

Irial ran one hand absently over the side of the marble fireplace. Like everything in his house, it was carved with an appreciation of textures. The sharp edges and smooth curves drew her attention, but she didn't approach the fireplace or the faery in front of it. Instead, she moved to one of the white leather chairs and traced a finger over the raised gray fleurs-de-lis barely visible on the walls.

"I know this is . . . difficult for you, pup." Irial kept his distance, but he let her taste all of his emotions, giving her nourishment to make up for what she'd lost.

Ani caught his gaze. "Do you apologize to Gabriel when he punishes faeries who need it?"

The play of firelight and shadows made the former Dark King appear ominous, but his temper was not stirred. "No."

"Then drop it. I'll do what's necessary for my court." She fought the urge to fold her arms, forced herself to be calm, even though he knew exactly how unsettled she was. Dark Court faeries couldn't feed on mortal emotions, but Ani wasn't entirely mortal.

If Irial had not been there for her when she'd come to live with the Hounds, she wasn't sure what she would've done. He helped her cope with her changes, nourished her enough to keep true starvation at bay. In truth, if not for him she might have died forever ago. He'd protected her—and Tish and Rabbit—for almost all of their lives.

She let him feel the surge of gratitude and whispered, "I serve the will of the Dark Court. I know you have reasons."

"If we can find a way to filter out your blood, our court will be unstoppable; Niall will be safe; and . . ." His words faded, but the hope was undeniable. Unlike many faeries, Irial was comfortable with modern science. If they could identify the anomalous component within her, replicate it, and introduce it to others, Dark Court faeries would be able to feed on both faery and mortal emotions. They'd be sated. They'd tried another plan, binding mortal to faery as conduits with tattoos, but those ink exchanges had presented unexpected complications.

"Right." Ani stood. She'd heard his theories before; there was little Irial could say that would be new.

"You can save us," he said yet again.

Ani wasn't sure if his words were truth. Faeries couldn't lie, but belief was a tricky thing. If Irial believed the words, they were utterable, and he did believe that her blood was the solution they needed to save the Dark Court.

"I'll be back later. You'll tell me"—she folded her arms over her chest as if it would still the shivering—"when you need me?"

"Your court needs you every day, Ani. No one else can feed on both touch and emotion; no one else can feed on both faery and mortal. You are the key." Irial wrapped his arms around her and kissed the top of her head. It wasn't much, but small touches from such a strong faery fed her skin hunger more than a lot of touch from a weak faery or a mortal would.

Ani stayed still, grateful for even the scant contact.

Irial stroked her hair. "You let me keep my promises to stop the ink exchanges, to protect my king. . . . We *do* need you, pup."

She looked up at him. "As long as Gabriel and Niall don't find out, right?"

"For now." Irial stepped away, his hands still on her shoulders, and then he unfolded her arms and took her hands in his as he repeated the same assurances he had the past few months. "Just for now. Once we figure out what's in your blood, they'll understand why we did this."

She nodded.

He led her to the door. "Do you need anything else?"

All sorts of things no one will give me.

Ani said nothing. Instead, she hugged him, knowing from other rejections that his offer didn't include the other things she needed. Irial—for all of his love for court and king, for all his protection for family and beloved—didn't want to hear what she truly needed. He wouldn't share his bed with her or force her father to let her run free with the Hounds.

"I need to go," Ani murmured, and then she turned her back on him before she gave in to the temptation to beg. He gave her enough to keep her from starvation, but the former Dark King wouldn't help her fully sate her hungers. She would have to find a few tastes here and there to silence the gnawing inside her.

Again.

CHAPTER 4

Rae walked into the image of a tiny kitchen. Ani stood in the doorway, leaning against the doorframe. A memory played out in the adjoining room. The tableau was set in a different era than the one where Rae had lived. It was familiar though: it was a memory that Ani replayed over and over in her dreams. So, Rae waited for the memory to run its course.

"Tell me about her?" Ani asked her sister.

"Who?" Tish paused mid-math, pencil held in the air.

"You know. Her." Ani practiced cartwheels on the sofa. Until Rabbit came up from the shop to remind her she wasn't to do it, she'd cartwheel and flip in their tiny living room.

"I was six. How would I know?" Tish rolled her eyes. "I remember she was nice. She read books. There was a blanket Dad gave her. Her

hair was light brown like yours."

"Dad visited her?"

"Uh-huh." Tish was done talking. She was filled with sadness that she was trying to hide. "Go read or something, Ani."

Tish's pencil was making scratching noises on the paper, like the sounds cockroaches made when all of their feet brushed the floor or walls. It was one of the many reasons Ani hated schoolwork. Tish never heard how loud her pencil was though. Her ears didn't work right.

Ani flipped over and snatched the pencil. "Tag."

"Give it back."

"Sure . . . if you catch me."

Tish looked at the clock, just a little glance. Then she snorted. "Like you could ever outrun me."

And Ani was off, not as fast as she could run because that would make Tish sad, and making Tish sad was the one thing Ani never ever did on purpose.

Ani's thinking of Tish so protectively wasn't unusual, but more and more often, the memories of difference, of awareness of the sisters' dissimilarities, had become central in Ani's dreams.

"She is well? Your sister?" Rae asked, drawing Ani's attention away from the memory.

Ani turned to face Rae. "Yeah, Tish is good. I miss her."

"And you? Are you well?" Rae materialized a sofa that was reminiscent of one from her own long-gone sitting room.

Ani sat on the arm of the sofa, balanced there with no effort. Even in dreams, Ani had innate animal grace.

"I'm mostly okay." Ani's gaze skittered away from Rae.

Her words weren't a lie; if they were, the Hound wouldn't be able to speak them. *Even here.* They were together in a dream, but because Rae was a dreamwalker, this, too, was a sort of reality. *And some rules,* faery *rules, are inescapable in every reality.*

"Mostly okay?" Rae envisioned a nice cup of tea and a tray of finger sandwiches, pastries, and other assorted treats. In dreams, she could adjust the world around her, so the imagined treats appeared as quickly as the thought had. "Scone?"

Absently, Ani took one. "It's weird to dream about eating."

"You needed comfort, so you dreamed of food," Rae said. Unlike faeries, Rae *could* lie at will. "You were stressed over thinking about your sister. It makes sense."

The Hound slid from the arm of the sofa into the seat. "I guess."

As Ani sat silently and ate, Rae enjoyed the semblance of normalcy. If Ani realized Rae wasn't a figment of her imagination, they'd stop talking, but Rae had been visiting her dreams since Ani was a child. Ani rationalized Rae's presence.

"I think I'm lonely." Ani pulled her knees up to her chest, hugging them to her. "Plus, being apart from Tish is . . . *wrong*. What if she needs me? What if—"

"Is she alone?"

"No, but still . . ." Ani's voice drifted off as distorted images from her fears formed around them.

A faceless faery reached for Tish.

Hands covered in blood swung at Rabbit.

Ani's mother, Jillian, lay dead outside a cupboard.

Ani was trapped behind a too-small barrier as a faceless faery reached for her.

Unlike the tea and food, these weren't things Rae created. They were the terrors of Ani's imaginings. Here, where Ani felt safe, she envisioned a mix of memories and fears. Rae could alter reality, but the dreamer's mind also held sway.

"These aren't real memories," Rae reminded. "This is *not* what happened. You don't even know—"

"She was there, and then she was gone." Ani glared at Rae. "There *was* a monster. There had to be. He took her and . . . did something. Hurt her. Killed her. He *had* to have. If she was alive, she'd have come home. She wouldn't have left us. She *loved* us."

"You're a creature that creates fear in others, not one who should dwell in it." Rae concentrated on remaking the landscape around her. She removed the faceless faery, the dead mother, and the trembling girls. She wiped it all away, and—hopefully—Ani's fear with it. "Tell me about your court. Think about that. Tell me how things go with the Hunt."

"I rode again. The wolves were at our feet; the steeds were like shadows. . . . It's perfect when it happens. I want it always like that. . . . I want a steed; I want to be stronger; I want . . . oh . . . I want everything." Ani's eyes glimmered the strange green of the Hunt's beasts. Despite her mixed parentage, she was meant to be among faeries; it had been obvious to Rae since she first met the girl.

Ani had no awareness of the vows they'd made and broken so Ani could live. Rae did. She remembered it each time Devlin refused to talk about the Hound, each time he refused to go check on her. They'd spared Ani. The time was coming when they'd have to deal with the inevitable consequences.

Rae reached out and squeezed Ani's hand. In the dreamscape where Rae walked, she could do that, touch another body. "You're too impatient."

Ani pointed at herself. "Hound. What do you expect?"

"Exactly what you are," Rae said.

Ani wandered into the dreamscape. To her, this was just another dream where her mind worked through fears and worries. And, just then, Ani didn't want to work through them—so she walked away.

Rae followed in what was now a vast shadowed forest.

Time was running out, and neither Devlin nor Ani was any closer to finding their rightful places. *And I can't tell them without undoing everything.*

From the depths of the forest, wolves' songs rose. A space between the trees opened up, and as Rae walked she could hear the pad of their feet on the needle-covered trail. Rae shuddered as the wolves drew near. Beside her, Ani sighed: the wolves were a comfort to her.

Ani spun to face Rae and blurted, "Do *you* think the monster was High Court? They hate my court. They steal halflings. They *are* monsters."

"Monsters are called such by those who are doing the naming." Rae tensed as a sulfurous green glow illuminated all of the wolves' eyes in the forest. "Mortals write stories of the beauty of Faerie, of the delicate fey creatures of other courts, and *your* court's creatures are the fiends."

"He wasn't *my* court. That's for sure." Ani crouched on the path and the wolves began to slip from among the woods. Their muzzles butted against Ani and Rae. Furred sides brushed against them. Howls rose into a cacophony.

Ani opened her arms to the wolves. The creatures began circling them in a blur of white teeth and green eyes, musky fur and growling throats. They ran faster and faster, pressing against Ani.

Rae visualized herself outside the circle, at a far distance up the path.

One by one, each wolf dove into the center of Ani and disappeared there. They were a part of her, the part that would wake and change the world.

If. That was the worst part of knowing: the knowledge that the future Rae so desperately wanted was only an

"if." She didn't know what the other possibilities were, but she did know that the future she had glimpsed was one she wanted, one where she would have autonomy for the first time. *Please, Ani.*

"I hope you are able to forgive him," Rae whispered. "He's not a monster. Neither are you."

And then she was gone from Ani's mind.

After being in the dream forest, her cave felt even more restrictive. Rae paced around the perimeter, counting out steps as if the murmuring of numbers would make the small space seem somehow larger. It didn't work.

Darkness, the time of dreams, was Rae's rightful place, but the past few weeks, Sorcha had insisted that there were but a few dark hours in Faerie. The moon did not go through normal phases; instead, it almost always stayed full in the sky, casting silvered light over them as if they were caught in one endless day. And without the dark, Rae was caught, trapped in the small cave that was her prison.

"Rae?" Devlin was in the doorway of the cave. The light from outside shone around him, illuminating him and adding to his otherworldly appearance. His coarse white hair, loosened from restraints, offset the harshness of his features a little, but not so much that the sharp angles of his cheeks looked human.

"You're here." Rae shifted her attire to match Devlin's more formal garb. Her dress was pale rose with a hem that swept the ground, and although the waist was narrow, the bodice was demure. Her almost floor-length hair was swept up with gilt combs. The only ornament beyond her combs was a black band around her throat that held a cameo. If Devlin looked closely, he'd see that it was his image in the ivory.

The stern set of his mouth softened. "You need not change for me."

"I know," she lied. She *did* need to change if it brought her the smile she'd sought. His stress was heavy enough that his straightened shoulders were rigid with it.

"I must go over to the mortal world again."

Rae stilled. "Again?"

Devlin stepped farther into the shadows of the cave. "I am not sure how long I'll be gone this time."

"Something is wrong with the High Queen. She barely lowers the light." Rae couldn't see beyond the crevice where Devlin had entered. The brightness that seeped through the small fissure was painful to her. Facing it full on would be blinding.

"Light soothes her; darkness reminds her of her twin." He was out of the light now, comforting in his presence as none other had ever been. The High Court's assassin was her friend, her companion, her only solace in a world that—even after decades—still made little sense to her.

Rae leaned against a flat stone on one side of the cave. "I could come with you."

Devlin kept his distance. "And if you were drawn back to your body by being in the mortal world?"

"*If* I was drawn into my body, which I don't think I would

be, I suspect I'd die." She stepped a little closer to him.

Devlin didn't move away. "Which I do not want."

For a moment, they stood in silence. She hated being left alone in Faerie, feared the High Queen, worried about Devlin, and wished she could go to the mortal world.

With careful deliberation, Rae stepped closer to him again. Were she solid, her skirt would be atop his feet. "Will you check on her? Ani is important. Just once go seek her out."

"Don't do this." Devlin's voice held the edge that it always did when Rae broached forbidden topics.

"You're making a mistake," she whispered. "You saved her. You ought to—"

"Don't." Devlin turned his back to her and walked away, retreating almost to the sunlight at the mouth of the cave. "I did as you wished. She lives. Nothing more is required."

Rae lifted one hand, but didn't follow. It wouldn't matter: she couldn't touch him, couldn't force him to face her. Without his help, she had no physical substance.

Without him, I have nothing.

"Can I take a walk? Before you go?" Rae tried to make her invitation sound casual. It was one of the things she'd realized early on: she couldn't act like it was important.

To either of us.

He turned. A flash of relief, so brief that it barely registered before vanishing, slid across Devlin's impassive face. "If it would calm you . . ."

"It would," Rae assured him. She didn't give voice to

the fact that it would calm *both* of them. Devlin wouldn't have stood so pensively if he didn't seek the reprieve. He needed an excuse, and he needed an invitation. Unless it was for political maneuvers, for the ability to lie, Devlin never admitted wanting the respite that Rae's possession allowed them both. Letting her close to him, letting her possess him, gave him freedom from the stifling rules of Faerie. It gave him an excuse to enjoy his *other* sister's heritage without consequences.

"Fine." Devlin stood still, motionless as only a faery could be.

She walked across the cave as if she could touch the stone floor. She measured each step as she'd been doing earlier for peace, counting them out as if at one of the long-ago dances she'd attended when she still had a body. Her skirts swayed, and the illusion made her feel closer to being tangible.

Devlin's lips parted enough that a sigh could escape as Rae stood face-to-face with him. His body tensed in anticipation. His pupils dilated in the flood of adrenaline released by fear and excitement.

She slipped into his body, pushing Devlin to the back of his own mind and animating the body as if it were her own. She could feel him, talk to him inside their body, but he didn't control the movements. *Not now.* After so many times inside Devlin, it felt as familiar as her own body had. *More perhaps.*

She didn't ask where he wanted to go. If she did, he would pretend not to have any interest in what she did with his body, but she felt him, watching and riding out the emotions they both felt during their shared occupation. It was the only time within Faerie that he could revel in passions—because he was not the one choosing to indulge.

"In the mortal world, you are not so cautious," she whispered. "I know your secrets, Devlin. I've seen the memories. The indulgences . . ."

What I do there is of no consequence, he muttered. *I do as my queen bids first. I serve my—*

"I'm not chastising. I think you *should* take pleasure for yourself." Rae stretched, enjoying the heaviness of wearing bone and muscle again. She reached her hands out and touched the rocks that jutted unevenly in the cave. It was within the side of a mountain, not visible to the High Queen or perhaps simply not worthy of her notice. Devlin had made the cave where Rae hid. Like the queen, Devlin could bend reality in Faerie if he wanted to, but no one—save Rae—knew that Devlin could remake the world at his will. Out of respect for his queen, he'd hidden that truth from everyone.

"Oh, the things we could do if you weren't so obstinate, Dev," she said. "The world could be ours. No limits. Think about the freedom, the pleasures. . . ."

I'm not going to spend all day like this, Rae, he said. *Or discussing* that *again.*

"Only because you know I'm right, and you're going to have to admit it or lie to me . . . which you can't do." Rae grinned and kicked off the sandals that Devlin had worn. They were too utilitarian, too restrictive. Feet bare,

Rae stepped out the doorway into the brightness of Faerie. It felt deliciously scandalous to have her feet naked. Such a thing would've shocked everyone she'd known in the mortal world.

I serve the High Queen. It's the choice I made, he repeated as usual.

"Some choices can be traps. Do you honestly think that staying the course just because you once thought it was right is wise? There are other choices."

Enough, Rae. He raised his voice inside their body. *Can we not . . . argue? Take the body where you will, Rae.* Devlin sounded both wearied and hopeful.

Rae heard the hope in his voice. It was small progress, but it was progress.

Chapter 5

Ani and Tish flung themselves down the street toward the Crow's Nest. It wasn't quite running, but it was far faster than walking. Ani had to pace herself, force her feet to move slower to keep beside Tish. It didn't used to be like that, but over the last year, Ani had changed more every month. Tish hadn't.

Ani had always been a little different, but not enough to matter. She was just part of Ani-and-Tish, the "Trouble Twins"—even though Tish was really almost three years older. They had a difficult time being apart, so Tish stayed home a couple years extra before starting school. She helped Ani with book stuff and following mortal world rules, and Ani kept Tish safe from dangers and boredom. That was how it worked. And it *did* work—until Ani had changed too much.

"Ani?" Tish's voice was breathless. "Slower?"

"Sorry." Ani slowed down, looking up ahead at the

cluster of people outside the Crow's Nest. Mortals. Almost everyone there was mortal, but that was fine by Ani. All the delectable faeries were afraid of Gabriel *and* of Irial, but mortals weren't aware of the Dark Court. Most weren't aware of the existence of faeries—which made them the best game in town.

". . . Rabbit's worried about money." Tish was breathing heavily, despite Ani slowing down even more.

"Money?"

"Things are tight, but he's still talking like I should"—Tish sent a pleading look at Ani—"go to college next year. Not far away or anything, but just . . . *away.*"

Ani kept her face as expressionless as she could. "Oh . . . so you want to . . . I mean . . . if that's what you want, good."

"I do, but I don't like being far from you or Rab or Iri or Dad, especially lately. I hated when Winter was constant, but at least then you knew what to expect. With the courts all snarling at one another . . . I'm not sure I want to be away." Tish looked down briefly, not saying the things they couldn't, not admitting that she was too weak to defend herself.

Ani slowed to a casual stroll. Tish being out of reach scared Ani, but Tish being out of the growing conflict in Huntsdale was appealing. Ani didn't voice that. No one—least of all Ani—was going to let Tish go where she was unprotected.

"I could come," Ani suggested. "Not to *school*, but I could get a job or something. We can get an apartment.

Oooh, maybe in Pittsburgh near Leslie? Or in Atlanta? You could totally pass there if you wanted."

"*You* couldn't." Tish said it softly. "Not anymore."

"Whatever." Ani didn't want to talk about *that*. She wasn't able to pass as mortal: any faery seeing her would know, but she was also under the protection of the strongest of the Dark Court faeries. Outside Huntsdale, she'd be vulnerable.

"Maybe in a few years I could go." Tish hugged her. "You'll get better at being what you are, Ani. I know you will. It'll get easier."

"Whichever is best for you is what we'll do." Ani forced a smile to her lips.

It was a matter of time until they'd end up apart. Halflings were sometimes strong, but strong Dark Court halflings were often targeted by solitaries or kidnapped by the High Court. *Not strong enough to be truly in the Dark Court, but too threatening to live outside it.* Irial's protection had kept them safe—and well hidden—for most of her life. Then Ani had changed and had to move away from her family. Rabbit and Tish were not fey enough to need to be within the court, and Ani was too fey to live outside it. Rabbit was able to pass; Tish was able to pass; and now that Ani lived with the Hounds, Rabbit could relocate to somewhere away from Huntsdale. *So Tish is safe.*

Ani wasn't book smart, but she understood a few things she hadn't when they were pups: Tish was almost mortal, and Rabbit had known how different the two girls were from each other long before they did. He didn't talk about those things, and Ani didn't do anything that demonstrated how different she was from Tish. She'd kept that as secret as she could, for as long as she could. Life was about secrets and pretending. It had been that way since Jillian died.

Jillian wasn't even a face in Ani's memories; she was hands and too-fast words trying to get Ani-and-Tish—their names were already just one word then—to hide and "stay quiet, please quiet like you're bunnies. For Mama?"

And after, when it was just Ani and Tish, when Jillian never came back to open the cupboard where the girls stayed still and waiting, Ani remembered that part too. Tish was sad, broken somewhere inside that Ani couldn't fix. She pretended though, for Ani. Tish held on to Ani, and late that night Tish pushed the buttons they had on the phone to the "special number for trouble." That was when Irial came and took them to Rabbit; that was when Irial made them safe in a new home.

Tish didn't remember that day. She'd erased it from her memory, locked it away somewhere. The *before* and the *after* was what Tish remembered: Irial, Rabbit, and a new home. Tish never remembered the other parts.

Ani did.

Remembering Jillian not coming back made Ani feel raw inside. The day when Jillian was gone and Tish was sad was the first complete memory that Ani had. Life, as she remembered it, began for Ani in that moment.

"Hey, you okay?" Tish grabbed Ani's hand and pulled her to the side of a group of guys headed into the club. "You weren't listening to a thing I said, were you?"

"Sorry, Sis." Ani flashed a fake smile. "The whole nonsense with Gabr—"

"Dad," Tish corrected.

"With *Gabriel* not letting me relax with any of the Hounds has me all out of sorts." Ani had found lying increasingly impossible the older she got, but she'd picked up the importance of misdirection years ago. She was out of sorts with Gabriel. That might not be what she'd just been thinking, but it was a true statement.

"He's a good person. Give him a chance."

"He's never been a father, not like Rabbit." Ani didn't want to admit that being in the Dark Court wasn't everything she dreamed of, not even to Tish. Being surrounded by the Hounds and the Dark Court should make her feel less alone, but the exact opposite had happened. "It's not like I'm a pup. And his not letting you and me live in the same place, keeping me away from you and Rab, is no good."

"I miss you too." Tish always gave voice to the stuff Ani couldn't deal with or even admit she needed to deal with.

Ani leaned her shoulder against the wall, enjoying the way the rough edges of brick felt against her bare back. It anchored her in the *now*—which was where she needed to be, not dwelling on memories best kept boxed up.

"Are you coping?" Tish gestured vaguely. They never

really talked about the way Ani craved contact—or the consequences of her getting too much of it.

"Sure." Ani watched a group of guys head toward the door. They weren't faery-pretty or emotional feasts, but they were on the prowl. For her, right then, that was good enough. *It has to be.* She could take a taste from each of them, a touch here and an emotion there, to keep the hungers at bay.

Not both. Never both from the same person.

She linked her arm through Tish's. "Come on."

Glenn was working the door. He winced as they approached. "And here it was looking like such a good night."

"Jerk." Tish cuddled into his open arms. "You'd miss me if I didn't stop in."

"Sure, but when you have your partner in chaos . . ." He wrapped an arm familiarly around Tish's waist and lifted her into his lap.

Ani tilted her head inquiringly. *This is new.* And Ani hadn't seen it because living with the Hounds meant not seeing her sister but once or so every other week.

Tish smiled contently as Glenn held her.

"Hey." Glenn kissed Tish's forehead, and then swept his gaze around the people and shadows in the lot. He didn't get involved in whatever business people took out of sight, but dealing inside was banned.

"Aren't you going to give Glenn a hug?" Tish played coy and silly, slipping into her role as easily as if their outings were still a daily thing. "It's been, like, weeks."

"You heard her. C'mere." Glenn held out the other arm.

Ani leaned in close, enjoying the feel of bare arm and partly bare chest. Glenn had a sleeveless shirt on, fastened with only one button. He'd taken to the surprising return of Summer like most mortals—exposing a good amount of skin.

Glenn released Ani, but held on to Tish. "You be careful in there. Both of you." He stared at Ani. "I mean it."

Tish kissed him. "We'll do our best."

"That's what I worry about," Glenn muttered.

"Just dancing, Glenn." Ani took her sister's hand and pushed open the door. "I promise she'll be fine."

"You too," Glenn said.

But the door was open and the crowd of bodies was right there, and all Ani could do was call back, "Sure."

The band was old-school punk, and there was a pit. *Perfect.* With a gleeful squeal, Tish shoved Ani forward into the mass.

Chapter 6

Devlin watched for Seth as he walked through the crush of mortals in the Crow's Nest. It was less complicated to await Seth here; the alternative was going to the Dark Court, and dealing with the Dark King could be fraught with difficulties. Niall, the Gancanagh who'd once lived in Faerie and now ruled the Dark Court, had changed. His years with Irial, his centuries advising the Summer King, and his recent ascension to the Dark Court's throne all combined to create a faery monarch who should not be trusted.

Not that Seth should be trusted either.

Seth was loved by the Summer Queen, had been gifted with Sight by the Winter Queen, and had been declared "brother" to the Dark King. Rather than nullify the threat of a mortal walking among all the courts—as Sorcha should've done—the High Queen had remade Seth as a faery and invited him into her court. Devlin couldn't help but wonder at the logic in some of the decisions she was making of late.

Mortals pushed against Devlin, and he had to remind himself that physically relocating them was considered aggressive in the mortal realm—*and* that aggression was not a quality he was supposed to embrace. He threaded his way through the crowd.

With the noise and blaring music, the shadows and flashing lights, the Crow's Nest called to the discordant side of his ancestry.

"I am looking for Seth," he told the barmaid.

"Not here yet." She glanced at his wrist, seeking the age band that would indicate whether or not he was allowed to order alcoholic drinks.

Devlin shifted his appearance so that she saw a glowing strip of plastic, white under the black lights hanging over the bar.

"Wine. White." He dropped a bill on the bar.

"Change?"

He shook his head. Exchanging funds for alcohol was odd; in Faerie such transactions were unnecessary. What one required was simply provided.

The barmaid grabbed a bottle of chardonnay, filled a cocktail glass, and set it on the bar. It was the wrong glass and cheap wine, but he didn't expect much else from the Crow's Nest. Her hand was still cradling the short glass when Devlin wrapped his hand around the other side, interlacing his fingers with hers, holding her attention. "I'm Devlin."

She paused. "I remember you."

"Good. You'll tell him I'm here," Devlin said.

She nodded and turned to the next customer.

Neither the doorman nor the barmaid had seen Seth, but between the two, Devlin was assured that Seth would know Devlin was looking for him the moment he arrived.

Drink in hand, Devlin retreated to the periphery. Something in the club was making Devlin want the release of a fight.

He looked over the crowd, but it wasn't Niall or Seth that he saw on the floor: Bananach stood in the shadows across the room. Her presence explained the extra urge to violence. Just as being near Sorcha made him feel calmer, being near Bananach made him feel disorderly urges.

If Sorcha knew that her mad twin was in the club favored by Seth, the illogical anxiety the High Queen had experienced of late would worsen. If Bananach injured Seth, Sorcha would be . . . He couldn't fathom *what* she would be. However, he was certain that he needed to convince Bananach to leave before Seth arrived. It would be preferable if Seth returned to Faerie—at least until the likelihood of true war in the mortal world was past. If Seth were injured, Sorcha might very well involve herself in battle with Bananach, and *that* could not end well for anyone.

Devlin didn't observe social niceties as he went toward Bananach. Instead, he pulled his glamour around him like a shadow to hide his presence and shoved mortals from his path.

Necessary logical aggression.

"Brother!" Bananach smiled at him and casually knocked a mortal to the ground.

A small fight broke out as two guys both blamed the other. One threw a punch. The one on the floor came up swinging.

"How are you, Sister?"

"I am well." She flicked her wrist out and cut a thin line on a mortal who wasn't in the squabble yet. It wasn't much of an injury, but her talon-tipped fingers were bloodied. Neither her presence nor the quarrel were random, but he wasn't yet sure what her agenda was just then, only that she had one. War might start in madness, but to flourish it must be calculating—and Bananach was the embodiment of war.

Her intermittent madness was increasingly absent as she became more powerful. The visible presence of her strength was in her shadowed wings—which were shadows no more. They'd been made manifest. Bananach drew strength from the growing intercourt conflicts and mistrusts, and her strength enabled her to increase the conflicts. It was a deadly cycle—one he didn't know how to end. Bananach had manipulated the courts, inner-court factions, and her sister until they were on the precipice of war. He'd seen her do so over the centuries, but this time he was afraid that they wouldn't escape without more deaths than he could comfortably sanction. The last time she'd been so effective was when the now-dead Winter Queen, Beira, had killed the last Summer King, Miach. Miach had been Beira's opposition, her lover, and father to her child. The consequences of his death had set the courts off balance for nine centuries.

Devlin pulled out a chair for his sister. Once she sat, he dragged another chair over and sat beside her. "Had you wanted to quarrel?"

"Not with you, dear." She patted his hand absently as she watched the mortals fighting. "If the Dark Court could feed from mortals' emotions and faeries' emotions . . . that would *change* things, wouldn't it? Imagine if I could make it so."

"They can't. *You* can't," Devlin pointed out. The Dark Court thrived in times of discord, but they were denied access to the throngs of emotional mortals all around them.

"Perhaps." She traced a jagged line down her forearm with one talon-tipped finger. "Or perhaps I just need the right sacrifice." She stretched her arm out, turning it so the blood dripped into his glass. "Blood makes Faerie stronger. *She* forgets, pretends she's not like us."

Devlin wrapped his hand around the glass of wine and

blood now swirling together. "Sorcha is *not* like you, and you"—Devlin lifted his glass in a toast—"are not like her."

War stabbed a passing mortal. "We are all—faeries, mortals, and *other* creatures—alike." She stood and stabbed the mortal a second time. "We fight. We bleed." She looked across the room at someone and smiled. "And some of us will die."

The mortal pressed a hand to his side, but the blood wasn't slowed.

"Stop by for dinner soon, precious one." Bananach leaned over and cupped Devlin's cheek with her bloody hand. She straightened. "Hello, my pretty lamb."

Seth came up to them, glaring at Bananach. "Get out *now*."

Devlin stepped in front of Seth, blocking his access to Bananach. He pointed to the mortal on the floor. "That one is injured."

Seth raised a fist. "Because of her."

"You can help him or argue with War," Devlin said. "You cannot do both."

Seth scowled. "And you won't do either."

"That is not my function." For an unexpected moment, Devlin wondered if the sometimes-mortal-sometimes-fey boy would fight Bananach or save the injured mortal. He hoped that he'd not have to try to wrest Seth from Bananach's grasp tonight.

Is he logical enough to sacrifice one mortal to strike

Bananach or compassionate enough to save the mortal and plan to confront Bananach later?

After a lingering disdainful look at Devlin, Seth lifted the injured mortal. "At least help me get him to the door."

Bananach stood to the side and watched, a bemused smile on her lips. She, undoubtedly, had weighed the possibilities too. The knowledge of Seth's actions would be factored into her next maneuver. The strategy behind maximizing conflict required skill and patience.

Devlin cleared a path so they weren't jostled. It wasn't quite the way he'd hoped the evening would proceed, but his primary goal was met: Seth was uninjured. All things considered, everything was as fine as it could be.

Then he saw *her.*

Seth stepped past Devlin, blocking the sight of everything else for a moment.

"Wait here?" Seth shifted his hold on the injured mortal. "I'm going to get him to the . . ."

But the rest of the words he said were lost on Devlin: the girl laughed, joyous and unfettered. Absently, he nodded and stepped closer to the crowd, closer to her.

Ani.

She had shorter hair: close-cropped in the back so that it framed her face, longer toward the front so the pink-tinted tips brushed the edge of her jawline. Her features were too common to be truly beautiful, yet too faery to be truly common. If he hadn't already known she was a halfling, a look at her overlarge eyes and angular bone structure would be sufficient reason to suspect faery ancestry.

Ani. Here.

Beside her stood her brother, the tattooist who'd bound mortals to faeries in the ill-fated ink exchanges and raised his halfling sisters as if they were his own children.

"Rabbit! Where did you come from?" Ani grinned at him.

"You were to call an hour ago."

"Really?" She tilted her head and widened her eyes beseechingly. "Maybe I forgot."

"Ani." Rabbit glared at his sister. "We talked about this. You need to check in with me when Tish is with you."

"I know." She was completely unapologetic. Her chin lifted; her shoulders squared. In a pack, she'd be an obvious alpha. Even with her older brother, she was trying to challenge the dominance order. "I wanted you to come out with us though, and if I didn't call, I knew you—"

"I ought to drag you out of here," Rabbit growled at her.

She went up on her toes to kiss his chin. "I miss you. Stay and dance?"

Rabbit's expression softened. "One song. I have work yet tonight."

"'Kay." Ani grabbed the hands of her sister, Tish. They shoved another girl toward Rabbit, and then pulled several mortals toward themselves, and they all writhed like fire burned in their skin. Their dancing was joyous and free in a way that Devlin admired.

I want to join her. He realized it with a start. The Hound was Dark Court, mortal, predator, any variety of things he should not find tempting. *Or beautiful.* He did, though. Her freedom and her aggression made her seem like the most beautiful faery he'd ever glimpsed. If only for a moment, Devlin wished he could step into her world. It was a deviant urge: Ani shouldn't hold his attention as she did in that instant. *No one should. It is illogical.*

When the song ended, a mortal girl whispered in Rabbit's ear. He dropped an arm around her shoulders, but before he left, he paused to tell his sisters, "Be good. I mean it."

They both nodded.

"Call if you need me," Rabbit added. Then, he led the mortal into the crowd.

The music resumed, and Tish bumped into Ani's shoulder and said, "Dance, silly."

Ani mock-growled, and they both giggled.

Devlin watched Ani, transfixed as he'd never been before. She shouldn't even be alive. If he'd obeyed his queen, she'd be long dead. But here she was, alive and *vibrant*.

After the first time, he'd never sought her out. He'd seen her in passing, but he'd kept away from her. His only intentional encounter with her had been when he was sent to kill her—and didn't—but as he watched her just then, he wondered if he should correct his oversight.

The request Rae made was to spare Ani, not to let her live for always.

The loophole was there; it had always been there. Ani was the proof of Devlin's deceit, the evidence of his failure, and the most captivating faery he'd ever seen.

Chapter 7

Ani lost herself in the music and the thrashing sea of bodies for hours. Club nights were essential as her hungers grew more intense. When Gabriel had taken her away from her home with Rabbit, her family and court acted like her ability to feed on mortals' emotions was a secret she'd hidden away. It wasn't: it was new. A matching hunger for touch had risen up over the last few months, and she couldn't reliably control both of them. She'd been trying—and failing—since she first noticed them.

"Do you mind if we step out again?" Tish yelled into Ani's ear.

Tish pointed to the edge of the crowd. Glenn was on another break, and as he had for every other break, he'd unerringly sought out Tish. Every time he headed their way, Tish asked, and every time, Ani shook her head. She'd never stand in the way of anything that made her family happy.

Before Tish could reach Glenn's hand, some guy with punk-for-the-night clothes grabbed Tish by the hips.

Ani snarled loud enough that Tish looked alarmed. "Ani!"

Forcing back her temper, Ani turned her gaze to her sister. The guy said something crass and moved on.

"Eyes!" Tish hissed. "Eyes. Now."

"Sorry." Ani closed her eyes, willing away the sulfurous green that she knew Tish suddenly saw there.

"I'm okay, NiNi," Tish assured. She leaned close and suggested, "But you should eat."

Here, in the crowd and surrounded by bodies, Ani could let go of her appetite control a little. She was Dark Court enough to ride the surge of emotions, Hound enough to swallow the sensation of touch, and peculiar enough to do so with mortal and faery both. The Crow's Nest offered her all of it.

Ani opened her once-more brown eyes.

"You okay?" Tish asked. "I can stay with you. Rab's going home now that he knows we're okay, and . . ."

Ani shook her head. "I'm good. Go on."

"If you—"

"Go." Ani shoved her sister gently into Glenn's embrace.

He gave her a questioning look. He might not know what she was or what she needed, but he'd known her long enough to recognize that she was on the verge of trouble.

How do any of the Hounds stand it? Gabriel dealt with his through fighting; Rabbit dealt through tattooing;

and Tish didn't seem to have a skin hunger. Maybe it was easier with just one appetite to suppress. Maybe it was easier with a pack to embrace. *Instead of being alone all the time.*

Ani moved farther into the crowd, hoping for enough of a crush that she would be able to lose herself again.

As she slid through the outstretched arms and gyrating hips, she saw him: a faery stood on the periphery of the crowd, just close enough that she could tell that he was someone altogether new. Solitaries passed through Huntsdale regularly. Having several regents in one place was an anomaly, and faeries were ever intrigued by anomalies.

The faery on the edge of the crowd was oblivious to the appraising looks he was getting, but he would've stood out even if they were at a faery club like the Rath and Ruins. His hair was so pale that it looked white, and Ani suspected that the shimmers of color weren't just the reflection of the club lights but a little bit of his true appearance. He was eye candy. *And he's staring at me.*

She stopped moving and asked, "Are you coming over or just looking?"

No one around her would hear her ask, but the eye candy in question was a faery. He heard her and answered, "I really don't think that's wise."

Ani laughed. "Who cares?"

Like many faeries she knew, he was sculpture-perfect, but instead of being wrought of shadows like those in her court, this faery had a tangled feel to him. *Shadow and radiance.* He didn't look much older than her, until she saw the arrogance in his posture. Then, he reminded her of Irial, of Bananach, of Keenan, of the faeries who walked through courts and crowds confident that they could slaughter everyone in the room. *Like chaos in a glass cage.*

"Come dance." She turned her back then and let herself be swept into the crowd. Hands and emotions were all around her; it was like drowning in euphoria and need.

And he's watching.

She glanced toward the shadows where he stood. He hadn't moved. So she held his gaze while she danced, not for the mortals in the room, not for the feelings that every brush of skin brought to the surface.

"Come dance with me," she whispered.

He stared at her, not even glancing at anyone else, even when they spoke to him or stood in his path. No one else in the room was there for him. *Just me.*

Twenty minutes later, the band took a break, and the floor cleared enough that there was more room to dance.

He was still in the same spot.

She considered going over to him, but she wasn't a pet to be summoned. She was a Hound. He could come to her.

"Hey!" Tish said.

Glenn had an arm protectively around Tish.

"You coming out with us?" Tish couldn't stand still. She might be more mortal than faery, but she had the Hound tendency to be always in motion.

Behind her, Glenn was immobile.

The club music came on to fill the silence while the band was on break.

Ani took her sister's hands, and they danced near Glenn as they always had. It was different now. Before, Glenn had always looked at them like they were about to consume everyone's good sense. Now, he watched Tish like she was his own personal heaven.

"I'm fine here," Ani said as she swung Tish around so that Glenn had her back in his arms. "Go on."

"Do you need my glasses?" Tish reached into the little bag she had slung over her shoulder. Emergency sunglasses had become a necessity since Ani started changing. The moment of green eyes earlier had been too close for Tish.

"Honest, I'm good." Ani kissed her sister on the tip of the nose. "Go"—she caught Glenn's gaze then—"and you take care of her, or else."

Glenn snorted.

Tish stepped between them. She pursed her lips as she looked back at Ani. "*You* be good. Glenn's our friend."

"If she's not treated like she's made of china, if she gets even the teeniest bit hurt"—Ani reached out and caught Tish's hand without looking—"it would be bad. That's all I'm saying. You don't want to meet my relatives."

"I've been watching her back—and yours—for years." Glenn's demeanor changed to something softer. "I'd sooner step in front of a fist or knife or *whatever* than let Tish get hurt. You gotta know that by now."

"Cool." Ani hugged him. "Get off my dance floor then."

Tish hesitated, so Ani grabbed the hand of a guy who was passing. "Dance?"

He nodded, and Ani led him into the center of the remaining crowd. She didn't need to look to know that *he* was still watching—or that he'd heard every word she'd said. The admonition had been for him as much as for Glenn.

Fair warning. Fair chance to flee.

If not for the gnawing ache inside of her, she might wonder why he was staring at her all night. If not for the fact that she had the former king of the Dark Court as her personal knight in shining armor, she might worry a little more. Tonight she wasn't sure she *could* worry. She needed to be lost in the music.

As the band took the stage again, her dance partner moved away, but she didn't follow.

"Come dance," she said again. "I know you're watching. Come out and play."

A few moments later, he came to stand—motionless—on the dance floor.

"About time." She spun so she was chest-to-chest with him and slid her hands up his chest slowly enough that she could feel the muscles under his shirt.

"I thought you were going to make me chase after you." She let her hands slip over his shoulders and around the back of his neck.

He stayed immobile as she did so. "You're a foolish one, aren't you?"

"Nope." She tilted her head so she could stare up at him.

All around, bodies crashed into them. The music was deafening, and if he'd been anything other than faery, she'd have had to yell over the noise.

"I could be anyone." He had his arms around her protectively in the writhing mass. "You're vulnerable here."

A faery she didn't know, a faery who wasn't being torn out of reach, had her in his arms—and the aching hunger inside her lessened. He was a strong faery, stronger perhaps than any she'd met, and bits of his energy were sinking into her skin where they touched. *I could die happy right now . . . or he could.* She tried not to think about the danger she would put him in if she fully gave in to her urges.

"You look dangerous . . . feel like it too," she answered both his question and her own musings.

He moved so they were closer to the edge of the crowd, maneuvering her toward the shadows along the wall. "So tell me: why are you holding on to me?" he asked.

"Because I'm dangerous too," she admitted.

He didn't say anything, but he didn't run either.

She went up onto her tiptoes and pressed her lips to his. A prism of energy flooded over her as he dropped whatever control he'd been using to hold his emotions at bay. *Need. Regret. Awe. Hunger. Confusion.* Ani let it all sink into her skin. She drew his breath and life into her body. She tensed like she was about to race something feral, like this was the only moment between her and starvation.

Despite the energy she took from him, he was steady as he held on to her. He slid an arm around her waist.

Her arms were still around his neck, and her fingers were clutching his hair. Her lips tingled. Her entire body pulsed with the energy she was stealing.

He broke the kiss. "You're . . . what *are* you doing, Ani?"

"Kissing you." She heard her voice as she said it. There wasn't anything mortal in those sounds. She was the Daughter of the Hunt, and he was her quarry.

I shouldn't.

She could hear every heartbeat in the room, feel the waves of sound pounding through the air, taste the breath of time itself escaping.

He stared at her. "This isn't why I came here."

"Is it reason to stay?"

When he didn't reply, she put her hands behind her and clasped them together so she couldn't touch him. "You can stop," she whispered. "When you want . . . you can just stop . . . or . . . not. . . ."

He took one step backward. His emotions were locked up now behind a wall she couldn't breach. Both his touch and his emotions were denied to her.

Ani bit her lip to keep her sob inside. To be so close to the energy that swirled inside him and be stopped felt criminal. She could taste blood, feel it welling up on her bottom lip.

He reached out one finger and took the drop of blood. She felt his breath warm on her face as she stared at him. He kept his hand raised between them.

Too many faeries could track with blood. She could. All Hounds could.

Can he?

She stared at her blood on his fingertip. "It's yours," she said, "for one more kiss."

He could be anyone. What am I doing?

But the wall he'd built vanished, and his emotions crashed down into her. He was excited, afraid, hungry. He leaned closer.

"Step away from her," a voice interrupted. Someone was pulling him out of reach. "Let her go."

"Let *her* go?" The faery Ani had been kissing slammed his walls back into place, denying her access to his emotions, cutting her off from the banquet again.

Ani blinked, trying to focus around the rainbows clouding her vision. Kissing him had made her hungers vanish. It made everything right.

"You need to take a walk, Ani." Her would-be rescuer had her arm in his hand and was stepping backward, propelling her away from the yummy kissable faery.

She focused her attention on the interruption. "*Seth.* What are you doing?"

Seth frowned at her and then directed his words at the faery. "He needs to leave. Now."

The faery watched the two of them with a bemused expression. "As you will."

And he vanished into the crowd.

"You are a pain in the ass, Seth." Ani shoved him. If it

wouldn't end up causing her far more complications than she could afford, she'd give in to the urge to bloody his nose. Instead, she pursued the pale faery across the club. She pushed her way through the crowd.

He paused at the door, and watching her as he did it, he lifted his finger to his lips.

Oh shit.

Ani froze—and he left.

With the taste of my blood.

Chapter 8

Devlin stood shivering in the alley outside the Crow's Nest. Much like his mother-sisters, he required blood, and none but his mother-sisters' blood had ever been truly sustaining.

Until now.

With one taste, he knew: Ani's blood was different. *She* was different.

He'd bled every species of fey there was; he'd bled mortals and halflings. Eternity had given him more than enough time to do so. He hated his need for blood, but he was made, not birthed, and that was the cost. His life wasn't natural, and being made of the twins had brought an unpleasant side effect: without absorbing blood, he would weaken. He took what he could in the violence that was his role in Faerie; it wasn't truly sustaining. Only the combination of the blood of both Order and Discord kept him strong—and getting their blood always had costs and complications.

As if bleeding Ani wouldn't present complications? How did one start that conversation? *Hello, I almost murdered you once, but I noticed that your blood—just a bit here or there—would be really useful.* Devlin shook his head. The shock of the cold rain that had begun while he was in the club helped him feel more alert, but his thoughts still felt muddled.

He tried to focus on the logical details: perhaps sparing Ani was going to change his life in positive ways—instead of the disastrous way he'd expected should his treachery be exposed to the High Queen. Until tonight, he'd thought Ani's was a brief mortal life. Considering the time difference between the mortal and faery worlds, such a span was easy enough to hide. As a mortal, Ani—the living proof of Devlin's disobedience to his queen—would exist for only a blink: Sorcha would not know he'd failed her.

Now, however, Devlin knew that the girl he'd not-killed was only barely mortal and becoming less so by the moment. He could taste it in the single droplet of blood she'd shed. Ani was something new, something unlike any other faery he'd met in all of eternity. He wasn't sure whether to be pleased or alarmed. He couldn't hide her from Sorcha forever, but he could be sustained by whatever irregularity her blood held.

Is she my salvation or damnation?

Seth suddenly stood across from him. Seth wasn't calm as he was within Faerie. Instead he looked ready to lash out at Devlin. "Do you have any idea who that girl was?"

I have all sorts of ideas.

Devlin didn't raise his voice or his hand—although the temptation was very much there. All he said was, "It is not your concern."

"It *is*, actually. Ani belongs to the Dark Court." Seth stepped closer and lowered his voice. "If Niall or Irial saw *you* with her, they would have questions about our queen's intentions and—"

"I know." Devlin's voice revealed his ire then. "Your tone is unappreciated nonetheless."

Seth stopped and took a deep breath.

"Sorry. It's been a long night." He wiped the raindrops from his face and smiled wryly. "Actually, it's been a long *year*. The guy from earlier is doing okay, I think."

Devlin nodded. He had no care over the injured mortal's state. He hadn't stabbed the mortal, hadn't done anything untoward. It mattered to Seth though. *He* was too recently mortal to understand that the deaths of mortals at Bananach's hands were merely a fact of being. Over the centuries to come—if Seth lived—he would grow used to it. War brought death and pain. It was who she was.

For several moments, the only sounds were the strains of music from inside the club and the conversations of mortals outside the building. The rain seemed to be making the edges of the world out of focus.

With practiced attention, Devlin forced himself to focus enough to visually examine Seth. "You are unharmed?"

"Yeah. I'm fine." Seth rolled his shoulders.

"Our queen asks after you," Devlin said. It wasn't the

message Sorcha had explicitly conveyed, but Devlin felt too tired to try to rephrase the truth as he probably should. "She . . . worries."

Seth's expression turned to blatant affection. "Will you tell her I'm fine? I miss her, but I'm fine. Things here are weird. Keenan's"—Seth lowered his voice—"missing."

"His court?" Devlin blinked as another peculiar wave of exhaustion washed over him, as if he'd been doing something strenuous. He stepped backward, bracing himself with a wider stance so as not to sway but not yet leaning on the wall.

"The Summer Court isn't just *his*, but it's . . . not doing as well as it should." Seth scowled. The calm he had within Faerie was absent out here. In the mortal world, Seth was not High Court.

Is that what happens to me? Devlin forced himself not to ponder personal things, forced his attention to political matters. "Are they weakened? The Summer Court?"

"Some, but . . ." Seth's words faded as he looked away. "The court's health is about the health of the regent, you know?"

"And neither the Summer King nor the Summer Queen is happy." Devlin gave in and leaned against the brick wall. *Just for a moment.* He ignored the curious feeling and asked, "And Winter?"

"It's that time of year soon, so Don's doing alright, I guess. Angry. Worried about Keenan, and pretending she's not hurting. I saw her and—"

Devlin slid down the wall a little.

"Whoa. Devlin!" Seth was beside him. "She should know better. Damn it."

"She?"

"Ani." Seth sighed and faded to invisibility as he spoke.

Devlin became invisible to mortals eyes as well. *Weakling*, he chastised himself as he stepped forward, away from the wall. *I am stronger than this. Duty demands it.* He needed to see Seth to safety and perhaps take some rest for himself—but all he wanted in that moment was to find Ani.

"I should go," he said. "See you home and tend t—" He stumbled.

"Come on." Seth helped Devlin to stand and offered himself as a crutch of sorts.

Devlin didn't lean on him, but he was grateful for his presence. The brief fantasy of leaving to find Ani was best not pursued in this state. He had her taste now, so he'd always be able to find her. *I'll find her again, and then I'll . . .* He couldn't keep his thoughts in order.

Devlin and Seth walked in silence for several minutes. A few times, Seth's arm went around Devlin's back to help steady him. It was far kinder than Devlin could understand. One of their first encounters had been Devlin choking Seth to unconsciousness. Such actions didn't inspire protectiveness—despite the number of times Devlin had come to verify Seth's state of being.

When they paused the fourth time, Seth frowned. "Sorcha's going to be upset."

"By what?"

Seth raised his silver-decorated brow. With a wisdom far more advanced than should be possible for his age, the former mortal gave Devlin a chiding look. "When she learns about Ani."

Devlin kept his features unreadable, but his anxiety rose. *Learns what?* Devlin had told no one of his deceit, and Rae spoke to none but him. *Maybe he means the kiss . . . my attention to her when I was to be looking in on Seth.* Devlin gave Seth his most disdainful look. "What I do for recreation would only be a concern if it caused complications for the court. Kissing isn't typically a court concern."

"True. Typically it wouldn't be." Seth directed them through the alley and toward his train-house. Since only the strongest fey could abide exposure to iron and steel, the rail yard was free of faeries, and the earth around the train cars was flourishing. Exotic vines twined around metal sculptures. It was Edenic, albeit in a strangely mechanized setting. At this time of year and in this part of the Earth, there were few ways to have such fecundity, but Seth's girlfriend was the embodiment of Summer.

Devlin nodded toward the greenery. "Your beloved seems to be trying to woo you."

"Don't change the subject." Seth opened the door.

Uncharacteristically, Devlin sank into the odd orange chair in the front portion of the room.

Seth went into his kitchen area, and momentarily, he brought over a mug of steamed liquid. He sat it on the wooden table beside Devlin's seat and said, "Drink it."

"I'm sure I'll be fine in a moment." He'd had both of his mother-sisters' blood of late; he should be at his best. "High Court faeries do not need coddling."

"You're too arrogant for your own good. Drink it." Seth moved a garish green chair back and sat. "Ani sucked down enough energy from you that you'll have a nasty headache and cold flashes if you don't get this in you. With your impending trip, you need to be stronger."

"She . . . drank my energy? She's a halfling, Seth."

"Don't try it on me, Devlin. You aren't stupid. You're weakened by her, and you know it." Seth gestured at Devlin's hand. "You had her blood on your fingertip. Did you taste it?"

"Why would I taste blood?"

"Because of who you are." Seth leaned back and gave Devlin an unreadable look. "Do *any* faeries answer truthfully without trying to dodge questions?"

"You are faery." Devlin drank the silvery liquid in the mug and switched topics. "This isn't usually found in the mortal realm."

Seth shrugged. "Sorcha worries. She'd 'prefer I am healthy,' so I keep it on hand. It's easier than arguing with her."

The laughter that escaped Devlin was unexpected. "I could grow less irritated by you over time."

"You will. We're just not at that point in time yet." Seth stretched, revealing a bruised and cut forearm as he did so.

"I see." Devlin tried to process what Seth was saying, but the words lacked cohesion. "You are injured."

Seth lowered his arm. "I try to hide things from you too, Devlin. You're hers, and as much as I . . . want to trust you, I'm sure you come here only because she sends you. If you know anything, I suspect she will as well, and I'm not really into her knowing everything."

"Indeed." Devlin gave Seth an assessing look. He was a child, a creature with not quite two decades of living, but he had truth in his words. "The question is how *you* know things."

"I'm not the one who is meant to answer that." Seth grinned then. "Huh. I suppose I've become faery enough to dodge questions."

"Our queen worries, and"—Devlin weighed his words carefully as he emptied the cup of elixir—"I may need to be away from your side to deal with business matters for some time."

"I know." Seth stood and took the cup. "While you try to convince yourself you *don't* need to go deal with that 'business,' witnesses will see you with me. They'll carry word home to Sorcha. It'll calm her, and when you're gone, I'll be fine. The Dark Court will protect me, and I'm far stronger than our queen will admit to you. In time, you'll know that . . . and I think you'll forgive me . . . or perhaps not. I can't see which."

Devlin watched Seth with a hazy awareness that the things the newly made faery was saying were true, but that there was no logical way that he could know so much. *Unless he is a seer. Did Sorcha use the Eolas' energy when she remade Seth as a faery?* Creating a seer loyal only to her would be a logical move on Sorcha's part.

I can ask him truths.

"You see the future."

"Some of it," Seth admitted. "I know where you go next."

Sleepily, Devlin asked, "And will I be safe?"

For a moment, Seth stared at him. Then, still silent, he turned and walked out of the room. Devlin thought to follow, but movement required more energy than he had. He closed his eyes.

When Seth returned, his footsteps the only sound, Devlin forced himself to open his eyes again. He watched as Seth piled a blanket and pillows at the foot of the too-short sofa. Then Seth turned off the lights and threw the bolt on the door. Every noise echoed loudly, and Devlin realized that he was no use as a protector that night.

"What else's in the draught?" His words were slurring. "Not jus' elixir, Seth."

"Something to help you rest and recover. I don't need guarding, Devlin. Once you realize why, you'll want to talk to Sorcha. . . . She didn't tell me your secrets, and I won't tell you hers."

Devlin closed his eyes again. Killing for his queen was far easier than dealing with seers. *She never told me what she'd used to remake Seth. More secrets. It had to be the Eolas.* Words swirled in Devlin's mind as he started to drift to sleep.

But Seth was still there. His words broke the silence. "You won't be safe, but I think you made the right choice."

"Haven't chosen . . . anything." Devlin tried to open his eyes, but they weighed too much. *Seers with sleeping draughts. All sorts of unacceptable.* "Thinking still. Logical paths . . . and such."

Seth's laughter wasn't aloud, but it was threaded in his voice as he said, "Of course. . . . Sleep now, brother."

Chapter 9

Not long before dawn, Ani stood on the stoop of an aging house. She pressed her palms against the dark wood of the front door, taking comfort in the simple pleasure of being welcome in Irial's home. It was still his, even though he now shared it with the new Dark King.

She extended her left hand to the yawning mouth of a brass gargoyle knocker. Lovely sharp pain drew a sigh from her as the gargoyle closed its mouth over her fingers. The bite was over before she saw it happen, but she was found to be acceptable. Only those Irial had permitted access were allowed to disturb him. She was on the list—even at this hour.

"Are you injured? Is someone else?" Irial looked like he was dressed for someone other than her: he was clad in deep-blue silk pajama pants and nothing else.

"No. I'm bored. Restless. You know, the usual." She sounded sulkier than she'd intended, and he smiled.

"Poor pup." He stepped back to allow her into his home.

Just inside the door, she slipped off her shoes. The foyer was slick under her feet and colder than seemed possible; walking over it was just this side of painful. She shivered at the sensation.

The door closed of its own volition, and Ani paused to let Irial precede her into the house. He was particular about where he met visitors, so it was better to follow than try to lead. Of course, following had the added benefit of allowing her to watch him.

"Are you . . . I mean, is he . . ." She wasn't sure of the right words when it came to Irial and Niall; no one in the court was. She settled on, "Is the king here?"

Irial glanced over his shoulder at her. "Niall is . . . out."

Ani could taste the sadness in her former king. He kept himself in control. The shadows shifted around him, stretching and creeping over walls, but his spectral abyss-guardians didn't appear.

"He's a fool." She didn't look away, despite the play of shadows around him.

"No," Irial murmured. "He's more forgiving than I will ever deserve."

The room they entered was the same one where he'd sat and held her when she tried not to cry after the pain of the thistle-fey's embrace. Irial had comforted her then. After the tests, he always stayed with her until she didn't want to scream or weep anymore.

Tonight, Irial kept his distance from her, moving over to an elegant mahogany bookshelf overfilled with tattered paperbacks. He ran a hand absently over the well-read books as he lowered the wall around his emotions, exposing his sorrow and longing, but his back was to her, hiding his expression.

She prowled the room. The rainbow pleasure of earlier had faded, but her nerves were too jangled to stay still. She paused beside him.

He turned.

Tentatively, Ani slid her arms around his neck. "Gabriel knows you help me. We could help each other."

He didn't move, so she leaned closer. It wasn't the first time she'd kissed him, but it was the first time she did so with the intention of *taking* more. Not even Gabriel would be fool enough to tell Irial that he couldn't have her if the former Dark King was willing.

For a few too-brief moments, he kissed her back, but when she pressed her hips tighter against him, Irial took her by the shoulders and set her away from him. His look of disapproval was one that still sent much of the Dark Court scrambling and cowering. "That won't happen, Ani."

"Maybe it would if you'd let me try. . . ." She could still taste dark chocolate on her lips, peat smoke in the air all around them. Irial tasted like sin, and she wanted more of it.

"No." Irial sat on the sofa and patted the middle cushion.

She flopped down on the opposite end of the sofa and stretched her legs out so her feet were in his lap.

He gave her a half-amused look, but he didn't tell her to move.

"So you're going to be celibate or something?" She leaned back, letting the sofa envelope her, and flung an arm behind her so that it dangled over the arm of the sofa.

"No, but I'm not taking Gabriel's daughter to my bed." He lifted one of her feet and idly rubbed circles on the bottom of it with his thumbs.

Ani thought she could melt at the simple touch. "*No one* will take Gabriel's daughter to bed, and I'm trying to follow the rules." She ticked them off on her fingers. "No taking both emotion and touch from mortals. Or faeries. No sex until I'm sure I won't kill them. No fighting with Hounds so they don't kill me. No. No. No. What am I supposed to do?"

"Are you asking for advice?" He looked gentle now, revealing the side he never shared in public, the side he showed her when she was ill or weak. This was why Leslie had loved him, why Niall loved him still. Irial would do anything for his loved ones, especially now that he didn't carry the responsibility of caring for the Dark Court. That kind of love was a once-in-a-lifetime thing; *nothing* should stand in the way when someone loved that intensely. Ani understood that, even if both her mortal friend, Leslie, and the new king were too daft to see it.

Ani couldn't understand anyone refusing him: he was perfect. *Okay, not* perfect, *but awfully close. That whole willingness-to-experiment-on-me thing isn't fun, but mostly perfect.* She'd had the worst crush on him growing up. *Maybe still do a little bit.* He had been the Dark King, the fiend that the nightmares feared. In her court, only Gabriel and Bananach were as terrifying.

"If advice is all you're passing out, I'll take it." Ani pulled her foot out of his hands and extended the other.

He laughed but commenced rubbing.

"I'm suffering here." She tilted her chin, widened her eyes, and let her foul mood show.

"Pouting doesn't work on me, pup." He pressed his thumbs harder into the bottom of her foot.

"It used to."

"No, it just made you happy to think you could play me." He ran a fingertip over her foot, taunting her with softness.

She pulled away and hugged her knees to her chest. "It's ridiculous, Iri."

"Gabe's just worried about keeping you safe." Irial reached out and squeezed her ankle. "The Vilas took the last batch of blood to a lab that specializes in nonmortal biology. If we can identify what you are, we can isolate your peculiar traits and—"

"It's been months of tests," Ani interrupted. "Just take some of it and do another ink exchange. I'm mortal enough to be bound to someone, and I am fey enough to feed. Instead of court tears, try my blood as the ink base. See if it works and—"

"No." Irial squeezed her ankle tight enough that it was painful. "Niall prefers that we don't do that. There is discord, and he can feed the court. If all else fails, my presence in his court and his anger at the Summer King and his frustration with Bananach upset him enough that he has emotion to spare. It isn't a forever solution, but it buys us time."

Ani rolled her eyes. Having an emotional king was proving useful to the faeries that needed to feed on emotions. That and the upheaval between the seasonal courts left the Dark Court nourished enough to survive—but not to thrive. It didn't help Ani's other need though. "I need more, Iri."

"Can you have unsupervised contact without weakening them? Without killing them? Without exposing what you are? Without endangering yourself?" Irial's gentleness was vanishing. "Tell me that you have the self-control to do so."

She couldn't lie, but she could avoid the question. "I don't hurt you, and no one is here to stop me."

He gave her a wry grin. "Sweetheart, I'm a Gancanagh again, *and* I have enough self-control to keep my emotions locked away from you when I need to. A mortal or a faery—even a strong faery—who lets you have both . . ."

Ani thought of him, the faery she'd met. It was just a brief flittering thought, but Irial caught her expression.

"What did you do?"

"Nothing really. He was fine . . . I mean, I think he was." Ani licked her lips unconsciously and then realized what she'd done. She looked away.

"Who?"

"I don't know. He wasn't a weak faery though . . . and he seemed fine when he walked away." Ani looked over at her former king. "He *did* walk away. No one saw, except Seth . . . and he wouldn't expose me. I don't think. Right? He wouldn't?"

"Tell me."

So she did. She told him every single detail about the faery she'd kissed at the Crow's Nest, and then she added, "He vanished afterward."

Irial said nothing for several moments. "He took your blood."

"Yeah, I know, but I was half out-of-it. If he's a problem, if he finds me and is a threat, I could . . . you know . . . *not stop.*" She pushed away the guilt at the thought of willingly killing the faery she'd met. She was Dark Court, and in the Dark Court, survival sometimes meant doing things that were unpalatable.

"If it's unavoidable, you *will* do exactly that." Irial's words weren't backed by kingship, but they both knew she'd obey him.

She folded her arms over her chest. "Hey, maybe I can be the permanent court punishment or a Trojan horse sent to the Summer Court to hurt the Summer King. 'You'll have to go kiss Ani, bad little faeries.' Faeries, mortals, half-lings . . . If I sat in Niall's place, I could feed the court. They could gorge. Would Niall hand the throne over if he knew? Or would he kill me so my monstrousness is—"

"Ani . . . stop. We'll sort it out. I know you don't *want*

to kill anyone like that." Irial paused, weighing the words even as his emotions drifted into sadness. "For some faeries, the tangling of affection and death is too *personal.* It's not a flaw. Niall isn't . . . he prefers . . ." The words started and stopped as the no-lying injunction interfered. Irial sighed. "Niall hasn't always been comfortable with the consequences of being a Gancanagh. Our touch addicts mortals; yours drains them. The cost for them is ultimately the same."

"And you?" Ani had wondered, more than a few times. Gancanaghs left mortals starving for affection, drove them mad with wanting and never being sated. Being Dark King made Irial safe for centuries, but now Niall was safe and Irial was once more addictive to mortals. *And had been before.* She held Irial's gaze and asked, "Did you . . . were you *okay* with the ones you killed?"

"Sometimes."

She swallowed against her dry mouth. "Oh."

"For most of my life, I've led the court of nightmares, Ani. I've damaged the two people I've loved." He let his emotions wash over her—sorrow, anger, but not regret. "I bound the Summer King, who was a *friend's son.* I've ordered more deaths than I could count, done things too perverse to speak of."

"Do you regret any of it?" she whispered.

"No." Irial paused at a sound. Heavy footsteps crossed the floor, stopped outside the door, but then turned away. "I made the best decisions I could. I took care of my court. I still do. Sometimes that means killing people. My court—and now my *king*—come first."

"I would do whatever my king ordered," she assured him. "I'd rather not kill with *this* though. Give me a fair fight and—"

"I know." Irial pulled her into his embrace, holding her carefully. "He wouldn't like using your hunger as a weapon any more than you would."

"You would. You still do the things Niall wouldn't want to."

Irial didn't answer, but it wasn't really a question. "We'll figure it out. You'll be strong *and* safe, Ani."

She lifted her head and looked up at him. "Can I crash here for a few?"

"Keep your clothes on, and you're welcome to stay."

CHAPTER 10

Ani felt like she'd just drifted off when she woke to snarls.

"Are you completely without any sense?" Niall stood above her, scowling. On either side of him, abyss-guardians swayed and patted him consolingly.

She blinked up at him, trying to understand why the Dark King was angry with her, but before she could answer, someone else did.

"What difference does it make to you?" Irial sounded nonplussed. His arm stayed around her, keeping her still as he spoke.

The cover that someone had tucked around them was pulled all the way up to her neck, and she was nestled against Irial's bare chest.

"She's Gabriel's daughter. She's half-mortal . . . and you—" Niall reached down as if to pull her out of Irial's embrace.

"Don't." Irial's voice wasn't the agreeable sound of a subject before his king.

Ani sighed. A bit of violence would be a perfect next step in an already pleasant morning.

If only . . .

"You're not the king anymore, Irial. Do you want to challenge me?"

There was laughter in Irial's voice when he answered, "Don't be foolish."

"You're a Gancanagh again." Niall sounded weary. "I don't know if her mortal side is dominant enough to make you addictive to her."

"Ani is barely mortal. Look at her. The only thing mortal about her is her strength . . . and with time and a little training, who knows?" Irial sounded irritated, but Ani couldn't tell if it was real. He'd locked his emotions down now that Niall was in the room.

"Are you going to tell Gabriel that?" Niall's voice dropped even lower, not that anyone in the house would spill the Dark King's secrets, but he was cautious. "Because I'm not going to tell him that you decided she was fey enough to fu—to *sleep* with."

Ani sighed again. Niall was actually kind of sexy now that he was furious instead of sulking. Shadows extended from him like the whispered suggestion of wings, and the lack of light made the lengthy scar on his face look menacing.

"He's tasty when he's like this," she whispered.

"Hop up, sweetheart." Irial didn't laugh, but it was just there under the edge of his voice.

"I'm comfortable and"—she glanced at the clock and then at her king—"who gets up at this hour? I just got to sleep."

"You can sleep in my room for a few more hours," Irial said.

Niall held out a hand; even in his anger, he was a gentleman.

Reluctantly, she took Niall's hand and stood up—thereby revealing just how clothed she was. At the confused look on her king's face, she leaned in and whispered, "Trust me: I tried, but he shot me down."

She glanced back at Irial, who was still stretched out on the sofa, topless and languid. If she hadn't been there, she'd think he'd truly had a night of indulgence from the look of him.

Niall followed her gaze, but he didn't soften at the sight. "I'm not in the mood to play games, Irial."

"Go upstairs, Ani." Irial swung his feet to the floor. He didn't glance her way. His attention was all for the Dark King now. "Tell me what you think I should've done differently, Niall. I spent the night talking and giving her a safe place to rest. I gave her the nourishment she can't find elsewhere without compromising her already absent virtue."

The Dark King didn't respond.

Several moments passed in a silent standoff. Ani crossed the room and slid open one of the ornately carved double doors that led to the most private part of the Dark King's home.

Behind her, Irial broke the silence. "What did you want to discuss? I heard you at the door last night."

He sounded perfectly calm. He might be half-lost over his feelings, but he didn't let that show. Both Niall and Irial were cloaking their emotions very efficiently.

Ani felt a curious mix of sadness that Irial felt the need to hide his feelings and pleasure that he'd trusted her enough to let her see them last night. If Niall was paying attention, he'd realize that Irial's gift of his court and his ongoing advice was a love sonnet.

The leather sofa creaked as Niall sat down. "I hate you sometimes."

As Ani left the room, she heard Irial ask, "And the rest of the time?"

She didn't stay to hear that answer. Sleep was more important than knowing secrets that weren't her concern. It was too early for anything other than crawling into bed.

Ani had only just drifted off to sleep when she found herself sitting in a cave. "What here doesn't belong? Stalactites, stalagmites, straw and organ formations, girl in *ball* dress? Hmmm."

Rae smiled. "Hello, Ani."

"Not in the mood for this." Ani walked out of the cave, away from the dark-haired girl she'd dreamed of for most of her life. "Dreaming you, *naming* you, a freaking figment of my imagination . . . it's a sign of insanity or something."

"You're certainly an odd one." Rae had followed her. "You're not crazy, though. Maybe I'm as real as you."

Ani glared at her, but didn't reply. There were times when Ani almost liked dreaming about her pretend friend, but this morning wasn't one of them. She was on edge, feeling a little worried, and just not in the mood for whatever nonsense she would think with a Rae Dream. Somewhere over the years, she'd decided that her Rae Dreams meant questioning herself or thinking about things in different ways than typically made sense. The first Rae Dream was when Jillian died, and since then, when Ani was out of sorts, she'd almost always dreamed about Rae.

"Poor thing," Rae whispered. "Are the restrictions too much? Can you talk to Gabr—"

"No. *Yes*, but that's not the point." Ani crossed her arms over her chest. "I met someone. He was . . . different."

Since it was a dream, Ani imagined him. Instantly, he appeared before her, as solid in appearance as her imagined confidante—but not wearing bizarre garb like Rae did.

Rae gasped. "Oh."

"I need to stay away from him." Ani looked away from the image. "I don't want to hurt him, Rae, and he has my blood. If he finds me, Irial will . . ." Even in a dream, the words weren't ones Ani wanted to say.

Rae took Ani's hands and held them tightly. "Trust yourself, Ani."

The world around them vanished, and Ani was standing in a white void with only Rae in front of her.

"Call your wolves, Ani." Rae's voice echoed in the white expanse.

For a moment, Ani couldn't respond. *My wolves?*

"Look for them, Ani," Rae insisted. "Why do you dream of wolves?"

The wolves appeared, growling.

"Now, let them in, Ani. They *are* a part of you."

"No. I'm the daughter of the Dark Court, so I dream of the Hunt." Ani watched the wolves solidify all around her. "They are dreams. I dream of the Hunt . . . but I don't belong there. I don't belong anywhere."

"You do belong. This is the *New* Hunt, Ani." Rae stayed away from the wolves. "Now that you've seen him again, everything will change."

One by one, the wolves dove into Ani's chest. They disappeared into her body as they had so many times before. It was an odd sensation, the fur and muscle entering her dream self.

"What are you, Rae?" Ani felt herself growling, felt the wolves inside of her snarling.

The wolves matter. Not Rae.

She pushed away the confusion of Rae's words and let the sensation of wolves overwhelm her. They wanted her in their pack. She belonged.

If only I could take them to the waking world . . .

CHAPTER 11

Rae returned to Faerie, to the cave that was her home. Unfortunately, she wasn't alone: the Eolas, the keepers of knowledge, were waiting. Rae shuddered. The Eolas had the ability to assure both endings and beginnings, to tie or to sever connections.

The three women glared at her. Each woman cycled through youth, adulthood, and seniority, as well as through species. On the left, a gray-skinned woman stood with her arms folded over her chest; in the middle, a transparent girl cocked her head assessingly; and on the right, a small leafy creature watched with no discernible expression.

"Do not interfere again—"

"—based on what you know—"

"—of what they are." They each spoke a part of the sentence.

Rae squared her shoulders to hide the shakes that threatened her.

They moved closer in tandem, as if they were parts of one body. "No one knows their own future."

"Not even him."

"Especially not him."

They all stepped back. Two retreated farther, so the translucent one stood in the forward point of their triangle. "We allowed *you* to know. That was more than fair exchange."

"It's *not*." Rae fisted her hands.

"Your knowing saved the Hound's life, and without her, he cannot become what he is to be." The leafy one rustled with each word. "If you speak what you know, you will die, and he will fail."

And they were gone again.

And I am not dead. For that, Rae was grateful.

The first time she'd met them had been after a day of experimenting. She and Devlin had not yet figured out the limits of possession and had spent the day in the cave. He was unconscious, and Rae—still inside him—saw a vision of a girl, Ani, whom he would be ordered to kill. Almost invisible threads wove Ani and Devlin's lives together. In a disquieting moment, while Devlin was asleep and Rae was awake, she'd seen the cave wall vanish.

Three creatures stood in the cave.

"He's not to know such things."

As one of them extended her hand, the other two matched the movement. Thread spindled out from Devlin's body, from the body that Rae was currently animating. It didn't hurt, not truly, but it felt curious. In the center of her, she could feel the tug as the fibrous strands of the vision were guided out of flesh and into a seemingly bottomless basket.

"Stop," she said.

They did. The fibers stretched between the basket and the body, suspended in the air.

"You are—"

"—not—"

"—him." They each spoke part of the words, but the voice from each tongue was the same.

Rae didn't answer. She reached a hand to the thread, feeling the truth in it, seeing the possibilities that Devlin hadn't.

"That's his future," she whispered. "The Hound . . . he is to"—she looked at them—"kill. Does the High Queen know? When she orders the death . . ."

"He cannot know that you know," one said.

The three exchanged a look. In perfect synchronicity, they nodded.

"You must never tell him—"

"—or her—"

"—what you know."

Rae wasn't sure what to say. These were the first creatures other than Devlin that she'd seen in Faerie—and they were nothing like him.

"Without you, he will fail—"

"—and if you tell either of them—"

"—you will die." The three women smiled, and it was not a comforting smile.

"Silence or death?"

"His success or his loss?"

"Your cooperation or not?"

So Rae had made her choice. When Devlin woke, she'd stayed silent. Knowing his future was a gift and a burden.

Years later, she begged him to spare Ani. She'd threatened to return to her mortal body. She'd threatened to expose herself—and him—to Sorcha.

"You are hiding something from me." Devlin faced her in the cave. "The Hound isn't anyone to you."

"She is," Rae insisted. "I ask one thing. You promised me years ago that I could have three wishes. I asked to be allowed to share your flesh; I asked to be kept safe. This is the last I will ask of you."

"You would ask me to disobey my queen? If she were to ever know . . ." Devlin crouched at Rae's feet. "Don't ask this of me, Rae."

Rae stretched out her hands, laying them atop his as if she could truly touch him. "She matters more than I can tell you. I need you to do this one last thing."

"Don't ask me to be foresworn. My honor. My vows . . . Don't ask this."

"You promised me." Rae felt tears slip down her cheeks. As insubstantial as she was, the tears vanished into air as they slid off her face. "Please, Devlin. This is my last wish."

"I cannot keep my vow to you and to my queen." He stood and looked down at her. "Don't ask me to choose."

She hated herself for doing the very thing that his sisters had done to him, but she lifted her gaze and said, "I am asking you to choose."

After he left, they hadn't spoken for months. He didn't come to her, didn't let her possess him. In time, he'd returned, but they'd never spoken of it without discord. She hated the secrecy, hated the Eolas for creating the conflict, and hated herself for not knowing a solution.

Without him, she would be alone in Faerie, ethereal without respite, never to have physical sensation again. She'd considered the possibility. It was impractical to ignore it.

Now the future that the High Queen had tried to stop was upon them, and Rae had to help assure that it came to pass as it was meant to be.

Without violating the Eolas' restriction.

With a fear she couldn't repress, Rae closed her eyes and let herself drift toward Devlin. She'd never told him she could visit dreams in the mortal world. Aside from Ani's dreams, she hadn't done so, but she could find Devlin anywhere. Following his threads was how she'd found Ani that first time: his emotions had cried out at the thought of killing Ani, at the choice Rae had foisted upon him. Without meaning to, Rae had gone to him, racing over some whisper-thin trail she hadn't known existed, but had been too afraid to slip into his mind. *His rejection would be only slightly less awful than his death. Either would mean losing him.*

But she couldn't sit and do nothing. She wasn't powerless in dreams. There she had voice and strength—so she slipped into the dream he was having far away from her in the mortal world.

"Rae? What are you doing?" Devlin watched Rae walk into his dream calmly—as if nothing were amiss. "Are you mad? You can't be here."

Instead of being cowed by his words, she smiled reassuringly. "It's not like I've never stepped into your dreams before."

"In *Faerie*. Not here." He took her hands in his. "Are you in danger?"

He studied Rae, but no signs of distress were obvious. In truth, she looked as lovely as she did in her true mortal form. Oddly, though, she was wearing the plain dress her mortal body wore. Her hair was as long as it was in reality, tightly bound in the long braid he'd woven it into.

"I'm fine."

"What are you doing?" He didn't let go of her hands. "What if dreamwalking here is fatal? What if being *here* means you return to your body?"

She paused. "I needed to see you."

"Rae . . ." He took one step back and caught her gaze. "Is that it? Is your body failing? Did you feel it? Some sickness? I can go to it—"

"No. I just needed to talk to you." She looked wistful and lost for a moment. Hesitantly, she asked, "Can I see it? My body?"

Devlin re-created the cave where she'd fallen asleep so long ago. Behind her, a glass and silver coffin appeared. It took no concentration to fashion the details with precision: he'd made it himself. Every mortal year he opened it and checked on her body, which remained in a state of stasis since she'd stepped out of it. She'd lived in Faerie for over a mortal century, and as a spectral being within Faerie, she seemed able to live without aging. Her body, without her dream self inside of it, did not age, but if she returned to her body, all of the years she'd lived would become *real*, and her body would age—and die.

"I look the same," she murmured, "but the cave has changed a bit."

"I added some stabilizing beams. It was logical." Devlin didn't look behind him. He visited the real thing often enough that seeing the image of her body encased in glass was unnecessary. "I think the dress is still looking fine."

"It will fall apart too. They all do." Tears glistened on her charcoal-dark lashes. "Maybe I should finally change it."

"If you prefer." He'd suggested as much for years, but Rae had always insisted on being re-dressed in replicas of the dress she'd worn when she'd lain down in the cave that day. He thought it an odd insistence, but Devlin didn't understand the mortal mind.

He had carried out her requests, refastening her into newer versions of the exact same dress when the old one fell to pieces, decaying like her body did not. They lasted longer since he'd picked her up from the damp cave floor and encased her frozen body in the glass box. Even though Rae and therefore her dresses were protected from the damp and the vermin in the cave, the material still fell apart over time, albeit slower.

Rae slipped her hands from his. "I have been visiting the mortal world for . . . what I think is fourteen mortal years." She paused and looked up at him. "I visit Ani."

He was suddenly grateful that this was a dream. In the waking world, he'd never allow himself the luxury of the extreme emotions that overtook his logical mind. Terror and envy and betrayal filled him.

A chair appeared behind him as he started to stumble. He sank into it. "You walk in the Hound's dreams? Why, Rae? How could you . . . I don't believe . . . *why*?"

Rae had removed the cave from his dreamscape and replaced it with a snowy field. "I want you happy. I want

you to have everything you need. I want to *tell you things* I . . . cannot."

"Rae?"

"I want to tell you so much," Rae whispered as she sank to the snowy ground that stretched as far as he could see and peered up at him. Tears rolled over her cheeks. "You must keep her safe, Devlin, from those who want to hurt you both."

Devlin brushed her hair back from her face. "Rae—"

Rae clutched his wrist in her cold hand. "Protect her, but be careful of yourself. Do you hear m—"

Her words stopped as Devlin startled awake. He was on the too-short sofa in the train, and something pressed on his throat. He felt like he was choking. He opened his eyes to see Seth's serpent. The reptile's attentive presence was disconcerting.

Devlin muttered, "Begone."

It watched him through unreadable eyes for another several heartbeats and then slithered to the floor.

He couldn't recall the last time he'd been drugged, and while the medicinal draught had rejuvenated him, it had apparently led him to have ridiculous dreams.

Devlin stood and took a clean shirt and jeans from the stack of clothes on the chair where Seth had obviously left them. *I'm here too often if he has extras of my clothes on hand.* He was the assassin of the High Court. For all of eternity, Faerie had feared him, yet a recently-made-fey creature had drugged him and apparently looked into his future.

A faery Sorcha hadn't told me was a seer.

Devlin hadn't ever responded well to surprises.

The door opened, and the seer in question stepped into the room. He dropped a threadbare satchel onto the kitchen table. "Good morning, brother."

"Stop calling me 'brother' and"—Devlin pointed at the coiled boa—"put that back in its cage. I dislike it crawling over me."

"Boomer likes you." Seth scooped the snake up into his arms and carried it to the terrarium. He glanced at Devlin assessingly. "You're looking much better. A few more days to recover before you leave would—"

"Cease." Devlin dropped the clothes back onto the chair and walked over to Seth. "I'm here to look after you."

"No, you're not. You were, but your purpose has changed." Seth closed Boomer's terrarium.

"You will not leave again," Devlin snarled. The urge to wrap his hand around Seth's throat was pressing, but violence was illogical at that point. *I am High Court.* He shoved those temptations back into the recesses of his mind.

Seth smiled placidly and walked over to the clothes. Without any visible indication that there was ill will between them, he set aside the ones on top and carried the rest to the table. "There's hot water by now."

"You will not leave the house while I bathe."

"Correct." Seth opened the satchel he had dropped on the table in his tiny kitchen and shoved the clothes into the

bag. "I went out for a few supplies while you were sleeping. They're in here too."

"Supplies?"

"Your trip. You'll be leaving sooner than I expected. Things change." Seth turned away, but not before Devlin saw the flash of worry on his face.

Chapter 12

Ani pushed the covers off and stretched. She was even less rested than when she'd arrived at Irial's. The house was silent as she went downstairs. At the door to the parlor, she paused. Inside, she heard the low murmur of voices. She felt the tangled threads of longing and disgust—and left.

She stood on the top step, with the gargoyle knocker sleeping behind her, and faltered. A Ly Erg was standing in the street.

"Where do you go?" he asked.

"Not with you." Shivering despite the midday sun, Ani turned the opposite direction from the Ly Erg.

The red-palmed faeries worked to support whatever machinations Bananach devised—to the point of regularly threatening mutiny in the Dark Court. It was inevitable: they were warriors, and any excuse to create true war pleased them. *Not the faeries for me.* Even if she had her doubts about the new Dark King, Ani had too much loyalty to Irial to support plots against the king he'd chosen for their court.

She went walking down the first shadowed alley; her court typically waited in such places. Instead of the faeries she found reassuring, another Ly Erg stood watching her. She turned down another and yet another alley until she was in what many deemed the least attractive part of the city. Oil and chemicals rolled through the puddles of brown water that collected in the dips and holes in the asphalt. The world was reflected back to her there—a bit less bright, a touch less sharply defined. To Ani, it was beautiful. Like her own court, the dark water could seem to make things ugly if a person didn't look closely, but she'd been born out of those shadows: she saw the beauty where some saw only grime.

Of course, not everything wrought of darkness was lovely, any more than everything in the light was. *That* truth was frighteningly clear as Bananach appeared. She stood in front of Ani like she'd stepped into existence, darkness given form in between an inhalation and a scream. The Ly Ergs had steered Ani toward her.

"Girl. Gabriel's child." The raven-faery tilted her head expectantly. "I require you. Come."

One of the Ly Ergs from earlier was standing behind Bananach.

Ani swallowed a cry of fear. Few faeries frightened her, but the raven-haired warrior did. Talons and beak, ashes and blood, Bananach unsettled the Dark King himself. The growing unease and mistrust between the faery courts had strengthened her enough that she could stand against even the strongest faeries.

"Lady War directs you to follow." The Ly Erg gestured. "Do you resist?"

The hopeful look on his face made clear to Ani that resisting wasn't likely to be a successful option. "No."

"Good pup," Bananach said.

Neither the raven-faery nor the Ly Erg spoke another word as they walked toward a building that looked as if it hadn't been inhabited during Ani's lifetime. The windows were painted black with iron fencing stretched over them like hurricane shutters. They weren't but a dozen blocks from Niall's house. *Would she kill me on his step?* The answer to that was, like all things with Bananach, impossible for Ani to fathom. War was both capricious and bold by nature.

Bananach pried back the metal and gestured Ani inside.

Ani's heart thundered so that she could feel it under her skin. What she couldn't feel was any emotion from Bananach. *That's no good.* Before she would cross the threshold, Ani asked, "Am I guest or prisoner?"

"Maybe." Bananach gave Ani an inscrutable look and motioned toward the window. "Go now before my soldiers' security is compromised."

The Ly Erg turned away, presumably to return to his post, and Ani crawled through the window and into a room that looked like it belonged in a medieval warlord's castle.

Swords and other sharp-edged weapons were being forged; others were being repaired. Yet as soon as Ani had started to process the odd anachronism of the inhabitants' activities, she caught sight of the curious contrast on the facing side of the room. Computer monitors and work stations sat on vast wooden tables. Ani stared at them.

"You are not part of the Hunt. You are not truly part of their court." Bananach's dark eyes were familiar enough to seem comforting even as her words were insulting.

"I am." Ani tilted her chin up. "Our king—"

"Your king. Not mine. I want no king."

"You made an oath," Ani whispered.

"I did. It's why Niall hasn't died at my hand. Why Irial has lived so long." Bananach looked beyond Ani to stare into emptiness. "Will *he* come for you, Gabriel's Daughter? Would he save you from my talons?"

Ani wasn't sure which "he" Bananach meant. *Gabriel? Niall? Irial? Some other "he"?* With Bananach, clarity was elusive.

Bananach was beside her then, her lips against Ani's ear. "Your father won't approve. You mustn't tell him. You mustn't tell them anything."

"Tell him I . . . I don't even know what you mean." Ani tried to keep her tone respectful and even, but following the raven-faery's comments was impossible.

"That's a good answer, Gabriel's Girl. You tell them that when they ask. Pretend ignorance. I'll speak for you." Bananach nodded once, as if to affirm something.

"Women's secrets. You give me what I want, and I will give you much."

"What *do* you want?" She was sure she was respectful now. Rabbit had taught her the importance of the right words and phrases, the right tones and gestures, all of the right ways to speak to the mad or the dangerous. Bananach was both mad and dangerous.

She cackled and tilted her head again. "I require your strength and your blood, little Hound."

"Would I be alive at the end?"

"Perhaps." Bananach crouched before her and gazed up at her. "I cannot see that clearly yet."

"Oh." Ani looked around for an exit. Fighting wasn't an option, not against Bananach. Ani could *run* though, not like the fastest Hounds, but faster than most faeries.

Faster than her?

Bananach petted Ani's arm like she was a stray dog. "There's something special inside you, and I need it. I'm offering you the chance to keep breathing while I take it."

"I—"

"First, you will kill Seth . . . and Niall. Perhaps Niall first. You aren't bound by fealty as I am. They won't suspect you." Bananach reached up and stroked Ani's face. "You will do this. Then you will come to me and give me your blood."

Ani shuddered. The sliver of mortality she carried wasn't just a limitation on her strength: despite her best efforts, it also meant she was less cruel than her court. Considering the murder of those she knew felt wrong. She forced herself not to flinch and asked, "Or?"

Bananach crowed. "No 'or.' There aren't choices, child. Disobeying me would be very . . . foolish. I will come for you."

The thoughts in Ani's mind, the threat to those she loved if Bananach came after Ani . . . it was more than Ani could process.

"You were born for this. If he'd killed you, it would be different, but he didn't, did he?" Bananach stood and stepped back. "He wants me to win. That's why he let you live. For me."

"If *who* killed me?"

"I am done with speech. Run along and do as I bid, or I will be displeased." Bananach turned away and left Ani sitting in the midst of forges and computers. The raven-faery wasn't even looking, so—half expecting resistance—Ani ran. She threw herself across the room with a speed she'd rarely found. In that instant, she was every bit the daughter of Hounds, every breath a Hound herself.

No mortality slowed her, and no one stopped her.

Chapter 13

Devlin stood at the mouth of the alley as the Hound left. With her blood as his guide, he'd followed her trail to Irial and Niall's house, and then to War's den. *What were you doing, Ani?* He wanted to follow. It was illogical that she should matter. *If she were dead, she wouldn't.* He'd thought about her death as he waited outside the Dark King's home, thought about the terror inside of him as he stood outside Bananach's nest.

Then Ani was gone.

"She's unpredictable," Bananach whispered into his ear. Her black feathers brushed against him as she embraced him.

Devlin stepped away.

She slid around the front of him, talon-tipped hands spearing into his sides. "Chaos sheathed in skin. Too much for you, darling Brother."

He took her wrist in his hand and squeezed enough to fracture her delicate bird bones, giving her the pain she enjoyed. "Must you try to provoke me?"

Bananach laughed, a grating caw that was accompanied by a congress of ravens on the rooftop above them. She cradled her wrist happily. "Have dinner with me, Brother. I am lonely."

"What business do you have with her?"

Bananach didn't pretend confusion. "She will free me. Her blood's the secret they didn't want us to know."

"What *about* her blood is import—"

"Tsk. Tsk." Bananach covered his mouth with her hand. "No questions. She's special, and I need her."

Devlin removed Bananach's hand. "You do?"

"Of course." She crowed, and the bevy of black-winged birds replied to her.

"You need the Hound," he repeated.

Bananach looked on him with pride. "And you know why, don't you? That's why you didn't kill her. I see it now. She's the key. With her blood, I can *win*. After all this time, Brother, I can defeat Reason."

"Why I didn't . . ."

"Kill her." Bananach caressed his cheek. "When they brought her to the Dark Court, brought her in like a little lamb among the wolves, I saw her difference. I listened. I know it was you who didn't end her life."

Devlin stared at his sister, mute and afraid. His hands did not tremble. *Could I silence her?* He couldn't kill her any more than he could kill Sorcha. *How do you eliminate problems you cannot kill?*

"Someone came in the night and slaughtered the little lamb's mother, and the Dark King himself has protected her all these years." Bananach's thumb stroked the skin under his eye. Her talon scraped the flesh so that a small cut trickled between his skin and her palm. "And you . . . I saw you *watching* her at their club. I knew."

He had no idea what to say. Truth or misdirection could go poorly, but leaving would end any chance of learning what she sought from Ani. "You notice much."

She smiled. "It was a test, but I—"

"Not a test." He reached up to Bananach's hand and pulled it away from his face. Entwining his fingers with hers, he added, "I would not test you."

Bananach sighed. "You did, but I figured it out. The little one's blood will give me strength they cannot fathom."

"Indeed." Devlin felt the stirrings of a fear that he'd never felt before, not for queen, or court, or Faerie itself. It was for Ani—but after an eternity of repressing emotions, he shoved the fear inside where his sister would not notice and gave her words she'd expect of him. "You would fight the High Queen then."

"Of course!"

He stared at Bananach, not arguing, not speaking.

She donned a glamour to look like Sorcha and laughed happily. "You're such a perverse child, Dev. I always knew you'd betray me. When I heard what you'd been doing"—Bananach paused, still dressed in the High Queen's image—"I was shocked. Disappointed. You're nothing like me, Devlin. You don't belong in Faerie. You never really did."

"Stop."

Bananach's own visage returned. "You've always liked *her* better, haven't you?"

She leaned heavily against a chain-link fence. The force of her body flopping against it made the metal rattle unpleasantly.

Devlin faced her. "Do I tell her where you hide?"

"If *she* hid, would you tell—"

"Stop." Devlin's calm was evaporating steadily. "She is my queen. She gives me home and life and reason to be."

"One day I'll take my rightful court or kill her, and then you'll swear loyalty to me." Bananach looked heartbroken as she said it. For centuries, she'd fixated on the same thing—not always, not even regularly, but when she was lost, her fallback plan was regency and sororicide. "You've used the Hound as a test, but I see what she can do for us. You doubted that I'd figure it out, but I did."

"I don't test you, Sister," he repeated. He didn't add that tests were their domain. Bananach's entire relationship with him was solely about competition with her twin, Sorcha. He was just an instrument to be wielded in their conflict.

"Where shall we dine?" he asked.

"We could stop for a bit of killing?"

"Perhaps." He'd done worse in her company—and not always at her behest.

And she was appeased. She linked her arm around his waist, and he obediently draped his arm across her shoulder. She adjusted the fall of her feather-hair so it wasn't pinned by his hold but fell like a solid cloak over his arm and down her back.

Afterward, he walked to the one house where he knew neither sister would want him to be, seeking not the king but the one in the Dark Court who'd best know how to deal with his sisters. A thistle-fey admitted him, led him to a room accessed by sliding a large surrealist painting to the side, sealed him in, and fled.

In the darkened room, Devlin found the faery he sought: Irial wasn't a monarch, but he retained enough power that if he truly wanted his court back, he could take it. He was not king, but not just a faery. *Like me.* There were some stronger faeries in the courts, but most of the truly strong ones were solitary—unless something more than power motivated them.

Two chairs sat on either side of the divan where the former Dark King now lounged.

Irial lifted a decanter from one of the alcoves in the wall. He poured a glass and held it up. "Drink with me?"

Devlin nodded, so Irial poured a second glass.

Irial held out a glass. "Many a good evening can start with a willing mortal . . . or a *halfling* perhaps."

Devlin ignored the intimation that Irial knew about Ani. He accepted the glass and took a seat on the chair to

Irial's right. "Perhaps, but that's not appropriate for those of my court."

"And which court would that be, Devlin?" Irial never missed a chance to ask that particular question. Like the Dark Kings and Dark Queens before him, Irial saw things that Devlin would rather keep locked away.

"I belong to Sorcha's court," he said.

"Why? You aren't like them. We both know that. If—"

"Stop." Devlin drank, keeping his expression bland as he watched Irial. "I have no interest in what you think you know."

"Aaah. You certainly are cruel enough to be High Court." Irial looked briefly wounded, but the momentary sadness faded under the faery's habitual wicked expression.

Devlin thought—not for the first time—how much different life would've been if he'd claimed the Dark Court when it was first created. Irial, like all the Dark Kings before him, was temptation personified. He had no need to repress his baser urges; he had no need to hide anything.

Unlike me.

Irial lifted his glass, peering into the amber liquid as if he'd see some truth waiting there. "You were at the Crow's Nest."

"I was sent to ensure that Seth is safe."

"I see." Irial took a drink and let the silence stretch out. "You could speak to my king if you have doubts of the boy's safety. Shall I see if he's in?"

Devlin weighed his words. It wasn't as if he'd never

conducted business without his queen's consent; eternity was a long time not to chafe against the bounds of being ruled. He'd only acted without orders when it was for his court or queen's best interests—or when there were no consequences to measure.

Except for Ani.

Devlin set his glass aside. "I'm not here about Seth, but I expect that you already know that."

"Indeed."

Devlin hated the necessity of speaking about it, of admitting to anyone that it mattered to him that Ani was vulnerable, but pride wasn't a luxury he could have just then. "Ani is in danger, and I would like to keep her safe."

The laughter that rolled out of Irial then held every dark thing that had once thrived in Faerie. "I doubt that *safe* is what Ani seeks."

Devlin ignored that truth and added, "Ani is of interest to my sister. I would like to take her away from Huntsdale, but I suspect if I did so without informing her court, we'd be pursued."

The guise of debauched layabout vanished. Irial's smile was akin to an animal's bared teeth. "Do you think I've hidden her only to have you take her to Faerie?"

"She is not being retrieved for Faerie. It would be best not to take her there. . . . Because of my involvement in Ani's life, Sorcha does not *See* her." Devlin said the words quietly.

Irial was silent.

"Now that Ani has come to your court, she is unsafe. Bananach has taken an interest in her too," Devlin added.

"And why does the High Queen's Bloody Hands involve himself in the safety of a Hound?" Irial swirled his drink. "It's a conundrum. Wouldn't you say?"

"Does it really matter?" Devlin asked.

"Perhaps. I suspect it matters to Bananach—and to Sorcha. It would matter to me if those I trusted were keeping such secrets. Do you suggest that it wouldn't matter to them? To your *queen* especially?"

Irial wasn't saying anything that Devlin didn't already know. All faeries knew the importance of fealty. Once sworn to a king or queen, obedience was to be absolute. Devlin was acting in direct opposition to his queen's orders—not only had he let Ani live, but he was working now to keep her alive instead of protecting Seth. Few faeries were likely to think that he would disobey his queen—except, of course, his queen herself.

Hasn't she always known the day would come?

Time passed without words or sounds. It was akin to being in the High Court, silence and contemplation.

Finally, Irial said, "If Ani goes with you by choice, I will dissuade Gabriel and Niall from pursuing you. If she refuses, we will protect her *here*. It's her choice though. Your vow on it."

Devlin stood. "You have my vow that the choice is hers."

Irial frowned up at him. "Be careful with her."

"She'll be safer than if she were in your court." Devlin turned to leave.

"Devlin?"

Devlin paused with one hand on the door.

"Be careful *with* her as well. Ani's not like any other faery." Irial's look was pitying.

"I am the High Queen's Bloodied Hands." Devlin straightened his shoulders and dropped enough of the control he'd held over his emotions to let the dark faery know that pity wasn't necessary. "In all of eternity, no faery born has overcome me in *anything*."

"Aaah. Pride goeth before the fall, my friend"—Irial stood and clasped Devlin's hand—"but you've already fallen, haven't you?"

And to that, Devlin had no answer.

Chapter 14

It was finally dark in Faerie, so Rae took advantage of the opportunity to leave the cave for a while. The world around her looked less full than usual, but Rae had long since grown used to the changing landscape of Faerie. The High Queen's moods determined reality, and some days the queen decided to create a new vista.

Rae drifted over a stream that had been a river previously. On either side, willows clung to the banks in clusters like groups of people in conversation. Thin branches swayed in a light breeze. Reclining on the soil with her bare feet dangling over the edge of the bank was a beautiful faery, one Rae hadn't met in dreams or in Devlin's body before. The faery slept on the mud-slick ground, a pile of moss under her cheek as if the earth had formed a pillow just for her. Bits of mud, twigs, and reeds were caught in a fiery mass of hair. Unlike the majority of the High Court faeries, this one looked like she belonged elsewhere, as if she had stepped from some Pre-Raphaelite painting of sensual women.

Rae entered the faery's dream.

"I don't know you," the faery said. In her dream, she was sitting on the bank of a much larger river. Lilacs bloomed at the edge of a lush garden that stretched into the distance.

Rae drew a deep breath. In dreams, her senses were as if real. The perfume of flowers lay heavy on her tongue, so thick that she was near to choking on it.

"Where do you come from?" the faery prompted.

"Perhaps you saw me in the streets, and you're remembering me." Rae was used to the High Court faeries resisting her presence in their minds. It wasn't logical to dream of strangers, so they often needed gentle guidance to accept that she was imagined.

"No." The faery shook her head. Her hair was unbound, tumbling down her back and trailing behind her onto a flower-dotted ground. There were no twigs or mud entangled in the curls here.

The faery turned away from Rae, staring into the water as if it were a giant mirror. Faces drifted under the surface like Ophelia drowned and tragic. *Has she lost someone?* Death was so much larger to faeries. When one had the promise of eternity, centuries seemed a blink. Rae had seen the reality of such loss when Devlin considered what he did for his queen. Her orders were blood on Devlin's hands.

"What do you dream of?" Rae whispered.

The faery didn't look away from the water. Silver veins like roots crept from the faery's skin and sank into the earth, anchoring her to the soil. Rae was transfixed by the sight: faeries weren't ever this unusual in their self-imaginings. They saw themselves much as they appeared in their waking world; their essential representation echoed reality. They were of the High Court, logical in this as in all things.

"My son is gone from me." The faery looked back at Rae. "He's *gone*, and I can't see him."

Rae's heart ached for her. Faeries had so few children that the loss of one must hurt even more than the loss of most faeries. Rae sat beside her, carefully not brushing the roots that extended from the faery's hands, arms, and feet. "I'm sorry."

"I miss him." Six tears slid down the faery's cheeks. They fell to the soil and rested on the ground like drops of mercury.

Rae gathered them into her hands and carried them to the edge of the river. With her words, she reshaped the water, stretching it and widening it until it became an ocean.

"Seven tears into the sea," she told the faery.

Then she returned to the faery's side and knelt. With one hand outstretched, Rae added, "Seven tears for a wish."

She caught a seventh tear as it fell.

The faery was silent as Rae flung it into the water.

"What do you wish for? As long as you're sleeping, you can have it." Rae stayed kneeling beside her. "Tell me what you wish for."

The faery woman stared at Rae. Her voice was as a

slight breeze, but she said the words, made her wish. "I want to see my son, my Seth."

Behind them the sea vanished, and in its place a mirror appeared. The glass was framed by vines hardened and blackened like they'd been darkened in fire. In the mirror, Rae could see a faery unlike any others she'd glimpsed and very unlike the austere appearance of most High Court faeries. Seth had silver jewelry decorating his eyebrows; a silver ring pierced his lower lip; and a long silver bar with arrow-like tips pierced the top curve of one ear. Blue-black hair framed a face that wasn't faery-pretty, but mortal-hungry. Seth didn't look anything like the son of the vibrant faery.

Is he why she sees herself with silvered anchors?

Seth was fighting with a group of faeries with moving ink on their forearms. If they'd been mortals, Rae would guess that they were the sort of people one should cross streets to avoid. In the mirror, Seth wrapped his arms around a muscular female faery and propelled the two of them through a window. Broken glass hit the cement floor inside of a bleak-looking room.

Where are they? Did she see her son die? Is that what this is?

Rae winced in sympathy at the thought that the faery had witnessed her son's death.

The faery didn't look away from the mirror at all. She raised one hand as if she'd touch the images. "My beautiful boy."

Seth was laughing at the scowl on the muscular female faery's face. "Got you," he said.

"Not bad, pup." The cruel-looking faery in the image plucked glass from a long gash in her shoulder. "Not bad at all."

Another faery tossed a water bottle at Seth. Only the inked arm was in the frame, but even without seeing the face, Rae knew that this was another fighter. His voice carried like a rumble of thunder: "Go another round with Chela?"

Seth shook his head. "Can't. Summer Court revels tonight. Ash . . . we're talking, and she wants me with her there."

"Keenan?"

"Still MIA." Seth grinned, but just as quickly looked away, as if his happiness was wrong.

"Pity."

"Do you know where he—"

"Don't," the female faery, Chela, interrupted. "It's not Gabe's place *or* mine to tell you things that we learn for *our* king."

Seth nodded. "Got it. Good fights today?"

"You're still broadcasting your next move too much," the voice, presumably Gabe, said.

"Tomorrow?"

"By the time you're awake, it'll be evening. *If* you do it right, pup"—Gabe stepped into the frame and grinned—"revels aren't the sort of thing one follows with early mornings."

The words spoken by the faeries in the frame felt far too

precise to be a memory. Moreover, this wasn't a scene that ended in Seth's death. *This is not good.* As Rae watched, she had the sinking suspicion that she'd done something new: she'd somehow given the dreaming faery a glimpse into the mortal world in that very instant. *How did I do that?*

"Your son isn't dead?" she asked.

"No. He is in the mortal world." The faery turned to stare at Rae with unblinking eyes. A clear lens slid over her inhuman pupils, reminding Rae of reptiles she'd seen. Faeries were *Other*. She'd known that from her first day in their world, but it was rarely made as obvious as it was in that instant.

"Where do you come from?" the faery demanded.

"I am but a dream," Rae said, as she had to so many other sleeping faeries. Her voice wavered though, making her words sound false. "This is all but a dream."

"No."

"Your imagination? Perhaps you've seen me in a painting, something you saw in the palace—"

"No." The faery crossed her arms and stared at Rae. "I know every detail of *every* painting in my palace. You are new. What you did here was . . . impossible. I cannot see the threads of those tied to me. I *saw* him."

Rae froze.

"My palace"? Threads of seeing? Sorcha.

Rae stood and stepped backward, away from Sorcha and the mirror where Seth was walking down a street that looked nothing like the mortal world Rae remembered.

Devlin's going to be furious . . . if I live through the next few hours. Words were suddenly far more dangerous than she'd imagined possible. Dreams were her domain. Here, she should be safe; here, she should be omnipotent. Sorcha, however, *was* omnipotent. Within Faerie, the world remade itself at her whim and will, and Rae wasn't sure if that extended to dreams.

Or the mortal world.

"Who are you?" Sorcha didn't rise from the ground. Even without a throne or trappings of power, she was fierce. The sea swelled in towering waves that did not fall. It hovered, threatening to crash yet frozen. The water iced over, capturing the waves in stasis. Sorcha's dreaming mind was taking control of the images Rae couldn't hold on to.

Except the mirror. It stayed in front of her, untouched by the shards of ice that were cracking from the waves and falling like rocks at the start of an avalanche.

"A dream. I'm merely the face you've called into being for your amusement. Nothing more." Rae hoped that the expectation of truth from faeries' lips was enough to buy her time to escape. "If you'd rather I vanish"—Rae turned her back as if to walk away—"it is your dream."

"Stop."

Rae paused mid-step. Then, resolute that the safest course of action, the *wisest* plan, was to keep going, she continued walking.

In a blink, Sorcha appeared directly in front of her. "I said, 'Stop.'"

"You can't control dreams, Sorcha," Rae whispered. "You can't control anything here."

"I control everything in Faerie." Her haughty look reminded Rae so much of Devlin that she wondered how she hadn't recognized Sorcha immediately.

"We aren't really in Faerie though. Dreams aren't your realm." Rae smiled at Sorcha as gently as she could. "There are mortals, *seanchaís*, with the ability to twist dreams. But you? You're just another faery in *my* land of dreams."

"You're not just another faery, though." Sorcha's gaze took in every detail of Rae's appearance. "Who has been hiding you from me?"

"No one," Rae lied. "I've always been here. You've simply not interested me before now."

And then, before the High Queen could learn dangerous secrets, Rae slipped out of the dream and back into Faerie.

Chapter 15

Ani was still shaken hours after she left Bananach—a situation only made worse by the fact that someone was following her. *Perhaps Bananach let me leave only to find out where I'd go?* Ani wasn't sure. The Barracuda's windows were tinted so dark that she couldn't see the driver, but she could tell that her stalker was arrogant. To follow someone in such a sweet ride spoke volumes about the driver's personality. In a faery, that sort of surety and egotism wouldn't be surprising, but most faeries didn't drive. It wasn't an option with so much steel, and having a custom car made of faery-friendly materials was foolish.

There are a few though.

She tried to think over the rare faeries who'd found beautiful machines appealing enough to have nonsteel machines constructed. It was a small list. Mostly, faeries would ride a beast glamoured to look like a motorcycle or even have a car fashioned out of magic and earthen materials. They wouldn't be able to create this. The engine growled with barely restrained energy, so much so that it appeared to shiver as it crawled after her.

She turned down the alley. *No, not a faery.* Odds were that a mortal drove the Barracuda; she could confront a mortal.

It turned in behind her. The typical heavy scent of exhaust was absent as the car eased up on her and paused. It sat—engine idling, body humming—but no one emerged. The windows stayed closed.

"Fine. If you won't reveal yourself"—she stepped toward the car—"we'll do it this way." She was beside the driver's door. Letting her fears and angers out on someone stupid enough to cross a daughter of the Hunt seemed pretty tempting, but she gave one more warning. "You really shouldn't try me."

The car didn't back up; the driver didn't get out or turn off the engine.

Ani grabbed the door handle—and froze. The material under her hand wasn't mere metal. She looked inside the now-transparent windows. *Empty.* The car in front of her wasn't faery-made. It was something far rarer, something out of children's tales that she'd long since stopped believing in.

A riderless steed.

Under her hand the car pulsed, like a purr. It vibrated through her body.

"Mine?" she asked.

Each other's. The words came unbidden into her mind.

It had a voice that she heard. Unlike when she rode another's steed, hers was in her mind, a part of her.

Of course, I am. The voice was genderless. *I am yours. You will not ride any other now.*

"Never again. Just you." She stroked the long sleek lines of the hood. It was everything a classic should be: power and beauty, strong lines and a great engine.

It shifted under her hand, becoming a black Ducati Monster with chrome-spoked rims.

"Daaamn." Ani felt it laughing as she all but drooled on motorcycle.

Then it was a horse, a skeletal steed capable of trampling every creature in their path. It lifted and lowered one leg, cracking the already-broken asphalt under a steel-sharp hoof. Like the most perfect Dark Court denizens, it was beautiful in its horror. "You're gorgeous."

And lethal, Ani.

"Yeah. That's what I said. Lethal *is* gorgeous." She stroked its neck. After the terror of facing Bananach, there was little that could ease her anxiety. This could. This did.

You needed me.

"I did," she whispered.

I felt your need to run *and so I'm here.* It closed its eyes and rested its head against her shoulder. *We can go from here.*

It had selected her, chosen her. She had her own steed, not Chela's, but her own. Halflings didn't have steeds;

unclaimed steeds didn't roam in the mortal realm. Yet, it was here.

Come, Ani. The steed became a car again. It opened a door. *Ride with me. Away from here.*

Ani slid into the driver's seat. The engine turned over with a satisfying growl.

"Oh." She breathed the word, and the car tore out of the alley with speed that made her heart race.

Take the wheel. I trust you, it assured her.

"Take it back if I fail you." She'd driven an actual car a couple of times, but not enough to be certain she could handle it.

Always. I'll keep you safe, Ani. Always. You're mine now.

"And you . . ." She couldn't say the sentence.

So her steed did. *I am yours. Always.*

After a few dizzying hours, Ani directed her steed into an alley near the tattoo shop. The riding had helped her settle her emotions, given her space to calm down, but Bananach's demands weren't something she could make sense of on her own. She couldn't kill her king, even if she wanted to. She had no desire to give Bananach her strength or her blood. And, despite her dislike of Seth, she wasn't sure she could kill him.

Would one of the three acts be enough to appease War?

Ani didn't know, but what she was certain of was that Niall, her king, would not be forgiving of Seth's murder. *But if he didn't know . . .* The possibilities were there. Ignoring

Bananach wasn't a viable plan; she was crazy, dangerous, and powerful.

Could I kill Seth?

He didn't really belong in the Dark Court. If he mattered to Irial, it would be different. On the other hand, he *was* of the High Court and loved by the Summer Queen. Angering them wasn't a great idea.

Neither is angering Bananach.

The engine stilled, and Ani slipped out of the driver's seat of the Barracuda and gently closed the door. It was a beautiful beast, but it was safe in the alley. The biggest risk was that it would eat some foolish mortal who tried to strip it or leaned on it, but the steed seemed tired enough that she didn't really expect any blood on the grill when she returned.

She leaned down to the hood of car and whispered, "Be back soon."

Its engine rumbled briefly, and then the interior lights shut off.

Ani walked up the sidewalk to Pins and Needles. She paused there. Once she crossed the threshold, there'd be questions. If she answered, there would be a lecture. Her brother hadn't survived on the borderland between Dark Court and mortals without a spine of steel. He'd taught her what she needed to survive—and not flinched at the inhumanity in her or at the mortal sweetness in Tish. Somehow, he'd loved them both, despite their differences.

"You going to come in?" Rabbit stood on the other side of the front window. His goatee was a braid in black and a garish shade of orange. The bone plugs she'd carved for him after one of her first hunts were in his ears. His clothes were his standard thrift-store fare: dark trousers and a mechanic's button-up falsely proclaiming him an employee of Joe's Stop and Go.

Home.

She put her palms on the glass pane of the door, covering the hours he was supposedly open for business.

Rabbit watched her with his usual taciturn expression. He'd ask her too many questions later, but just then, he saw what she didn't admit: she was afraid. Her brother had been the one to croon comforting words when she came home sobbing or raging; he'd taught her to cope with a world that confused her. He'd helped her come to the realization that the things that set her apart were strengths as much as weaknesses.

She opened the shop door and went into his arms.

He held her as carefully as he had when she was a little girl, and they'd thought she might turn out to be more mortal than not.

Like Tish did.

"Want to tell me what's wrong?"

"Maybe." She stepped away and wandered over to the red vinyl chair in the far corner.

Rabbit flipped the sign on the door to CLOSED and threw the bolt. "Well?"

"I saw Bananach." She picked at a loose thread caught under a piece of black electrical tape Rabbit had used in lieu of stitching one of the rips in the chair. "She wants some things from me."

"She's trouble." Rabbit pulled down the shades so that any passersby wouldn't see them sitting inside while the sign was turned.

"Aren't *we* trouble, Rabbit?" Ani looked up at him. He looked like trouble; stereotype or not, her family looked like the sort who'd be fine bending or breaking a few rules. They *had* broken both mortal laws and faery traditions. He'd hidden them from the brute that killed Jillian, the High Court, and most of the Dark Court. He'd stolen mortals' wills and freedom when he'd bound them to the Dark Court in ink exchanges.

"There's trouble, and then there's *her*." Rabbit sat down cross-legged on the immaculate floor of the tattoo shop. Even out here in the waiting room, he kept it as clean as he possibly could. When she was a child, she'd built Lego cars and Popsicle-stick towns on that waiting-room floor at night when Rabbit worked.

"She wants me to do some things . . . and . . ." Ani folded her hands together and clasped them tightly and then forced herself to meet his gaze. "I don't want to tell you."

"We don't cause trouble just for trouble's sake. Not real trouble. There needs to be a reason. You get that, Ani, right?" Rabbit scooted over so he was sitting at her feet. "I can't keep you safe now that you're in the court. You exposed what you are, and they won't let you live among mortals anymore . . . not for years to come."

She tilted her head defiantly. "Irial trusts me."

"So do I," Rabbit said before glaring at the door. Someone was trying the handle despite the turned sign and closed shutters. He lowered his voice and added, "So think about whatever she asked of you."

"I just . . . I'm scared. If I don't cooperate . . ." Her words faded as she thought about drawing War's anger.

"We'll figure it out. Come on." Rabbit stood and pulled her to her feet. "We can talk over dinner. I'll make dessert."

He draped an arm over her shoulder.

"Opening ice cream doesn't count." Ani tried to lighten her voice. It was what Rabbit did when there was stress: gave her space to relax while he teased out what was upsetting her. She took a steadying breath and added, "I want something you *make*."

"Deal." He opened the door to the private part of the shop, where they'd lived for most of her life. "I'll call Irial."

Ani stumbled a little. She didn't want to tell Irial she'd seen Bananach. *Which is why Rabbit's calling him. Taking care of me.* Her brother had always done what he could to keep her safe. That hadn't changed. His ability to do as much might've changed, but the desire to do all he could was still the same.

"I'll tell him, Rab." She stepped in front of him. "You don't need to get involved."

Rabbit looked older than he usually seemed. "If she

wants you in her plans, Irial needs to know. The new king needs to know . . . and you, Miss Impulsivity, need someone stronger than me to be by your side. You call, or I do."

She leaned on the wall, took out her cell, and pressed 6. The phone rang only a few times before Irial answered.

"Hey. Long time no chat." The nervousness in her voice was enough to let him know that it wasn't a social call.

"Where are you?"

"Home." She closed her eyes so she couldn't see the worry on her brother's face.

"Do I need to tell Gabe anything?" Irial asked.

"Not yet." She heard Rabbit walk away; his footsteps were solid thuds on the floor. She didn't open her eyes though; instead, she waited for the beep of the oven being preheated, the water as he washed his undoubtedly already-clean hands, and the cupboards opening and closing. Finally, she said, "I need to talk to you. There's a . . . problem, I guess. Situation? I don't know. I need help."

"Stay at home. I'm coming." Irial didn't hang up the phone. He kept the line open, a lifeline she didn't want to need, to talk while he headed her way. "Did someone hurt you?"

"I'm okay." She sat down on the floor, her back to the wall as the fear she'd resisted started to overwhelm her. "I'm cooking dinner."

"I'll help."

She smiled. "I'm not making something fancy like you would."

"Did you *hurt* someone?" he asked.

"No."

"Then it'll be okay." Irial's voice was the voice that she remembered from her childhood terrors. He was her savior, the one who'd brought her and Tish to safety, the one who made sure they were hidden away from the cruelty of the High Court and whoever killed Jillian. "*You'll* be okay."

"I'm not sure this time." Ani stood up and went to the kitchen. Rabbit kissed her forehead as she paused beside him at their tiny kitchen counter. "Bananach wants me."

CHAPTER 16

When Tish walked into the kitchen, she squealed as if it had been weeks since they'd seen each other.

"There's a sound I don't miss." Rabbit covered his ear and gave a mock wince. "I'm lucky I'm not deaf by now."

Ani tossed her phone to Rabbit. "Talk to Iri. I'm going to catch up with Tish."

"Stay in the house!" Rabbit yelled as they took off toward their room.

No.

Ani wished she could tell Rabbit everything, but the more she'd thought, the more she realized that this was too serious. She'd come running home, potentially endangering them. Leaving for a while was the best bet. *Especially now that I have the means to go.* Fleetingly, Ani wondered if that was part of why the steed had come to her. She needed to get away to where her presence wouldn't endanger her family.

"I love you." Ani hugged her sister. "More than anyone or anything. You know that?"

"You too." Tish frowned. "So . . . what did you do now?"

"Nothing yet." Ani flicked the stereo on, and the speakers immediately thumped to life. The bass was heavy, and the weight of it pushed on her skin.

Home.

She knew that Rabbit realized that the music was to keep him from hearing their words. Her brother might not be as much of a Hound as she was, but he had exceptionally keen hearing. She seemed to have gotten almost all of their father's traits. Rabbit had some—longevity, strength, hearing—and Tish . . . Tish had "Hound-light" qualities. That's what they'd called it growing up: a little stronger, a little faster, a little bit too interested in trouble.

They sat down on Tish's bed. Ani's bed was still there, unmade from the last visit, and looking like the haven she needed. She couldn't stay though, not here, not where her mostly mortal sister was.

"What's going on?" Tish crossed her legs and waited.

"I'm in a sort of situation," Ani started.

As quickly as she could, she explained everything about Bananach. Then she said, "Tell them. Tell Rab and Iri *everything.*"

"Ani?" Tish reached for her hand, but Ani was on her feet and backing up.

"I can't stay." Ani turned up the stereo. "If she comes after me—"

"No. You can't *go*," Tish whispered. "If she's watching for you . . . Come on, Ani. Just do that focus thing. That helps."

Ani glanced at the closed door. "If she comes, she'll hurt you and Rabbit. I shouldn't have come here. I need to go away from everyone before she does. It's safer and—"

"*Iri* knows now. He'll fix it. We can all go live with him." Tish stood and took Ani's hands and held on to her like she had when they were little and Ani was freaking out. "Come on. Just stay here."

"I can't, Tish. You stay with Iri, okay? Stay with Rabbit. Stay with Gabr—*Dad*." Ani felt like something prickly was swarming inside her skin. She needed to run. The thought of staying, of not getting away, made her feel like she was choking. Irial would keep Tish and Rabbit beside him; they'd be safer without her around. She couldn't stay trapped in the house or put them in danger.

"I need to get out for a while," she said.

"And go *where*?" Tish still held on to one of Ani's hands.

"I don't know yet." Ani pulled free of her sister's hold and opened their closet. Grabbing a duffle, she started shoving a few clothes into it.

Silently, Tish helped, giving permission by her actions if not by her words. Tish held out a brush. Tears were in her eyes. "Be careful, NiNi."

Ani hugged her, barely resisting tears at the sound of the pet name. "I'll call."

"Rab has your phone." Tish reached into her pocket and pulled out her glaringly pink phone. "Take it. I'll get yours when he's done talking to Iri."

Silently, Ani slipped Tish's phone into her front pocket. They'd switched often enough that they kept each other's contacts in both phones. "What about Glenn? I don't have his number in my phone."

Tish grinned. "I guess I need to go to the club then."

"No!" Ani shuddered at the thought of her sister out alone. She pulled the phone out and flipped through the contacts. "Copy it down. He can meet you at the shop. No going anywhere alone unless Iri clears it. Okay?"

Tish wrote down the number on her hand and then she slid open the top drawer of the nightstand between their beds. Nestled under the various bras and stockings was a *sgian dubh* that matched the one already on Ani's ankle.

Tish held out the black-handled knife and a black leg holster. "Take my lucky one."

"Are you sure?" Ani patted her other leg. "I already have the prickler."

"Take mine too. A girl can never be too careful . . . or too armed," Tish quipped.

"True." Ani lifted her pants leg and fastened the holster. She might be Dark Court enough to like carrying a traditional blade, but she wasn't a fan of shoving it into her stocking or boot. Tradition was important, but adapting was good too.

Ani slid the knife into the holster.

Tish opened the closet. "Holy irons?"

When they were in elementary school, Irial had taken them on a series of field trips to different houses of worship. At each place, a man or woman said prayer words over a handful of blades. By the end, the girls had a box of sharp things blessed by representatives of a number of the dominant mortal faiths. Like many of the gifts Irial had given them, the "holy irons" were practical presents. *One never knows,* Irial had said, *and we aren't the only things that go bump in the night.* Ani hated carrying the blessed steel because it was a deterrent to many faeries she'd like to get closer to, but she wasn't going to take chances. *Not now.*

She shucked off her shirt, slipped on a vertical shoulder holster, adjusted it, and then slipped one of the remaining blessed blades—an eight-inch partially serrated tanto blade—into the sheath that now rested on her side.

"Hold still." Tish straightened the holster straps. "Take it all. I'll get Iri to restock for us."

Ani nodded. Then she grabbed a punch knife, iron filings compressed in a pepper-spray-style container, and a spring billy. She shoved them all into her bag with her clothes. No amount of weapons would give her the strength to overcome Bananach, but overaccessorizing wasn't a bad idea when planning a road trip. *And Bananach isn't the only trouble out there.* The thought of hostile solitaries, of Ly

Ergs, of being alone without the Dark Court's protection made Ani pause—but the thought of endangering her family by remaining in town outweighed any hesitation. She grabbed a bang stick.

Tish absently folded and unfolded her hands. Her nerves were getting more unsettled, but she didn't want to add to Ani's stress. She never did. Her emotions said everything her words didn't. She was afraid—but so was Ani.

And neither of us need to talk about that.

The smile Tish offered was proof that she understood the impossibility of discussing those truths. Even more telling were her words: "Dad's going to be furious once he catches you."

"Who says he'll catch me? He's not the only one with a steed now." The thought of Gabriel hearing about her steed was all that made her happy just then. *He'll be proud.* She turned her back and, softly, whispered, "Love you."

Tish grabbed her and held on as tightly as she could. "Be careful. Please?"

"You too." Ani held her sister just as fiercely.

Tish squeezed her harder, and then stepped back.

Together, they popped the lock and hefted the window.

With her bag slung over her shoulder, Ani climbed out and to the street. Tish dropped the bang stick to her and then closed the window carefully. The curtains fell over the window, and Tish was gone.

Ani was halfway down the block within a breath of her feet touching the sidewalk. *This is for the best.* She knew that—especially as she wasn't a block from the shop before she was being followed again.

Without changing her stride, she headed toward a side street that would put her near where the Barracuda was parked. Calmly, she made her way toward the steed.

Can you hear me? She thought of the car, imagined the thrill of driving with it, and the warmth of its hood when she'd walked away. *Are you awake?*

Yes, but this would be easier if I had a name, Ani. Its voice had the same vibrating hum as its engine did. *I thought on it. I lack a name. Being a Steed With A Rider means I get a name.* It rumbled the words inside her mind. *It is important to be Named.*

Okay, but right now? Not the best time, she thought back.

Soon, it said.

She dropped her duffle, reached down, and slid a *sgian dubh* from its ankle holster. Then she turned around so she was facing her pursuer—and faltered. The faery from the Crow's Nest who'd kissed her and tasted her blood stood in the street.

"It's *you*," she said.

"It is."

You should not speak to this one, Ani, her steed rumbled. Ani felt it ease up behind her. Right now, it was a Hummer, oversized and bulky, looking like far more steel than most any faery could stand. Being a creature not a machine, there was no actual metal, but the illusion was convincing. It should be frightening.

Pretty Boy in front of her wasn't shying away though.

She didn't move any closer. "I thought you left."

"I did." He watched her with the same unflinching stare as at the club.

She shivered. Part of her wanted to ask if he'd tracked her, but another part of her preferred not knowing. "Do you know who I am?"

He gave her a thorough looking-over. "The faery from the club . . . or should I know something else about you?"

She straightened her shoulders and stared at him. It certainly wasn't a hardship to do so. "You were following me."

"Yes. Are you going to run?"

"Should I?"

"No." He walked past her, turning into a narrower alley that was heavy with shadows. "You should come with me."

She hoped that he'd followed because of their kiss, but she wasn't a fool. Everyone wanted to curry favor with Gabriel, or Irial, or Niall: he was likely here because of politics.

Or because of Bananach.

"Did . . . War send you here?" she asked, rather than following him.

He paused and glanced back. "No one sent me. I am here for my own interests."

She shivered. "Interest in what?"

"You," the faery said, his voice a whisper from within the shadows.

Ani stepped into the mouth of the alley.

He's not prey, her steed muttered.

Just a little fun, a little nourishment before we leave, Ani told her steed. *I won't kill him . . . unless I need to.*

The temptation to not tell the faery who she was warred with her inherent sense of good sportsmanship.

"I'm not solitary," she hedged.

He held his body with such easy grace—no tension, but awareness of her every move. She'd watched his reactions as she stepped closer. He tracked her like one accustomed to fighting.

"I know that." He almost smiled; one corner of his mouth quirked up. It wasn't Dark Court cruel, High Court bland, or Summer Court sweet.

"Are you Winter Court?" she asked. Her hand was behind her, holding her knife.

"No. The cold doesn't suit me." He did smile then. If he wasn't sin-pretty before then, the look on his face as she walked closer made him near irresistible.

She watched his eyes; storm-dark clouds were hidden there, but they weren't warm. "You're not Summer," she said.

"Neither are you."

If she didn't know better, she'd think he was Dark Court, but power like his didn't hide in the crowd, and between Irial and Gabriel, she'd had plenty of education on her own court's powers. "And you look like too much fun to be High Court."

"Indeed." His eyes told her what his words weren't admitting: he was dangerous. Every instinct she had whispered that he was formed of the same sort of shadows Irial was. He should be in her king's court.

I can't fit in the alley in this form, Ani. Her steed's voice was a muffled warning as she walked toward the faery.

"What are you? *Gancanagh?* Water fey? Help me out here. Solitary, but with enough juice to stroll through this place." She moved her other hand closer to the knife on her side. *Not that it will help much.* If she was right about how strong he was—and he must be to walk in Huntsdale so carelessly confident—she wasn't strong enough to take him. She held his gaze. "Who are you?"

"Devlin. Sorcha's order keeper, but—"

"Fuck." She stepped backward. "I'm not going to *her* world. I belong to Ir—to *Niall*'s Dark Court. I am protected. You can't take me."

Panic rose inside of her like a riot of winged things struggling to escape too-small spaces. She retreated farther, scurrying backward until a gust of sulfuric breath warmed her back. Her steed had transformed again.

I told *you,* her steed grumbled.

She glanced behind her. It wasn't a horse, but a reptilian thing that stood where the Hummer had been. Green scales covered a massive body. Claws the length of her forearm dug into the ground beside her. Feathered wings folded tightly together on her steed's back so as not to brush the buildings on either side of the alley. It parted its jaws to flick a thin black tongue.

The massive head lowered and for an instant she thought it was going to swallow her.

Don't be foolish. I wouldn't eat you—it paused, leaving a strange quiet in her mind that told her that it was still mid-thought—*no, not even if I were starving. Curious. I've never had a rider until you. . . . I might save you before me. Huh. That's—*

"Can we talk about that later?" She looked into one enormous, swirling eye.

Of course.

The faery pulled her to him then. One arm wrapped around her waist, the other held her from hip to throat. "I could kill it," he whispered, "or you. It's what I do, Ani. I kill those who are out of order."

She tugged at his wrist with her one free hand and simultaneously tried to fling her head back into his.

His hand tightened around her throat. "Stop."

"I am one of Gabriel's Hounds," she rasped. "I am a member of the Dark Court, not just some random halfling. There will be consequences if you—"

"Tell the beast to step back, or I will have fewer choices. I don't want that. Neither do you." Devlin squeezed. "Tell it to back off, and I can release you."

Ani looked up at her steed. Its eyes were swirling as though great storms of fire writhed inside them. Its claws had ripped furrows in the asphalt.

I'll kill him if you are harmed. It flicked its tongue again.

Drive my claws into his guts and—

"I'm not going to get hurt," she said, far more confidently than she felt, but saying the words felt true. Had they been a lie, they wouldn't have formed so easily. "He's going to let me go."

He didn't release her, but his grip on her throat loosened until the pressure of his fingertips was hardly noticeable. "I'll release you *if* . . ."

She tensed.

"You don't run from me." His words were a breath soft against her cheek. "I truly don't wish to kill you today."

She stayed still. "Or take me to Sorcha?"

He laughed, a delicious sound as shadow-heavy as any of the Dark Court's own. "No, definitely not that."

Then he relaxed his hold, letting her pull away.

Once she was several steps away from him, he held out a hand as if to shake hers. "As I said, I'm Devlin."

She stared at his outstretched hand and then lifted her gaze to his face. Her heartbeat thrummed in time to the cacophony of fear and anger inside her. "Am I to say 'pleased to meet you' or some social pleasantry?"

Heart still zinging, she turned her back and walked over to her steed.

She cuddled against it. It was a smaller beast now—not much more than double the mass of its equine form—with a leonine body, reptilian head, and feathered wings. It tucked its wings close to its side and lay flat on its belly, so she could climb astride its back if she wanted.

She didn't, but she did lean closer to it.

I'd like a name now, Ani, it murmured.

"After this," she promised her steed without pulling her gaze from Devlin. "I live here. Your queen has no business—"

"She didn't send me after you today." He stood stiffly, not lounging as comfortably as he'd been before he'd restrained her. He reminded her of things she usually found beautiful: deadly power and contemplative violence.

"I don't want anything to do with the *High* Court." She was screaming inside, but her voice was even. "Just go—"

"Are you planning to help Bananach?" Devlin asked. "Will you give her your blood?"

"No. I won't help her, or you, or the High Court." Ani had spent her life refusing to give in to fear; that wasn't going to change because of some genetic fluke that made everyone want her blood. She straightened. "You can kill me, but I won't *ever* betray Irial."

Devlin's expression softened for a moment, too briefly to notice if she hadn't been used to studying faeries who hid their expressions. The softness was gone just as suddenly as it had appeared. "I see."

Ani shivered. He'd said he wasn't there on Bananach's orders, but he knew about her blood, knew that Bananach wanted it. She didn't feel particularly inclined to stand around asking questions. Getting out of town sounded wiser by the moment.

"So if that's all, I'll be going," she said.

She started to turn, but his voice stopped her: "I'm the High Court Assassin. Trust me when I say that running from me is not in your best interest, Ani."

Chapter 17

Devlin waited to see how Ani would react. A sliver of excitement hummed inside him. If she ran, he'd chase. Despite an eternity of being bound to his sister's court, he still hadn't subdued that particular instinct. As the High Queen's Bloodied Hands, he could sometimes let loose that urge with impunity, but that was business—with killing at the end of the chase. Chasing for pleasure, chasing *Ani*, was exceedingly tempting.

She didn't run. Instead, she cocked her hip and glared at him. "Do you have *any* idea what would happen if you killed me?"

Bemused, he watched her face him with challenge clear in her every movement and word. "Tell me," he said.

"Irial, Gabriel, Niall—they'd all be after you." She had a hand on each hip, chin raised, shoulders back.

"You invite attack with that posture." He gestured at her hands. "The footing is good though."

"What?"

"Your feet. It's a steady stance if I were to attack you," he clarified. He wanted to train her. He'd tasted her blood: he knew she was well on her way to becoming equal to a Gabriel in strength.

"Are you planning on attacking me?"

"No, I'd like to speak with you. It's a bit more civilized," he said.

"Right. *Civilized* conversation after you track me, grab me, and suggest killing me. I guess you are High Court after all, huh?" She shook her head and glanced at her beast. It pressed its still-reptilian muzzle against her shoulder as she spoke. Whatever conversation they were having was locked from his hearing.

He waited.

"Fine . . . let's talk." She tensed, but other than that, her aggressive posture was unchanged.

"Come." He turned and walked into the brightness of the street. He didn't offer her his arm, didn't wait to see if she followed.

He repressed all of those untidy things he felt, hid them away, and kept his expression stoic as he'd long since learned to do. It was foolishness, his urge to protect her, but he very much wanted a solution that didn't involve Ani's death.

Especially by my hand.

He walked through the streets, following the twists of the poorly laid-out city design until he reached the warehouse district. The few faeries who saw him would undoubtedly report his presence to Niall and Irial. Most faeries wouldn't be foolish enough to carry the news to Gabriel, but would leave that to their king or former king. Hounds' tempers were easily sparked and slowly quelled. Only a faery looking to be injured would deliver news of Devlin's contact with Ani to Gabriel. As order keepers of opposing courts, Gabriel and Devlin didn't mesh well.

Devlin paused at an intersection. Mortal cars raced by, and he marveled at the appeal of traveling in the tangled cages of metal. Much of the mortal world seemed unnatural.

Unlike Faerie.

He wondered, as he had for centuries, if he could adjust to living in the world of mortals. Bananach had. Many faeries had adjusted when the Dark King pulled them out of Faerie so long ago. Others sickened. Some died or went mad. Still others flourished. Devlin, for his part, felt too closed-in by the pace of it.

Too much information was always bombarding the senses: horns and engines, neon glows and blinding lights from signs, smoke and perfumes from mortals. It was jarring, and when it wasn't, the peculiarity of visuals and weather left him off-kilter. It was a curious world where nothing but ice or water fell from clouds, where food tasted the same each time, where the climate was sorted by location and the spin of the planet. Faerie's fluidity made more sense to him.

He paused. Across from them, a window was filled with

brightly colored shoes. Cars were careening down the street. Voices clashed, and sirens shrilled.

"What are you looking at?" Ani was beside him then. She appeared tinier up close, or maybe she only seemed that way because she wasn't radiating aggression. The top of her head was level with his shoulder; the edges of her garish pink-tipped hair brushed against his upper arm as she turned her head to look down the street.

A woman too thin to be healthy stood on the other side of the window looking at shoes; her face was illuminated by the harsh lights inside the store. She glanced outside, but her gaze flickered away before fully settling on him.

Devlin turned his attention to Ani. Like Rae, she was unafraid of him. Even his queen found him frightening: it was the order of things. Faeries should fear him. Death in Faerie—or by order of Faerie—was his function. Ani seemed foolishly nonplussed by this. Once she'd learned that there was no immediate fatal threat, she'd become bold. *Is that why Rae wanted me to see Ani? Did she know?* It couldn't be. There was no way for Rae to know that Ani would be unafraid. Still, such fearlessness near him was rare, and he cherished it.

"Hell-o?" She nudged him. "What are you looking at?"

"We need to cross here." He wasn't sure how fast she could move, but he'd noticed that mortals were slower. She wasn't a true mortal, and her sire was one of the fastest sorts of faeries. Thinking of her getting crushed by the metal racing past them was disconcerting.

She matters.

He gripped her arm just above her elbow and started walking, forcing her to scurry to keep pace with his longer stride.

She yanked her arm free. "What are you doing?"

"Helping you cross the street." He narrowed his eyes at her tone. Boldness was only amusing so long. When it interfered with his objectives, it ceased being entertaining. "The vehicles speed, and you are still somewhat mortal. I'm not sure how fast mortals—"

"I am a *Hound*." She raced down the block.

From a distance, he could see her belligerent posture. It was foolhardy, but not unexpected. He should've kept a better grip on her.

She's unrestrained. It's— He froze. Thoughts, action, everything around him seemed to stop as he watched Bananach come up behind Ani and slide an arm around the Hound's shoulder.

NO.

Before the objection was a completed thought, Devlin stood in front of them. "Step away, Sister."

"For what coin?" She curled her hand around Ani's shoulder so that her talon-tipped fingers furrowed skin, not piercing but deep enough that the Hound would bruise.

He had chosen to be ruled by logic, and logic said there was an answer here that would get Ani safely out of War's reach, but it wasn't logic that rode in his words. "She's mine. I have taken her into my keeping."

"She's alive." Bananach rubbed her face against Ani's hair in a feline gesture that seemed peculiar for the raven-faery. "This is good. I find that I need her not-dead. She has a mission now. Don't you, puppy?"

Ani caught his gaze. She didn't look afraid, despite her situation, and Devlin wondered fleetingly if she was impaired. He'd seen that in some of the mortal-faery mixes, a lack of instinctual fear. *Has she no sense of self-preservation?*

She widened her eyes, as if she was willing thoughts to him.

Devlin stared at her, trying to make sense of whatever she was trying to convey.

She pursed her lips and almost imperceptibly tilted her head. Her gaze shot pointedly to the left.

Sitting on the curb beside him was her steed, looking like a car now. Her intention seemed to be to use the beast as a weapon. The results of such an attack weren't likely to be severe, but it would upset Bananach—which would lead to her striking Ani.

Which would result in my injuring my sister.

Devlin moved forward, putting himself between the steed and his sister. He didn't always like his sister-mothers, but he was sworn to keep them safe to the best of his ability.

Even from me.

Moving as close to his sister as he could get, he made himself a barrier to Bananach's injury.

Ani glared at him.

"You made mistakes. Sisters know." Bananach craned her neck forward so her cheek rubbed Ani's face. "I won't tell our secrets."

Devlin weighed and measured the words. He couldn't tell Bananach anything false. *I wish Rae was here.* Being possessed so as to allow his lips to form a lie would be incalculably useful just then.

"You won't tell secrets either; will you, little pup?" Bananach spun Ani so they were face-to-face. "You'll go to your court. He can help. Is that why you came, Brother? To help?"

Bananach looked over Ani's shoulder at Devlin.

He held her gaze and said, "Yes. I've come to help."

With most faeries, Bananach would press; she would insist on clarity of word—but it was not so with him. She believed him. Bananach kissed Ani's forehead. "Trust him, little one. He is wise."

Some part of Devlin's long-suppressed emotions cringed at those words. For everything she'd done, she was still his creator. Betraying her today—as he'd betrayed Sorcha fourteen years ago—wounded him.

For you, Ani.

The faery in question backed away from Bananach. She shot a glance at Devlin. Then she walked toward her steed. A tremble in her hand as she reached out to the door handle revealed her fear—or perhaps her anger.

Silently, he turned his back on his sister and followed Ani.

He slipped into the passenger seat and barely had the door closed before Ani peeled out. He could see his sister in the rearview mirror: she stood staring after them.

Ani cranked the stereo; angry guitars and shrieking voices came blasting out of the speakers.

He put a hand on hers.

She jerked away.

"Are you helping Bananach?" Ani didn't take her gaze from the road. She was speeding between cars and occasionally getting close enough that Devlin braced for the sound of scraping metal. "She said—"

"If I told her I wanted to remove you from her reach, do you think she'd have let us leave?"

She looked over at him. "Why should I trust you?"

"Maybe you shouldn't." He had just betrayed his second sister for Ani, but he couldn't say he wouldn't kill Ani. If the options were Ani's life or the good of Faerie, he'd act in Faerie's best interest. "I did not come seeking your death or injury, Ani."

Her hands tightened on the wheel. "But?"

He looked over at her, wishing that she'd stayed safely hidden, wishing she'd never attracted Sorcha's attention before or Bananach's now. He couldn't tell her those things, not at the moment, not when she was already so furious and frightened. He couldn't *not* tell her anything either, so he said, "But you have something she wants, something she believes will allow her to defeat Sorcha, to become more powerful than War should ever be, and I cannot let her have it."

"Why?"

He sighed. "Do you want to help her?"

"No, but—"

Devlin interrupted, "And I prefer not to have to kill you. If you help her, I will have to."

After that, neither of them spoke, not as she blared the music to obscene volumes, not as she drove carelessly enough that he was quite sure of her parentage, and not as she gunned the engine as they departed Huntsdale.

Please let me find a solution that isn't her death.

Chapter 18

Rae didn't truly sleep, but she could reach a meditative silence that felt very energizing. She felt as if she floated in a gray nothingness where the world couldn't reach her.

"You!"

Rae focused her attention on the cave, pulling herself back to the state in which she typically existed, staring at the rock walls she had called "home" these past years. In the shadowed alcove, the queen of Faerie stood waiting. Her left hand held a broken mirror. All around her feet shards of reflective glass were scattered like the bones of the dead on an abandoned battlefield.

"None of these work as the one you made did." Sorcha dropped the mirror to the floor, where the glass pieces joined the others already there. "You were in my mind."

How did she find me?

Rae winced. She feigned comfort as if she merely rested on an oblong rock on the floor of the cave. It was an illusion, but it was the sort that made her feel anchored in the waking world. She looked directly at Sorcha and said, "I was."

"I didn't give you leave to live in Faerie. You never came to ask my permission," Sorcha said. The words lilted at the end, a question that wasn't meant to be. Her eyes were unfocused, her gaze not centered on Rae but on something beyond. She wasn't as lovely here as she was in the dream world. Here, her imperiousness was off-putting; her rigidity was disconcerting. The flamelike vitality of her dream-self had been muted, like Rae was seeing her through a thick glass.

Rae would feel sympathy, but Sorcha was the queen Rae had feared, the faery who kept Devlin bound to a path that didn't suit him. At her word, Devlin could die; Rae could die. That reality nullified any sympathy Rae would otherwise feel.

She stood and walked deeper into the shadows, putting more distance between them, standing as if she were leaning against the cave wall. Distance wouldn't keep her safe, but it made her feel less unsettled by the High Queen's presence.

"Can I ask permission now?"

Sorcha paused. "I'm not sure. I don't know that I like your willingness to walk in my dreams. . . in anyone's dreams. It's indecorous."

Rae kept silent. Once, in her mortal life, being accused of indecorous behavior was a severe charge. Rae's long-ago instincts made her want to apologize for being inappropriate, but she hadn't done anything untoward: she'd tried to help ease the pain of a grieving faery. The apology she owed was to Devlin, for exposing herself. So Rae stayed silent, hands folded demurely, gaze lowered. The semblance of propriety seemed a fitting response.

"Yet, I'm not sure how to kill you. The lack of a body to bleed complicates the matter." Sorcha was as callous as Devlin appeared to most faeries, as unyielding as logic should be. It was chilling.

"I see." Rae nodded. "Have you tried wishing me dead?"

"No."

"May I ask—"

"No." Sorcha was suddenly seated on a silver throne that sat atop a dais. Neither had been there a heartbeat ago. The queen had willed a chair into being, and a floor, and marble pillars, and—

We aren't in the cave. Rae shivered. Obviously, Sorcha could relocate Rae. *Or did she move the world around us?*

"Fortunately for you, I have decided that I have use of you." Sorcha raised a hand in a beckoning motion. Two mortals came forward. They were both veiled. Diaphanous gray gauze hung over their faces and draped their shoulders. Shifts of a similar cloth covered their bodies. Their arms and feet were bare.

Rae wondered if she'd met them when she'd walked in dreams or worn Devlin's body, but she couldn't tell from the slight glimpse of bare arm or foot. She stayed silent before the High Queen.

"Sleep," Sorcha told the mortals. "Here."

The floor was undoubtedly beautiful; mosaic tiles created elaborate art that they trod on as if it were merely a base surface. It was not soft or inviting, however.

The mortals lowered themselves to the ground obediently. They crossed their bare ankles and folded their hands over their stomachs, looking like cloaked corpses at a wake. Still silent, they were stretched prone at their queen's feet. What they weren't doing, however, was sleeping.

Rae debated commenting. If she spoke, there was a chance Sorcha would be further displeased. If they slept, Rae suspected she'd be given direction to invade their dreams for some reason Sorcha had devised but not yet shared.

"Tell me what they dream," Sorcha demanded.

"They aren't asleep."

"Of course they are. I told them to sleep. They'll sleep." Sorcha's dispassionate gaze invited no disagreement, but the High Queen was wrong.

"I can't go into their dreams if they aren't dreaming," Rae lied. She *could* give them daydreams. It took far more concentration, but if they were creative—which most mortals in Faerie were—she could even entice them to sleep. She hadn't had much experience with that because Devlin kept her so carefully hidden, but there were a few tricks Rae had practiced covertly when mortals or faeries were within reach.

"Make them dream." Sorcha smoothed down her skirts as she sat on her uncomfortable throne. Her attention to the fall of her attire was more concentrated than her attention to the mortals at her feet.

"They're awake." Rae wasn't sure how much disappointment the High Queen would forgive. She wished that she'd told Devlin good-bye.

"Sleep," Sorcha repeated to the mortals, but they did not. The High Queen could change everything around them, but even she could not control the biological responses of sentient beings.

"Perhaps if you gave them pillows and something softer than the floor," Rae suggested.

Before the words were fully said, the room shifted. The mortals were now reclining on beds that were several feet thick, more pillow than mattress; thorny frames twisted up around the pillow-mattresses. From the thorns, Spanish moss hung down like curtains.

The mortals had not moved. The world around them had shifted, yet they remained in the same deathlike positions they'd assumed. Sorcha, for her part, had no reaction to any of it. This was the High Court that Devlin had sheltered Rae from; this was the High Queen in all of her disdainful glory.

Rae, however, was not of the High Court. She was in Faerie by accident, and at first she was only with Devlin out of happenstance. Over time, that had changed: Devlin mattered.

And would be quite welcome right now.

The queen of Faerie lifted her gaze and stared at Rae. "Tell me what they dream. Now."

On the bed, the mortals breathed slowly and evenly.

They fell into sleep, and Rae followed the first one into her dreaming world.

The mortal was a worker of fabrics. In her dream, she was in a great open warehouse. It was piled high with bolts of fabric, swaths of fur, and vats of odd items. Uncut stones and sinuous metals were piled at the ready.

The mortal sat at a table that spanned the length of the room. On it, sketches were illuminated by backlighting, so that the parchment they were drawn upon seemed to glow. Some of the illustrations were already pinned to model forms. Others were cut from the fabrics, but not pinned or stitched together.

The dream wasn't particularly interesting to Rae. It was simply an artist wishing for more tools with which to create new art. Such dreams were not the most tedious ones in Faerie, but they weren't particularly fun to tweak either. Mortals were resistant to dream alteration. Artists were worse still. They'd been brought to Faerie for their creativity, and that creativity was their essence.

Rae pulled herself from the artist's dream.

"Wake." Sorcha nudged the mortal and then motioned to Rae. "Well?"

"She dreams of her art. Fabrics, a warehouse, some odd accoutrements for the attires she sketches in her dream," Rae said.

The mortal nodded, and Sorcha smiled.

But Rae felt dirty. It wasn't that the content was scandalous. It was the sense that she was violating a trust by reporting to Sorcha. She'd never relayed dreams to anyone.

"The other." The High Queen gestured to the still-sleeping mortal. "What does she dream?"

Rae hesitated, and something in her posture must have revealed that resistance.

Sorcha was beside her, close enough that Rae was tempted to try wearing her body as she'd worn Devlin's so often. It was a last resort though, a measure to take when she had no other options. It wasn't a secret she would reveal yet.

"What is your name?" the High Queen asked.

"Rae."

"I rule Faerie, Rae," Sorcha breathed, her words so soft that they weren't even a true whisper. "All here bend to my will. Air, form, everything. You will obey me, or I will not allow you to continue to exist within Faerie."

Rae stayed silent.

"What does she dream?" Sorcha repeated.

And Rae slipped into the mortal's mind, hoping that the girl wasn't harboring secrets the queen would want to know. Inside the dream, the mortal was waiting expectantly. She sat upright in what looked to be the exact room they'd left.

"Return," a disembodied voice said. In the waking world, Sorcha was speaking to the dreamer.

"What?" Rae asked the girl.

"The queen is summoning you. Remove yourself from my dream." The mortal was motionless, but then she glanced left and right as if someone else could come into her dream. With a look of alarm in her eyes, the mortal added, "Hurry now. She is not to be ignored of late. The Queen of Reason has become something other than rational."

Rae nodded and stepped back into the room where Sorcha was. "You summoned me?"

The High Queen's entire posture shifted. Her arrogance faded under unmistakable excitement. Her silvered eyes glimmered as if full moons hid there. She smiled at Rae, not affectionately, but with pleasure.

And Rae had rarely felt as frightened as she did in that instant.

"It works." Sorcha looked at the mortals and said, "Make ready."

The two girls sat up. One came to take the High Queen's outer garment. The other arranged the pillows on an ornate bed that was suddenly there in front of them. The frame was cut of stone, and on it thick quilts were piled in lieu of a mattress.

Sorcha leaned close to Rae and whispered, "I will see my son. You will make it so."

Rae couldn't move for fear.

"You will depart from my dream once I can see him." Sorcha ascended the half-dozen stone stairs to the bed. After she reclined on it, clear glass walls raised up on either side of her. "Only Devlin or Seth will have the ability to wake me. Tell him—when he returns—that I am safe in my bed."

Both mortals curtsied. Neither spoke.

"You will do as ordered, and each day, you, Rae, will visit

me to tell me what my ears and eyes"—she looked at the two mortals—"report."

"Your Highness—"

"*My Queen*," Sorcha corrected. "I am the queen of all in Faerie. Do you wish to live in Faerie?"

"I do."

Sorcha raised one delicate eyebrow.

Rae curtsied. "I do, *my queen*, but what if there is danger? Shouldn't *we* be able to awaken you?"

"No." The High Queen closed her eyes, and the glass expanded over her, encasing her. "I have spoken. You will obey."

Chapter 19

As Ani worked through her anger, Devlin stayed as silent as he could be—which after centuries in Faerie was akin to the stillness of the earth. However, unlike his experience in Faerie, staying still with Ani beside him was challenging. The more the car raced forward, slipping in and out of small spaces between vehicles, the more Ani radiated calm.

Unlike me.

Devlin found the steed's resemblance to a mortal car unnerving. Being trapped in a steel cage wouldn't make him physically ill as it would many faeries, but it was disquieting nonetheless. Moreover, the steed's choice of a smaller vehicle meant he was physically uncomfortable. Gone was the spacious Barracuda, and in its place was a ridiculously tiny Austin Mini. It was cherry-red, convertible, and, according to Ani, "a 1969 classic." Nothing about it was subtle or designed to blend in—or fit anyone above average height. Added to that was Ani's need to play music at a volume that undoubtedly would cause permanent damage to mortal ears. It was the final aspect in a trifecta of discomfort.

"Ani?" He raised his voice over the din of someone singing about being "tired of cheap and cheerful."

She ignored him, so he turned down the volume.

"Ani, I'd like to discuss our plan." His voice revealed none of his frustration or worry.

"*Our* plan?"

"Yes. *Our* plan. Do you think you could stand against my sister alone?" Devlin tightened his grip on the door as she sped up again.

"I might as well be alone. You were absolutely *no help* when I wanted to attack her." Ani glanced his way and bared her teeth. "You were useless. I ought to just leave you along the road somewhere. Maybe if we'd tried—"

"You would've been taken or killed." He closed his eyes for three seconds, opened them, and tried to find a sentence that wouldn't reveal how disquieting both of those possibilities were to him. He settled on, "This was the best decision. We need to keep moving, find a place reasonably free of faeries if we rest for long. Perhaps if we are gone, my sister will redirect her attention. She is not always *constant* in her interests, and there is much discord in Huntsdale to distract her."

Ani was silent, staring ahead at the increasingly congested road in front of them. She downshifted and then slammed through the gears as she darted past a large truck. Devlin wondered what she'd have been like if she'd been raised by the Hounds. Her temper was less fierce than Hounds', but her impetuousness was more extreme.

She broke the silence. "She asked me to kill Niall, and I considered it."

His calm faltered. "You probably shouldn't tell this to many people."

"I know. I didn't consider it *much.* Niall being gone would upset Iri." She frowned. "I'm Dark Court so I should be okay with the murder thing, but even if it *wouldn't* upset Iri, I don't think I could kill Niall. He doesn't deserve death."

"Could you kill to protect Irial?" Devlin prompted.

"Sure."

He continued, "Wouldn't killing Niall be betraying your court?"

"I suppose so, but I never swore fealty. Hounds don't. Mortals don't." She swerved into a minuscule space between two cars and then back out, passing a sports car going too slow for her taste. "He's not really my king then, so I mean, *technically—*"

"You're not really a mortal," he interrupted. "Hounds are loyal. Irial has earned your loyalty, so your choices are perfectly rational *and* within the expected parameters for a Hound of the Dark Court."

"Riiight. The parameters." She pulled her attention from the road and scowled at him. "Your court must be a nonstop party."

"Indeed." Devlin couldn't repress a smile at her fluctuating mood.

Ani directed the car onto an exit ramp without slowing. "Thing is, I'm trying to make sense of it, but the part I don't get is that she wants me to kill *Seth* too."

Devlin stilled. Of all of the things Ani could do, striking Seth would be one guaranteed to result in her death. *Is this what Sorcha had foreseen?* Devlin stared at Ani, pondering. *She* didn't *kill Seth though.* If Seth was in danger, Devlin should return to Huntsdale. However, Seth was with Niall and Irial. It wasn't as if he was unprotected—or defenseless in his own right. Sorcha wouldn't see it that way, of course: Devlin's failures to his queen were multiplying.

Midway through a sharp S-turn, Ani turned to look at him rather than the road. "Why kill Seth? You have the logic skills, so help me figure it out."

"To increase hostilities," Devlin murmured. "It's why she does all that she does, to position us for greater discord."

"And Seth is that important? Huh."

As are you, Devlin thought, but couldn't say aloud. *Not to her. Not right now.* Letting Ani know that she was important enough that the first two faeries both noticed her, that her death had been ordered, that her death was still very possible, that assuring her continued life had been his greatest betrayal—of both sisters—and a betrayal he would continue as long as possible . . . it all felt too weighty to say. Instead, he sat silently.

Ani slid into a parking space, and the engine cut off.

Outside the car, a bustle of mortals milled around at

what the signs had proclaimed as a highway "rest stop." No one appeared to be resting despite the early hour. Mortals walked over to nondescript buildings, returning with as little notice of the world as they had when they entered. A few faeries perched in the boughs of trees in a dusty area where some mortals let their pets relieve themselves. One black-and-white dog snarled at a rowan-man who swiped at it for trying to urinate on him.

"I'm stretching while you think or ignore me or whatever you're doing." Ani opened the door and left.

Which isn't safe. He thought of the possibilities: of their being followed, of Sorcha—or Bananach—knowing that Ani was fleeing, of solitaries knowing she mattered, of random faeries trying to attack her because she was thought to be fair game. The world suddenly looked more menacing than it ever had before.

He was out of the tiny car and following her in a heartbeat, but she was already across the parking lot and headed into a building. She was Hound-fast, especially when displeased. He followed her through a heavy door—and was greeted by angry expressions from several mortal women and girls standing at a row of washbasins.

"Are you okay, sugar?" one older mortal asked Ani. The woman clutched a small black canister with a spray nozzle.

"Devlin." Ani took his hand. She walked the several steps to the door. "You can't follow me into the ladies' room. Out."

He looked around, assessing everyone in the room—most

of whom were staring at him. He nodded. "I'll be outside the door. If there is a danger—"

"I know." Her voice was free of emotion, but the look in her eyes wasn't. She was inordinately pleased by something.

While he pondered the curious way she looked at him, Devlin stood outside the washroom, positioning himself as close to the door as he could be without blocking it.

And he listened to the mortals talking to Ani.

"Are you in trouble, sugar? He seems awfully worried." The same mortal woman spoke.

"He's shaken up over a scare earlier." Ani undoubtedly knew that he was listening, but her voice was at a normal volume. "He's sensitive like that, but I'm not—I'm not *as* afraid as he is."

"Bless your heart, you poor things," the woman replied. "Well, I'll wait right here while you use the facilities. He can't come in here, but you're not alone."

Outside the door, Devlin smiled to himself at the woman's kindness. Her efforts would be futile if there were a threat to Ani, but if the Hound was the mortal she appeared to be, the woman's kindness *could* be an asset. It was the sort of mortal selflessness that had astounded Devlin over the centuries.

The other mortals, who'd kept a distance from Ani at hearing her words, weren't the only sort found in the world. Unlike so many faeries, mortals were unpredictable. *Like Ani.* It confounded him—and made him strangely awed.

When Ani walked out, the mortal woman stood protectively beside her. They stopped in front of him, and before the woman could speak, Ani hugged her. "You're a good person."

"Well . . ." The woman looked a little startled, but she still reached forward and squeezed Ani's hand. "You be safe."

Ani nodded, and cuddled against Devlin as if they were something more than strangers. "I will. He'll take care of me. Right, Dev?"

"One can hope," Devlin murmured.

After a few moments of chatter, the woman walked over to a mortal man who was standing several feet away waiting for her.

Ani stayed pressed against Devlin's side and sighed in a way that evoked a number of inappropriate thoughts. He held his emotions as close to even as he could. He didn't share his secrets or his emotions with anyone. *Except Rae.* A stray worry for his bodiless friend assailed him. With it came the curious realization that he wished he could introduce Rae to Ani.

The Hound in question had her fingertips grazing the bare skin under the edge of his shirt. She was still leaning into him as they walked back toward the car.

"Ani?"

"Mmmm?" She stayed near him, acting as if they were . . . *something.*

"What are you doing?" He was loath to ask, fearing that

any answer she offered would be disappointing. He had no business allowing himself fond thoughts of the Hound. He'd known for years that it was inappropriate to let emotion cloud his judgment.

She looked up at him with a mischievous expression on her face. "How High Court are you, Devlin?"

He couldn't answer, not truthfully. *Or maybe because I don't know anymore.* Reluctantly, he stepped away from her. "I am the High Queen's Bloody Hands, Ani. How High Court do *you* think that makes me?"

She hopped up onto the hood of the car, which had shifted form while they were away from it. Once more, it had become a Barracuda. Idly, she patted its hood. "Honestly? I think you're a lot more like my court than you're admitting."

He stepped closer, so that he was beside her. He lowered his voice and said, "You're a child. I wouldn't expect you to—"

"A child?" Her voice was dangerously soft, and the glint in her eyes was one he recognized.

Part of his mind—*the reasonable part*—warned him away from answering her, but instincts he typically repressed urged him forward. The two responses warred momentarily, but despite centuries of choosing logic, he knew that logic wasn't what he wanted. If he were truly logical, he'd put her in the earth before he went even further from sanity. His queen might overlook his lapse in obedience. Rae would have to forgive him in time. He needed to put things back in order.

I can't.

"Are you trying to tell me that I imagined your interest when we met?" She straightened one denim-clad leg in front of her. The other leg was bent, so that her right foot was flat on the hood of the car. "No parsed words. Tell me why you're helping me, or tell me why you won't admit the urge that went with the look back there. You were honestly worried for me."

He wanted to take the openings in her sentences to mislead her—almost as much as he wanted to tell her the truth. "Does it matter?"

"I just met you, but you seem more worried about my safety that most everyone I know . . . and that's saying something." She put a hand on either side of her hips, bracing herself. "Yeah, I think it must matter."

He watched her get ready to spring at him. "I'm stronger than you. It's logical that I keep you safe."

"It's not logical." She tilted her head and widened her eyes beseechingly. "You know what I am, Devlin. Do you expect me to just sit next to the strongest faery I've met outside my court and *not* wonder why he's appeared out of nowhere and worrying over my safety?"

"My motives shouldn't matter." Devlin couldn't say they *didn't* matter: that would be a lie.

"Tell me why." Her words weren't a request, but an order. "Tell me why if it isn't personal. I almost believed it was just business, but you weren't looking at me like business when you followed me, and you sure as hell weren't thinking High

Court thoughts when I touched your skin. Tell me why you want me with you."

He wasn't going to answer that, not now, and possibly not ever. He held out a hand. "Come. We need to go. Just get in the car—"

"Trouble!" she interrupted. Ani slid off the hood of the car. Her gaze was no longer on him.

He turned so they were side-by-side.

Two Ly Ergs approached, one from either side. Another faery, a female thistle-fey, stood a slight distance away. They were Dark Court faeries, but the Ly Ergs often allied with Bananach. Devlin didn't know whether they were sent in pursuit or had simply come upon them. What he *did* know, however, was that they were a problem that needed to be resolved quickly.

"I'll take the Ly Ergs," Ani said.

"Not both." He saw Ani out of the corner of his eye and was aware that the car had shifted into a great reptilian beast. The steed and all of the faeries were invisible to the mortals in the parking lot.

"Come *on*." She didn't look away from them, but her tone was as good as a glare. "There's only two. You go after *her*."

"One." He tracked the Ly Ergs, watching the calmness evident in the muscles not yet tensed, the heartbeats not accelerating. They were trained fighters, unlike the thistle-fey, who stayed back watching.

"You're as bad as Irial," she muttered as she lunged at

one Ly Erg, and Devlin was torn between instinct and an unfamiliar urge to watch her. Logic won.

Or maybe a hunger for discord.

When it came to fighting, it wasn't logic that ruled him. Then, he accepted both sides of his heritage: the precision in eliminating his opponents balanced with glee in the bloodletting.

"Come and get it," Ani challenged. A long knife was in her hand as she advanced on her target; a second short knife was in the other hand.

Devlin scanned the woods: several other faeries became clear among the trees. He wanted to tell Ani, wished briefly that he could speak to her as her steed did, but as he glanced at her, she tilted her head, sniffed, and smiled. She was more Hound than not. His sight allowed him to know the same thing her sense of scent revealed to her.

"More fun, Dev," she called as she tried again to skewer the Ly Erg in front of her. "I'll get at least two after all."

Devlin reached out, grabbed the Ly Erg in front of him, and before the faery could respond, slit his throat.

"We need to go." Devlin watched as at least four more faeries approached from their left. The thistle-fey turned and ran—which felt more ominous than victorious. Even if the faeries weren't there at Bananach's behest, the fleeing faery would likely report back to her. He needed to get Ani farther away.

The steed bit the Ly Erg, pinning him in one place. Ani darted forward and sliced through the muscles at the faery's knees, bringing him to the ground.

As she stepped backward, the steed was a car once more, with both doors open. Without a second look at the bleeding Ly Erg, Ani slid into the driver's seat.

She shot a glance at Devlin. "We could've taken them."

He paused, looking at her, realizing as he did so that she was every bit as capable as a young Gabriel would be—and wondered briefly if they should've done so, if they should've pursued the thistle-fey. "Perhaps, we might've. You're a worthy partner, Ani."

Her answering grin was more exhilarating than the fight. "Damn right, I am."

Chapter 20

The fight earlier that morning had left Ani edgy. She shifted in the seat, tapped her hands on the wheel, and could not sit still. Being caged in small spaces had never worked for her. It was worse when she was restless.

Would you like to stop? the steed asked.

He won't agree, Ani murmured. Devlin sat beside her, silent and unapproachable.

Several turns later, they were on a smaller road. Devlin still did not rouse from whatever contemplation he was in. His eyes were closed.

A thumping noise came from the engine as the steed pulled over alongside the road; beside them a stretch of woods extended into the darkness. *Imply that it's a mechanical thing,* the steed suggested. *You need a proper run.*

"What are we doing?" Devlin opened his eyes and leveled a suspicious glare at her.

"Stopping." She opened the door and stepped onto the

gravel. No cars were in sight. The moon was high in the sky, and the only sounds in the darkness were animals.

Ani took a deep breath.

Devlin opened his door. "Ani?"

She stretched.

"Ani," he repeated.

"You can come or stay here. I'll be right back," she assured him, and then she darted into the woods.

It had been forever since she'd run, and when she *had* run, Gabriel always kept her carefully surrounded by Hounds. She hadn't been able to decide her own course. The freedom of running as she wanted was unprecedented in her life—and so was being chased.

Ani wasn't surprised that he followed. In truth, she was glad. It was unexpectedly thrilling to feel like prey.

Devlin kept pace almost as well as a Hound. It made her wonder what his lineage was.

After about twenty minutes, she stopped, stretched, and waited for him. His emotions were still securely tamped down, unreadable to her.

"You're exhausting," he said.

"I'm what?" She leaned against a tree, watching him close the last few yards between them.

"Exhausting, tiring, capable of wearing on my very last bit of peace." He faced her, as if his attention was only on her, but she had no doubt that he knew where every faery near them was. *Because he is a predator too.* Most of those faeries had vanished as she and Devlin raced through the woods and along the highway.

"What were you thinking?" His voice lowered enough that she had to suppress a shiver. He was hiding something—several somethings if her instincts were right.

"That I needed a run. You chose to come with *me*, so don't go thinking that you're the one calling all the shots." She swung her leg to kick him in the face.

He caught her foot. "No. You had your play. We need to go."

Ani jerked her foot free. She wasn't very good at taking orders, not even when instinct told her that he was right. "It's not *your* life in dang—"

"Don't." He held her gaze, and it wasn't frustration in his eyes. Anger burned there, intense enough that she didn't need to be Dark Court to feel it.

It was exhilarating. Despite being a creature of the High Court, Devlin had a shadowed core that was everything her own court was supposed to be. He was everything she had wanted to find in her own court: he saw her as an equal, yet he still wanted to keep her safe. He didn't dismiss her challenges or bow to them.

"Go back to the steed," he started.

"No." She leaned closer. "I want answers before I go anywhere with you."

He jerked a hand through his hair and narrowed his gaze. "Gods. Maybe I *should* have killed you when you were still a mewling pup."

Ani froze. "Say that again."

He turned away.

She grabbed his arm. "Say. It. Again. *Now.*"

He shook her off with as much effort as he'd need to brush away a moth. "Let it go, Ani."

"It was you. At our house. You . . ." Ani stumbled backward and dropped to the ground. She stared up at him. "You killed my dam."

His marble-white face showed no remorse, no pain for taking away the mortal who'd birthed her. "I keep order for the High Queen. It is my purpose."

My mother.

"You killed Gabriel's lover. My mother . . . *Why?*"

"It's what I do, Ani. I put things back in order. My queen has enough trouble with the half-breeds of other courts. Dark Court progeny are unpredictable. Some"—he looked at her pointedly—"are more a threat than others. I was sent to correct the problem."

"Progeny?" She stared at him.

"Yes." He stood as motionless as a sculpture, seeming unaware of the awkwardness of his unchanging position, unwilling to sully himself by joining her on the ground.

Feeling like a guest in her own body, Ani stood. Vaguely, she was aware that her hands were dirty from pushing herself off the ground. Every detail felt too crisp then, too *real.*

Devlin still didn't move. "You were important enough to attract the High Queen's attention, and now—" His words ended as Ani stepped closer to him.

She tilted her head so she could stare into his face, and then she slapped him as hard as she could with her dirt-covered hand. "So you killed Jillian? Because her *progeny* are a threat?"

She lifted her hand a second time, but he didn't let her strike him again.

"No. Just you were the threat." He caught her wrist and simultaneously dropped his ridiculous self-control to the point that she could feel his emotions for the first time.

Sorrow-sweet. Afraid. Protective. Longing.

She paused. He didn't feel like someone who wanted to hurt her. He felt like someone who wanted her safe.

What am I missing here?

She stared at him, letting his emotions roll through her, drinking them down to sate her hunger. "You didn't kill me before. You won't now. . . . Would you kill me if they ordered you to?"

"Bananach does not order me."

Ani almost smiled at the idea that he could play word games with her. "Nice dodge. Try again. Would you kill me if Sorcha ordered it?"

He didn't move. "If she ordered me to end your life and I disobeyed, I would be cast out of my court. My vow of fealty"—he held Ani's gaze—"would be corrupt. I would be foresworn."

"You *are*. You're hiding things from her, hiding *me*." She understood then. "You've known where I was my whole life."

He nodded once.

Ani tucked her hands in her back jeans pocket and rocked on her heels. "Why not tell Sorcha where I was? Why spare me? Why not save Jillian too?"

He stared at her for several very even breaths, silent in word, but his emotions ricocheted from excitement to fear to hope. Now that he was off-kilter, she could be nourished to the point of gluttony on only a taste of his feelings.

Like feeding from a king.

Devlin reached out and cupped her cheek in his hand. "Take your taste, Ani. It won't make you understand."

Her mouth opened at that. No one outside the court was to know what the Dark Court took for nourishment. Sharing that secret was punishable by starvation up to the point of death.

He lowered his hand from her cheek to her collarbone, so it rested just there on the edge of her throat, above her heart.

Ani wasn't sure if it was a threat or a caress.

He stood perfectly still, hand motionless against her skin, inhaling and exhaling slowly. "Ask me again." His voice was soft. "Ask me your question."

She paused. He wasn't shutting down his emotions. *Where's the trap?*

"Would you kill me?" she asked.

"Not that one." He brushed a thumb over her bare throat. "Ask the other one."

She'd been waiting her whole life to ask this question, in this moment, of this faery. "Why did you kill Jillian?"

He leaned in and whispered in her ear, "I didn't. She's hidden away in Faerie."

Ani felt herself stumble, but Devlin caught her before she could fall. He lowered her to the ground. A lifetime of certainty, everything she thought she knew about her past, had shifted. Her mother was alive. It was almost too beautiful to believe. Her vision blurred as tears filled her eyes. The monster she'd feared had saved her, saved Jillian, and risked himself to do so. After all these years of fearing the faery that had changed her life, Ani looked up at him and knew that he was why she was alive. *Why Jillian lives.* She couldn't make all of those changes fit into her mind. All she could say was, "My mother."

He knelt beside her. "She didn't want you to know, but . . . I won't have you hate me. I can't keep you safe if you hate me."

"She's . . . *where*? Where is she? Is that where we're going?"

"No. She's safe, but we can't go to her," he said.

"I thought . . ." Ani tried to find words for the years of fear and loss, but there weren't any. "I thought she was dead. That you . . ."

"It was for the best."

"Help me understand how. Because of not knowing, I've spent my life thinking she died and fearing someone—apparently *you*—would come back to hurt Tish." Ani felt tears sliding down her cheeks.

"I had few choices. Sorcha can see everyone but those

closest to her or those whose lives matter in *her* life," he started.

Ani couldn't speak, couldn't do much other than stare at him and wait for the rest.

"If I hid Jill, she wouldn't be important enough to draw Sorcha's attention . . . especially if Jill didn't remember having children." Devlin's emotions went several different directions, but his inflection was unchanged. "The alternative was her death."

"Do you save many people Sorcha wants killed?"

Suddenly, his emotions were completely blocked from her. "Only you."

"And Jillian."

"No. Jillian's death wasn't ordered, but . . . her vanishing would make Irial put you under his care. It was her idea. She would've done anything to keep you and your sister safe."

Ani sat there. She considered reaching out to him, telling him that he'd given her everything by not killing Jillian.

Or me.

Almost an hour passed while they stayed silent beside each other, and then Ani looked up and caught his gaze. "You're a traditional faery; aren't you, Devlin? Three questions. That's the rule, isn't it?"

"It is, but I've already—"

"I want a third question," she interrupted. "And I want you to promise to answer it."

He didn't look away or tell her that she had no right. Instead, he nodded.

"Tell me who you are, Devlin. You know *everything* about me." She caught his hand in hers. "You've seen every step of my life."

He startled. "I *didn't*. I stayed away. . . . I only saw you in passing until the other night. I wouldn't stalk you like that. It's . . . unseemly."

His expression begged for her understanding. The High Court was about restraint, not desire; it was about reason, not impulse. And Ani was realizing that Devlin was violating every trait of his court to be with her, to save her, and to hide her. What she didn't know was *why*.

"You know me, my history, my family, and I *need* to know you." She didn't let go of his hand, as if holding on to him was the only thing that would keep either of them from falling apart. It wasn't about skin hunger; it was about things making sense. Holding on to him made sense. "Tell me who you are. There's more to what's going on here."

His already volatile emotions became so intense she shivered again.

He looked—and tasted—frightened. "In all of eternity, I have acted in the best interests of my queen . . . until you. And now, War tells me that you are the key to my queen's death. I should kill you, Ani. I should've killed you then. I should kill you now."

"I'm glad you didn't."

"As am I," he admitted, "but if your living means her death . . . I cannot sacrifice everything."

"I know." Ani didn't have words that would make

things make sense for either of them. That wasn't really her strength. She went up on her knees so she was face-to-face with him.

He didn't back away. His heartbeat didn't race, not really, but she heard it speed.

For me.

Slowly, as if he were spun glass she could break, she leaned in and brushed her lips over his. It wasn't even really a kiss, just a butterfly brush, but it felt like the sort of kiss that made the world stop turning—which made her even less able to speak.

What follows those sorts of sentences? Or emotions?

Ani started back toward her steed. "Let's go."

"Where?" He looked and felt alarmed. "I can't take you to Jill. She's in Faer—"

"I know," she said. Whatever reason the High Queen had for ordering her death presumably hadn't vanished, and the last thing she wanted was to have Sorcha actively pursuing her too. It hurt to realize that her mother being alive didn't make her any less *gone.*

"What are the odds of my surviving? I mean, really?"

Devlin scowled. "Numbers are not what you need to think about. The probability is that Bananach will not stop thinking of you. The statistically likely results are—"

She held up her free hand. "Right. My odds are not good."

They walked in silence until they reached the road.

"Camping," she announced. "Rabbit used to take us

camping, but only with a host of guards and just for a couple of days."

"You're a peculiar creature, Ani." Devlin started to pull his hand free, but she held on. *Just a little longer.* She was pretty certain that this wasn't a side of Devlin she'd be seeing very often.

She walked to the passenger side of the car. "I want to just go roam in the woods."

"Cities are probably safer."

Reluctantly, she let go of his hand. "So that's the predictable answer, right? Bananach would figure you'd be predictable, what with the whole High Court thing. Let's not be predictable."

Devlin paused. "If I insist that cities are the better choice? Will you run?"

"No." She kissed his cheek before she walked away. "You saved my mother and me. You're deadly enough to keep me safe. And whether you like admitting it or know why, you are all sorts of interested in me. I'm not High Court, but I'm practical enough to sort out the reasons to stay together. I think I'll keep you for now."

"You'll *keep* me?" He gave her a look that she suspected was intended to be intimidating, but a faery who'd grown up with the Hunt and the King of Nightmares as playmates wasn't easily browbeaten.

"For now." She suppressed a smile at the sliver of arrogance in his voice. "You're not nearly as boring as you pretend, and considering my family, that's high praise."

"Indeed." He put his hand on the passenger door of what was currently an ostentatious red Lexus.

Ani walked around to the driver's side and looked over the roof at him. A part of her insufficiently used conscience warned her away from him, but for one of the only times in her life, it wasn't just hunger driving her interest. She *liked* Devlin.

Chapter 21

Devlin chastised himself as they sped along the freeway. He was becoming far too close to Ani. He'd lived forever, and she'd had barely a blink of existence. She was a Hound unlike any other, a faery unlike any he'd known.

And she's vulnerable.

And she really shouldn't even be alive.

And losing her would destroy me.

He didn't believe in inescapable fate. He'd watched both of his sisters sort through threads of possibilities frequently enough to know that few things in the world were certainties. He'd seen threads himself, watched their fluidity, and marveled at their transience. Where Bananach saw the threads that could further discord, Sorcha saw the threads that could further order. Devlin often saw both, but as he looked at Ani, he realized that he saw nothing. Her entire tapestry was blank to him.

Some fragment of a memory of Ani's life niggled at his

mind, but he couldn't focus on it. *Rae.* She knew something. He remembered that. *What's the rest?* His head throbbed as he tried to make the memory come clear. *Why I was sent to kill Ani?* If the threat was to Sorcha, he'd have been willing to kill Ani, but despite what Bananach intimated, Devlin didn't believe that Ani would help Bananach. Ani wouldn't give her blood to War or kill Sorcha.

Because she isn't that cruel.

Devlin wondered if the threads had changed because of his actions, if his telling Ani what he'd done had changed her path. *Have my choices changed things, or were these choices already ordained?* There was no way to ask Sorcha what she had seen before Ani was tied to Devlin, and there was no way to tell if Bananach had interpreted the possibilities truly. The thinnest thread of possibility was enough for War to embrace as fated truth. Her desires clouded her interpretation. It was a perverted sort of hopefulness.

The one truth that was inevitable was that Sorcha had *stopped* seeing Ani when her life was tied to his and to their lives. He realized it in an awful moment of clarity: Sorcha had known then that Ani's thread was to be entwined with his.

The insight became so clear to him so suddenly that he felt sick with it. He had no doubt at all that both of his sisters were jealous or cruel enough to change his life for their interest. That's who they were. Sorcha reshaped the world to bend to her will; Bananach manipulated faeries to bring about destruction. Perhaps it wasn't ever that Ani was meant to be entangled in their lives, but always in his. *Was that how her blood would kill Sorcha? By his refusing to shed it? By his* not *killing her?* Such interpretations would not be out of character for Bananach.

But her blood is different. I tasted it. She *is different.*

"Are you okay?" Ani's voice startled him. "You're, ummm, locking down your emotions again."

"Tell me what *exactly* Bananach wants from you."

"Kill Seth. Kill Niall. And to give her my blood because"—Ani took a deep breath—"if you tell anyone what I tell you next, Irial *will* want you dead. So you can't. Ever."

He nodded.

"Irial's overprotective, but . . . he . . ." She paused, took another breath, and continued, "I can trust you?"

He hesitated. The weight of that decision was unexpected. Devlin had never willfully chosen to put another before his queen.

Until now. I would. For you.

"You can trust me," Devlin assured her. He considered telling her then that he'd spoken to Irial about her, but mentioning that Irial had given consent for him to take Ani wasn't something he wanted to do. The premeditation might anger her, and that wouldn't help matters.

It would also lead to more things I don't want to discuss. The former Dark King's taste of Devlin's emotions apparently had revealed enough of his concern to convince Irial that Ani was safe in his care. Devlin would get her to safety and then find a way to extricate himself from her life. It was the logical choice, the appropriate path.

"Tell me," he prompted Ani.

"So you know how I can feed off your emotions?" She paused only a fraction before saying, "That's a Dark Court thing."

"I know."

"But I can do the same with mortals." She accelerated the car, whether consciously or not. "I really shouldn't be able to do either."

Devlin struggled to keep his own emotions in check. The more Ani revealed, the more he realized how rare she was. *If Sorcha realizes Ani lives, she will hunt her.* The chances of Bananach telling Sorcha, of letting slip that he was with Ani, were strong. War needled. It was her way.

Neither sister will rest until one of them possesses or destroys Ani.

Ani didn't look his way. She drove the car faster still. There were things she was not saying, things she obviously worried that she should not say, so he waited.

After several quiet minutes, she continued, "You know, *Hounds* don't feed like that anyhow. We aren't about emotions. They're what we evoke, not what we consume."

"Hounds need touch, not emotion," he said, realizing then what she hadn't said earlier, what she was admitting now: she required touch. He reached out and covered her hand where it was on the gearshift. "I've been insensitive. Forgive me?"

She sped up faster still. "What do—"

"Skin hunger. Hounds have skin hunger." He slipped his fingers between hers. "That's why you were wanting near me. It makes sense now. I should've thought of that. I apologize."

He watched her draw several breaths as if she were afraid. Hounds typically had skin hunger, not emotional appetites, and in all of his looking at her as a mortal and as Dark Court, he hadn't been thinking about her father's lineage. Few Hounds so young could handle it well enough to hide it all. They didn't travel without their pack because of it, and Devlin had assumed—erroneously—that her independence meant she did not carry that trait.

"I won't take advantage," he whispered. "You can hold my hand or . . . embrace me as you did if you are in need of nourishment. I should've—"

"I didn't want to touch you for that reason." She blushed a little.

It was so out of character that it made him falter. "Oh. Should I remove my hand?"

Ani laughed. "Gods, *no*. I'm afraid. I'm hungry as hell. I'm wondering if I'm going to die. Hounds need touch. . . . I'm not sure if it usually gets easier with practice, but for me nothing seems quite right. I'm getting worse."

Devlin looked out the window, not at her, but he lowered his control so some of his emotions were there for her to taste. He let her in further.

"Dev?"

He looked over, but he couldn't speak. The rules he'd lived by for all of eternity were all vanishing. He'd nourished his need for blood over the years, reveled in fighting. He'd taken other pleasures that he knew weren't High Court. But at the core of himself, he chose to live as if High Court was his instinct. Every day, he had made that choice.

"Can I keep hold of your hand?" she asked. "Please? I want to, and you . . . and I think *you* want me to." The last words were rushed together, and now she paused. She turned her hand so it was palm up, and the car adjusted around them so it was suddenly an automatic. The gearshift had vanished. "Am I wrong?"

"No." He squeezed her hand in his.

In all of his life, he'd never had a relationship. It was occasionally done in the High Court that two faeries chose to entwine their lives, but no one had ever looked at Devlin that way. He was deemed inapproachable, too fearsome to want, as if they recognized that he was not truly of their court. *I am the innocent in this.* The thought amused him: only two faeries had existed before him, and yet he was inexperienced in relationships.

What does it matter? I cannot stay with her. I cannot have a relationship.

Devlin stared out the window as they crossed the landscape. If Ani survived, Devlin would return her to the Dark Court, to Irial and Niall's care, to the Hounds. They were her court and family. And he would return to Faerie. That was the order of the world. An aberration of emotion wasn't going to change logical order.

Focus on Ani's situation.

He pushed his emotions back under layers of High Court control and began to think through what Ani had revealed. Somewhere in the details he'd find the answer; it was simple logic. He just needed to focus.

The reasons Bananach had were serious enough that her interest wouldn't wane. Murdering Bananach would be catastrophic, and killing Ani was untenable. *So where does that leave us?* They couldn't spend Ani's life running, but he had no better plan.

Ani watched Devlin close her out. She felt the walls go up, and if not for his hand in hers, she'd wonder if she were alone in the car.

He's frightened of you, her steed suggested.

Ani didn't want to talk about that. Instead she thought, *What do you think of* Barry *for a name?*

There was silence.

It's short for Barracuda. *It can be male or female.* She switched lanes again and accelerated.

I like it, the steed growled happily. *It's mine. I am Barry.*

She smiled to herself. *One problem resolved, a few more to go. . . .*

Unfortunately, the rest of the day was spent in silence. Eventually, Barry whispered, *Sleep, Ani. I will drive.*

The next four days and nights were spent in much the

same way—brief stops for food, hours of silence, and fitful rest while Barry carried her farther and farther away from everyone she knew. They passed through the middle of the States, headed west to where there were wide-open parks, natural areas where camping and running were possible. They drove through every city or remotely steel-filled town they could, slowing their progress with mortal traffic, but hiding themselves more fully from faeries. If not for the threat behind them, it would be the start of a great trip. *It still could be if he would let me in.* She had found Devlin impossibly tempting when she'd met him, and her opinion of him had only gone up after fighting next to him. The revelations he'd shared made her like him, but the passion he hid—and revealed during fighting and running—made her want him.

But, as they traveled, Devlin kept his walls up. He spoke less and less, and when he did, it was polite but distant. The silence and distance in such close quarters was maddening. After their brief revelations, she hoped there was something happening between them, but his actions implied otherwise.

Late on what Ani thought was the sixth day of driving, she pulled into a motel parking lot. The building was surrounded by a thick steel fence; the balconies on the rooms each had steel rails; and the windows had steel safety bars. With the faery aversion to iron and, consequently, to steel, it was the ideal place for them to rest. As long as the building didn't catch fire, they were safe from faery and mortal dangers.

"I'll stay with Barry while you get a room." Ani touched Devlin's hand briefly, drawing him out of whatever contemplation he was in.

He looked at her in confusion. "What?"

She gestured to the humming lights that said VACANCY and wondered if he'd ever stayed in a motel. Somehow, she doubted that this was what things looked like in Faerie. "A room. Do you have money or a credit card?"

"Yes, but . . ." Devlin frowned. "Barry?"

"My steed"—she ran a hand over the dash—"has been Named."

"I could've given it a name," Devlin grumbled.

He's still upset over the seat adjustments, Barry said with marked amusement. *His knees . . . and head . . . and perhaps arms are a bit sore, I expect.*

Ani wisely didn't respond to either of them. All she said was, "I'll be right here. Just outside the door, inside Barry the whole time."

Helpfully, Barry opened Devlin's door.

"Why are we stopping? It can—" His seat fell backward. "*Barry* can drive while you rest."

"I want a shower. Pillow. Bed." Ani gestured. "Please? A room for the night."

"I don't suppose it matters." He sounded as exhausted as she felt, and Ani knew then that he was no closer to figuring out a plan beyond "stay moving" than he'd been when they left.

We could kill the raven one, Barry suggested.

Privately, Ani agreed, but she didn't know if Devlin would go for that plan. Bananach was who she was. If moving and hiding for a while would be enough to make her forget about Ani, that was a better plan than asking Devlin to murder his sister.

Ani closed her eyes to wait for Devlin to return. The grungiest of rooms sounded like a treat just then. Hot water and an actual bed were rarely as tempting as they were in that moment.

They'd be even better if he'd share them. . . .

Chapter 22

Rae had thought that being trapped in the cave was frustrating, but being caught inside Sorcha's palace made her realize how very fortunate she'd been. In the cave, Rae had been alone, but she'd not been at anyone's mercy. Here, she was Sorcha's prisoner; here, she was the only link between Faerie itself and the queen who was to keep the world in order.

And has lost interest in doing so.

Sorcha had retreated to a dream so she could watch her absent son.

One of the veiled mortals sat observing the sleeping queen; the other had left the room to speak to whomever she consulted to find information for the queen. Neither spoke to Rae unless it was unavoidable. They kept themselves far from her, sitting on the step of the dais. Even with the room empty of faeries, they didn't step on the top of the dais or near the chair of twisted strands of silver that sat there. They remained silent and distant.

Fear of her or me?

The room in which Rae waited was far larger than the cave. It was vast, fading to shadowed reaches on one side and enormous arched windows on the opposite side. The farthest corner of the room was lined with barred doorways, some covered by ancient tapestries. Beyond the mosaics that surrounded the sleeping queen's glass bed, the floor was of slick black rock, and the whole of the room was interspersed with white pillars supporting a star-scattered ceiling.

Rae stood and approached the queen. The glass had taken on a deep-blue tint; it darkened the longer Sorcha slept. And as it darkened, more and more faeries drifted into sleeps from which they would not awaken. Rae could feel them, feel their dreams beyond the room where she attended the sleeping queen.

Where are you, Devlin? Please, please, come home. But wishes didn't change the waking world, and hoping to be rescued was as futile now as it had been in her mortal life.

"It is time again." The mortal spoke. "You must check on our queen."

Rae had no idea how the girl knew the time or could keep count of the moments that had passed. It didn't matter. What mattered was that Rae needed to go to the High Queen.

"I hate this," she muttered as she stepped up to the blue glass chrysalis and into Sorcha's dream.

Sorcha didn't look away from the mirror. It was the same cloudy glass framed by fire-blackened vines as in the first dream. In it, Rae could see Sorcha's son, Seth. He sat in a strange green chair drawing in a notepad. As far as interesting visions went, this one didn't rate at all, but Sorcha was transfixed by it. The High Queen's expression was one of utter rapture.

"He creates such beauty." Sorcha lifted her hand and made as if to trace the sketch. "Would that I were so skilled."

"You create the entire world. That's—"

"*Nothing* compared to him." Sorcha pulled her gaze away to scowl at Rae.

And Rae knew that openly disagreeing was unwise. "Yes, my queen."

Like Faerie itself, the landscape around Sorcha's dream was shrinking. In the dream only the two walls of the small room where she sat with the mirror were in full detail. Beyond that, it was as if they were in a painting only partially completed. The dreamscape was a darkening blue void, as if it were some sort of endless sky or sea that wasn't yet in focus.

Rae began envisioning the fields of Faerie, rebuilding the landscape as it had been when the dream began. The emptiness of the dream was unsettling, more so because the dreamer was the one who built and maintained Faerie.

"No. I want none of that." Sorcha waved her hand, blanking it all out before the vista was truly even there. It was her dream, so such an alteration was possible—more so, perhaps, because the High Queen understood the particulars of remaking reality.

If she cannot look beyond the mirror in her dream, what does that mean for Faerie?

Rae stood uselessly in the dream room, not quite in the nothingness beyond it, but close enough to that abyss that she had to struggle against her instinct to form worlds there. It was an empty plane with no one's desires, no one's horrors, no one's fingerprints to alter. *This must be how Faerie looked before Sorcha.* The High Queen, however, was oblivious to the things around her. All that she saw was the image of her son in the mortal world.

Sorcha did not look away from the mirror a second time. "Leave me."

Rae started, "Perhaps you might wake. The world is falling apart—"

"I will wake when my son returns." The High Queen waved her fingers. Suddenly three winged leonine creatures wrought of moonlight and lightning stood between them, guarding the queen, keeping her out of reach. The animals' translucent bodies flickered with the lightning that flashed inside them. As one opened its mouth, sparks escaped. It didn't advance, but it watched Rae. The second creature stretched out at Sorcha's side. Its wings spread wide and blocked the sight of both the High Queen and the mirror. The third snarled as it crouched down.

Rae wasn't sure what would happen if she were to be bitten by them, but she didn't care to stay and find out. With a barely proper curtsy, Rae turned and stepped from Sorcha's dream into the deteriorating world of Faerie.

She needs to wake.

Rae had given Sorcha the window into the mortal world. It was an anomaly, but the High Queen was the embodiment of logic. She shouldn't be so fascinated. Something was amiss, and the cause of it was beyond Rae's understanding.

I need to reach Devlin.

Of course, he hadn't even told Rae that he had a nephew. The High Queen had a son who lived in the mortal world. It explained Devlin's frequent secretive visits there, but it didn't explain why the Queen of Order would behave so irrationally.

Something here is wrong.

Silently, Rae drifted across the throne room and stopped.

One of the mortals was weeping.

"What happened?" Rae asked.

The other mortal pointed toward one of the tall arched windows. Rae couldn't approach it, not as bright as the sky was, but she could see even from a distance that the mountain was partially gone. Faerie was shifting, unmaking itself more and more. As the queen's mind noticed only the images in the mirror, the landscape of Faerie was no longer real to her. Some faeries could not adjust to the lack of logic and were following her, retreating into their own dreams. *The truly High Court faeries are lost without her.* In the street outside, those faeries stretched out in odd positions, fallen to sleep where they'd been. Faerie was going dormant.

The weeping mortal lifted her veil and stared at Rae. "The world is ending."

Behind Rae, the High Queen slept. She wore a smile, looking more at peace than she appeared in waking or in her dreams.

"Go back." The mortal sank to the floor and stared up at Rae with a tear-wet face. "Talk to her. She needs to wake."

And Rae had no choice. Outside the palace, faeries were apparently either sickening or sleeping. Within the palace, there were few faeries left awake. Rae could feel the tendrils of all of their dreams like whispered summonses. For the first time since she'd entered Faerie, there were dreamers all around.

Rae slipped back into Sorcha's dream.

The High Queen hadn't moved; she remained crouched at the mirror.

"My queen?" Rae tried to keep the tremble from her voice.

"How long has it been?"

"Your court needs you. I think it's time to awaken."

"*You* think?" Sorcha laughed. "No. You are to only interrupt if there is a crisis."

"There is." Rae knelt beside the queen. "Faerie seems to be . . . falling apart. Parts of it are vanishing."

Sorcha glanced down at her long enough to give her an indulgent look. "It's large enough that it'll be fine, child. Leave quietly. My son is resting. He sleeps so fitfully sometimes. I wonder at his health."

The High Queen had no interest in Rae's remarks, her own court, or Faerie itself. Rae debated removing the mirror, but there was no one around capable of dealing with an angry queen who would be forcefully brought back to Faerie. *What I need is Devlin . . . which means I need to reach him . . . which means . . .*

Sorcha leaned closer to the mirror. "I can't see what books he prefers to read. He stacks them haphazardly rather than shelving them."

And with that, the High Queen's attention was gone from Rae, from Faerie, from the crisis that her sleep was causing.

Silently, Rae stepped back into Faerie—hoping that it hadn't unraveled further still.

The room was lit by several candles, and the scant light was barely enough to make out the area immediately around the sleeping queen. One of the mortals was missing.

Before Rae could ask, the other said, "She has gone to the kitchens."

"I need to go for help." Rae wished she could take the mortal with her or promise her that things would get better, but she had no words of comfort.

Sleep soon, Devlin. I need you.

"She doesn't wake." The mortal rested a hand on the darkening blue glass. She caught and held Rae's gaze as she asked, "Where will we go if Faerie vanishes? Will we fade away with it?"

"Faerie won't disappear. Neither will you." But even as Rae spoke those words, she wasn't sure if they were truth or lie. Without the High Queen to direct the world, Rae suspected that Faerie *would* unravel—and she had no idea what that meant for the faeries and mortals living there.

CHAPTER 23

Devlin slid the key into the door of the motel room with a gratitude that he felt almost embarrassed to admit. It wasn't that Ani's driving was bad. *There is appeal in chaos.* The car, however, had periodically slid the passenger seat so far forward that he was forced to sit with his legs folded into uncomfortable positions. When it wasn't cramming him into too-tight spaces, it was dropping the seat back so that he was lying completely prone.

Ani, of course, smiled each time—which was probably the only reason the car needed to repeat it over the past several days' drive at illegal speeds. Neither the Hound nor her steed understood the concept of avoiding attention.

"You speaking to me yet?" Ani's tone was confrontational, as was her posture. She leaned against the wall next to the doorway. One hand clutched the strap of the bag slung over her shoulder, and the other hand rested on her hip. "Or are you still pretending you're alone?"

He stared at the angry tilt of her chin. "What do you mean?"

"You haven't said a word in at least eight hours." She walked past him and dropped her bag on the bed.

"Eight hours?"

"Yeah." She spun and glared at him. "Eight silent hours."

"I was contemplating our situation."

"Short version? It sucks." Ani folded her arms.

"I . . ." He watched her with an affection he needed to quash. All of his High Court traits seemed to vanish in her presence.

And I like it.

She turned her back to him, unzipped her bag, and then added, "You are caught between Banan—"

"No." He was beside her with a hand over her mouth before the next syllable could be spoken. "Don't name her *or* the other one anymore. For safety. Do you understand?"

Ani nodded, and he lowered his hand from over her mouth.

"Why?" She resumed sorting through her bag as if nothing had transpired. Perhaps for a daughter of the Hounds, it wasn't odd.

"Not only Hounds hear well. We were already found once. They will carry news to her, and there are others who want what she wants."

"*Which* 'she'?"

"Both have their followers. And I'd rather not kill anyone

tonight. I could enjoy a fight but . . ." He glanced at the closed curtains and then back at her.

"Me too." She smiled at him as if he was something amazing.

It was unnerving to have anyone look at him with such intensity. Devlin forced himself to lift his gaze to meet hers. "I'll keep you as safe as I can."

"And?"

"And nothing." Devlin turned the lock on the door. It wouldn't stop faeries, but it would keep any wandering mortals out. "If you go nearer my sister without doing her bidding, you'll die by her hand. If you do that sister's bidding, you'll die by order of the *other* sister. I'll be the one ordered to kill you . . . and for some reason I dislike the idea of your death."

He kept his distance, staying close to the door, out of her reach.

And keeping her out of my reach.

She pulled a change of clothes and a hairbrush from her bag. "Wouldn't it be more logical to just kill me and get it over with? You know they're both going to be furious with you, and somehow I don't think they're the forgiving sort. You could go back to Faerie, go back to the way things were—"

"No. I don't want that. I don't want you hurt, and I don't want to go back." He paused and shook his head as soon he realized what he'd said. "I don't want . . ."

"What?"

But Devlin couldn't respond. He stared at her.

Silently, she walked into the bathroom and closed the door.

Could I go back? Could I hurt her? Why does she matter? Rae had answers; she'd pressured him so often to go see Ani that he was sure now that she knew something. He just didn't know what it was—or why she kept the reason from him.

When Ani returned, she set her bag on the floor on the opposite side of the bed from where he sat, but didn't speak. Instead, she stayed there and turned her back to him and contorted her body into several muscle-loosening positions. The shirt she wore lifted up, exposing her midriff.

Devlin stared at her bare skin.

She is not mine to keep.

He wanted to, though; for the first time in all of eternity, he looked on another faery and thought about relationships, futures, fighting alongside her. *Hounds are not inclined toward relationships.* He reminded himself of that truth, as if it was somehow more important than the fact that she would likely die because of one of his sisters.

She continued stretching for several more moments, and then came to stand in front of him—hands on her hips again—and asked, "Is this more contemplation or are you going to say something?"

The expression in her eyes was telling: she was frightened, tired, and hungry. Her response was that of most Dark Court fey when weakened—irrational attacks.

Devlin took her hands in his. "Time is different for me. If I am silent too long for your comfort, speak to me. I've never been in a place where regular conversation is required of me."

"Well, that just . . ." She clearly wanted to say something hostile, and for a moment, she looked like she would, but instead she stared at his hands holding on to hers. Her shoulders relaxed a little.

And he realized that not only had he not spoken, he hadn't touched even her hand. In four days, Ani hadn't even had a brush of skin until she'd tapped his hand to send him to acquire their room.

He released her left hand and unfastened his shirt.

Ani didn't move, didn't look at his face, didn't respond at all.

It's not personal for her. It is merely a physical need. He stared at her, watching her reaction, wishing he could taste her emotions. *It is not logical that I want this to mean something.*

Still without speaking, he released his hold on her right hand and removed his shirt.

She lifted her gaze to his. "What are you doing?"

"You need nourishment." He slid farther onto the bed. "I am here."

Ani stayed where she was. She turned to watch him in a predatory way. In a very low voice, she asked, "What are you offering?"

"Skin contact."

"Are you sure?" She took two steps forward so that the edge of the bed was against her. "I mean . . ."

He dropped his walls, so she could feel the things he would prefer she didn't know. *Craving. Fear. Doubt. Joy. Hope. Excitement.* It was all there, emotion to feed her second appetite.

She knelt on the bed. "If you want me, why not—"

"You are not mine to keep, Ani." He held out a hand. "If you were someone else . . . but you're not."

She removed her shirt and then took his hand. "I don't get you, Dev."

With a sigh of some emotion he didn't know how to name, he wrapped his arms around her and pulled her to him. Her hand was splayed out on his stomach, and her cheek rested on his shoulder. Tendrils of damp pink-tipped hair brushed against his chest.

Devlin remained immobile. The only indication that he was alive was the rise and fall of his chest. He concentrated on keeping it this way and on hiding his emotions again. Her nearness frightened him, and he couldn't bear the idea of her knowing how afraid or how happy he suddenly was.

Ani, however, seemed oblivious. After an hour or more of being silently curled into his arms, she pressed a single kiss to his chest—directly over his heart. "You confuse me."

"You require contact. It's a logical thing to supply it." He relaxed a little though, his body and mind refusing to follow the reasonable path. Just for a moment, he let his fingertips graze her skin.

She sighed and pressed closer. "If we were in Faerie, and I wasn't *me*, but just a faery . . . what would you say?"

"About?"

"If I was in your arms like this."

"You wouldn't be." He smiled at her curiosity. "This isn't done."

"Being near each other? Are you saying there's no sex in Faerie?" She lifted her head to stare at his face. "For real?"

"Of course there's sex, but *this*"—he gestured at the two of them—"is not sex. Sex is a very different thing than what we are doing."

"What about after?"

"After sex one bathes and dresses." Devlin repressed a sigh of pleasure as she snuggled back into his arms. He'd never simply held anyone, not for pleasure or need or emotion.

"Faerie sounds horrible." Ani shuddered a little. Absently, she began to trace some sort of pattern on his stomach.

"No, not horrible, just out of balance," Devlin admitted the truth he hadn't ever spoken aloud. His frequent trips to the mortal world had made him increasingly aware that the beauty of Faerie was missing something. Without shadows, the brightness was insufficient. The Dark Court's prolonged absence from Faerie had created a void. Faerie was out of balance and had been for centuries.

Is that why Sorcha acts so unwell? He felt guilt at the thought, but it seemed shameful that the Queen of Order kept sending him off to check on a newly made faery.

"Dev?" Ani lifted her head to look at him. "You're doing that not-really-here thing again."

"I'm sorry," he said, and strangely, he was—not just for being aloof, but for the moments he'd missed over eternity by doing that very thing. Being reserved wasn't something he enjoyed; being Sorcha's creature wasn't something he enjoyed. His pleasures were almost all found in the mortal world, where he could lower his self-control for a heartbeat here or there. *What would Faerie be like if the Dark Court returned?* The thought of it gave him an unfamiliar jolt. If the Dark Court returned home, there would be change in Faerie. *And maybe . . . Ani.* If not, if he couldn't go to Faerie with her, maybe he could stay in the mortal world. Sorcha had remade Seth; she could make him her assassin. If not Seth, someone else. *I could be free.*

Devlin lifted one hand to caress Ani's cheek. "I don't want to be distant. I want to be near to you."

She stilled, holding her breath for a moment.

He hadn't had a plan beyond removing her from Bananach's reach. "Until I know you're safe, how am I to leave you?"

"Irial could keep me safe. He's not bound to the court . . . Maybe he'd move, or I could hide. You don't have to—"

"But I *want* to." He traced the line of her jaw, pausing just under her lips.

"Want to what?"

"Everything." He felt an unfamiliar nervousness.

"What are you offering?" she asked again, just as she had when he removed his shirt.

"Asking," he corrected. "I'm *asking* to kiss you. May I?"

"Yes please," she whispered.

It wasn't the sort of consuming kiss they'd shared at the Crow's Nest, not at first. For a brief few moments, it was the sort of kiss that he'd never had: exploring and careful, tasting and gentle. Then, Ani pressed against him like she was starving.

No logic. No negotiations.

She was stretched out beside him, and he rolled onto his hip so they were face-to-face.

No discussion.

He had no idea where they were going, but in that instant, he set aside all thought. As long as she was alive, she was his responsibility.

My reason.

Mine.

As she wrapped a leg over him, his emotions slipped free from the last restraint. Letting down the walls that kept his very un–High Court emotions repressed had become easy around Ani. He liked it. It felt natural.

It is. With Ani, it's the way it should be. With Ani is the way I . . . An untried emotion filled him. It wasn't appreciation or lust; it wasn't worry or protectiveness. Those were all threaded into it, but it was something else.

He felt her pulse race faster as they kissed.

A wave of exhaustion washed over him then, and he couldn't focus his thoughts.

Abruptly, she pulled back. "No."

She scrambled backward off the bed.

"Ani?" He held out a hand. "Have I offended—"

"No." Her eyes were shimmering with the vivid green of the Hunt. She was the Hunt, and she could consume him.

He felt a thrill of terror.

She held her hands out as if to warn him off. "I can't if you . . . just . . . *no* . . . not with you. You're not safe if . . . You don't know what I am."

She ran into the bathroom and slammed the door behind her.

Ani sat on the dingy floor and tried not to shiver. She reached up and locked the door. It wouldn't matter: neither of them would be even slowed by the lock—or the door, for that matter.

I won't hurt him.

She could hear him on the opposite of the door; she could feel his emotions. *Guilt. Shame. Fear. Worry.* If she didn't explain, he'd think he'd done something wrong.

"I can do this; I can tell him," she whispered. Then she raised her voice and said, "Go to the other side of the room. Please?"

She waited for a couple moments, listening to him walking away. In the still of the room, she could hear his heartbeat racing. *Like prey.* It didn't make her self-control any easier.

Slowly, she opened the door and took two steps forward.

He stood on the opposite side of the tiny room. His dangerous emotions were walled up again. "Did I injure you?"

Without meaning to, Ani let out a laugh. "No."

His face didn't betray anything. "I would never force—"

"I know that." She sat on the floor with her back to the edge of the door frame. "It's not you . . . I . . ."

Devlin stayed standing. "You don't need to explain."

Neither his voice nor his posture revealed any of the emotions she'd felt so clearly when she sat with the door between them, but she knew what he'd felt. He *knew* that she was aware of every emotion that had flooded him. Part of her wanted to pretend ignorance, but she wasn't selfish enough to let him believe he was at fault.

To most people, yes, but not you, Devlin.

She sighed and started the conversation she didn't want to have. "How did you feel after I kissed you at the Crow's Nest?"

"It had been a long—"

"Exhausted?" She paused long enough to see him nod, and then continued, "Dizzy? Weak?"

"I am the High Queen's Bloody Hands. I am not weak." He scowled at her. "I'd had much to do of late, but—"

She interrupted again. "I drain the energy from faeries . . . and mortals."

Devlin watched her, but he'd locked down his emotions. She hated the fact that he'd done so, almost as much as she hated that he hadn't done so when they were kissing.

She pulled her knees to her chest and wrapped her arms around her folded legs. "If it's emotion, but no touch, I do okay. If it's touch, but no emotion, I do fine. Sometimes, though, when it's both . . . I was drinking your energy that night, Devlin."

For a long moment, he didn't respond, and then he asked, "And tonight?"

Ani took a deep breath. "I could feel your emotions, so I stopped."

"I see." Devlin walked toward her. When he was directly in front of her, he knelt down on the carpet.

She lifted her gaze. "I don't want to hurt you."

"I do need to be well to keep you safe." His voice was emotionless.

"That's not why." She closed her eyes. Having him so close was cruel.

His hand stroked her hair. "I am sorry I caused you upset."

She opened her eyes to look at him. "I could *kill* you."

"You could've just now," Devlin whispered. "I don't

think I would've stopped you."

She shivered. "I don't want to hurt you," she repeated. "I want . . . you."

His emotions remained locked down as he ran his hand down her arm. "I talked to Irial."

Few sentences could've startled her as much as that did. She stared at Devlin. "You . . ."

"He told me to be careful, but not *why*," Devlin whispered. "I told him I wanted to take you away, to make you safe, and . . . he said only if it was your choice."

"Oh."

He leaned in and kissed her lightly, lips closed. "How deadly are you?"

"I could drain every faery I touch if they don't know how to keep their emotions contained. I could funnel that energy to my court; I could feed them all." Ani couldn't hide her shudder. The idea of drinking down lives, of feeling bodies grow cold in her arms, was horrific. "Banan—*she* probably wants my blood for that reason. I'm not sure how, but if she could use it, she could feed on mortals, halflings, faeries. . . . Killing would be a way to feed the court. She likes killing."

Devlin held her gaze. "I won't let her use you."

"Iri would use me too. He told me to kill you if I needed to."

"And would you kill me, Ani?" Devlin held out his hand.

Ani slipped her hand into his, and he stood and pulled her to her feet and into his arms. "I don't want to."

"But if your kings ordered it?" he prompted.

"Disobeying my king . . . *or Iri* would mean leaving my court." She stepped out of his reach. "But I'd rather not kill you."

"And I you." He kissed her forehead, and then he walked over to the bed.

She stood motionless.

"Come. I will keep my emotions hidden away so I can be next to you." He folded the covers back.

Tears threatened. "Are you sure?"

"Never more in my life." He held out a hand again. "Rest now, Ani. Even potential murderesses need their sleep."

Chapter 24

Rae walked through the palace, peering out windows at Faerie. It was like an abandoned city, but with the unpleasant addition of having bits of the world fading away. A mountain had vanished, and the sea seemed to be draining. The glimmer of soft violet water was faint. In the streets, faeries, mortals, and half-fey slept. Not everyone was asleep, and most of the world was still in place, but there was no doubt that Faerie was destabilizing.

As she walked openly through palace corridors, she kept reaching out for the thread that unmistakably led her to Devlin. Finally, somewhere in the mortal world, she felt him sleeping.

Forgive me, Devlin, for what I come to tell you.

There was no doubt that it was Rae's fault that Sorcha had abandoned her court; it was her fault that Devlin's home was in danger—and she had to tell him.

As she entered his dream, she saw him leaning against a

wall, staring at a closed door on a small stone building. The top was covered with jagged metal bars. The whole building was wrapped in thorns. It was an edifice designed to be foreboding, inviting no approach.

Rae wondered if the building existed in the real world: Devlin was resistant to flights of whimsy or indulgence. It was a High Court trait he clung to willfully, as if pretending to be like them would make it so. It had been more than a century since Rae had walked in the mortal realm anywhere other than Ani's dreams, but she had a difficult time imagining that such a fairy-tale construct was representative of modern architecture.

What hides in that building?

Rae walked over to him. "Devlin?"

He turned and frowned at her. "What are you doing, Rae? Do you know how dangerous it is to come here? You must go—"

"You must come back," she interrupted. "Sorcha has gone into a dream, and she doesn't want to awaken. She's . . . unwell, only interested in watching her son within the dreamscape. I can't change her dream enough to force her to wake. The first time I went into her dream, she was able to resist me, and—"

"Her son?" Devlin's brow furrowed; his lips pursed. *"Seth."*

"You need to bring him back," Rae repeated. "Faerie is fading. Things are vanishing. Faeries are asleep and won't wake."

Devlin glanced at the stone building. "She knows what you do . . . and now Faerie is unraveling while she stays in a dream watching her *son*. She would destroy Faerie mourning his absence. Such a thing is not logical."

The lack of emotion in Devlin's voice made Rae cringe.

"I'm sorry," she said. "She made it so only her son or her brother could wake her. I don't know him . . . and she's so obsessed with watching him. I'm not sure she'll wake without him."

Devlin scowled. "Seth shall be made to come to Faerie."

"Do you know where he is?" Rae asked.

"I do. He's the one she sends me to see." Devlin's emotions, usually so clear to her when they were together in a dream or in his body, were locked away as he spoke.

"Dev?"

"He'll be there whether or not he wants to." Devlin glanced again at the stone building. "Sorcha never told me."

Rae reached out and touched his arm.

He looked at her.

"Told you what?" Rae asked.

"Her secrets." Devlin looked at Rae's hand and then at the building. "But I never told her mine either."

Rae reached out with her other hand and touched his cheek. "I'm sorry. I didn't know it was Sorcha when I met her. I'm so sorry."

He shook his head. "She was already unwell. That's why she ordered me to stay in the mortal world. I should have—I don't know. I don't know what I should've done. How did I not know she had a *son*?"

He sounded lost as he spoke, and Rae felt useless to help. She couldn't lie and promise that all would be well, not to him.

"I would fix it all if I could," she murmured. Her hand was still on his face, and he was not pushing her away as he had done before when she offered him her affection. "I can't fix this. She instructed that only you or Seth could awaken her. I tried to talk to her. I went to her and . . . she doesn't care. She's the Queen of Order, and she doesn't seem to care at all."

"Is it wrong to want something other than the life one has?" Devlin leaned his head against hers. "That's what Sorcha has done, isn't it?"

"Yes." Rae kept her voice gentle. "But she's not thinking of the lives dependent on her."

Devlin laughed mirthlessly. "I won't fail Faerie. I never have."

"I know." Rae smiled at him. "You are different from her. Stronger."

"No, I'm not. I understand what Sorcha is doing. Love makes you foolish. It makes you throw every bit of logic away, do stupid things, dangerous things." His eyes flashed shimmers of color as he spoke. "It's her. Ani. She's the new life I want. For her, I might throw the world into chaos."

"No." Rae put her hands on his shoulders before he could retreat. "Even now, you would think of the good of Faerie.

Unlike Sorcha, you've spent eternity balancing passion and your practicality. If you were a king, you'd still protect your court. She would too, if she wasn't unwell."

Devlin caught Rae's gaze. He stared at her silently for several moments before saying, "You came to me in a dream in the mortal world . . . because of Ani."

Rae stepped backward, putting distance between them.

"You keep secrets from me, Rae," he said.

She opened her mouth to reply, but he held up a hand. "I know you do, and I'm not asking what they are. What I need to know is whether Ani is safer with me in Faerie or here without me."

"I can't tell you that," Rae whispered. "She is important. Forgive me for what I cannot say, but . . . treasure her. She *is* dangerous, lethal, but she's also essential. I would give my life . . . what there is of it . . . to keep her at your side. Treat her with the care I know you harbor for me."

Devlin stared at her as if he would read secrets from her skin. Then he nodded. "What happens when you return to Faerie?"

"It depends on if there's anything to return *to*," Rae admitted. "It's disappearing too quickly to predict. I'm not sure how long Faerie will last if she doesn't wake."

"I'll retrieve her . . . son." Devlin's tone was no longer unreadable: he was angry now. "Go back and try to talk to her. Tell her that Seth is on his way home, that her brother brings the child she wants. Tell her that if Faerie isn't as it should be, her son might not be able to reach her."

Rae couldn't respond to whatever anger drove Devlin. She knew that the High Queen had done plenty to push Devlin away from her, but this was new; the anger was unfamiliar. Things were shifting, and while Rae didn't understand them all, she nursed hope that they were leading to the future she'd glimpsed so briefly.

Devlin walked over to the stone building. One wall became glass. Inside Ani slept. She was holding a black-handled knife in her closed fist. He put a hand up as if to touch the barrier. "She's . . . ferocious and strong. My sisters want her death, but I need her to live."

"You always have," Rae murmured.

He looked over his shoulder at Rae. "I hope you are there when I return to Faerie."

Rae nodded, and then she reached out and took Devlin's hand.

He pulled her into an embrace and held her tightly. "I wish I could keep you here or bring Ani there. I wish we were all hidden away in your cave, that you were safe with Sorcha, that Ani was safe from Bananach."

"Be careful?" she asked.

"No." He shook his head. "I think I'd like to be truly *not*-careful. Not for just a few hidden moments, but often. I was made of order and discord. Perhaps it's time I let myself know both sides."

Rae stretched up on her tiptoes and kissed his cheek. "I love both sides, Devlin. I always have."

He said nothing for a moment, just held her carefully.

Then he said, "I will bring Seth to Faerie, wake the queen, but after that . . . I am not sure."

Rae wanted to tell him that there was another path, but she could not speak that. She could only hope that he would see it. "If there is a way, I would always be where you are."

Devlin's voice was muffled as he held her close. "I'll be home soon."

After he turned away, Rae created a mist in his dream to hide her presence and whispered, "Forgive me, Devlin."

And then she reached for the thread of Ani's dream and held the two faeries' dreaming minds in her hands. She stitched the two sleeping faeries' dreams together. If Rae wasn't dead, she could unstitch them later, but if Faerie was gone and her with it, Devlin would need some other way to give in to his emotions. Rae could give him—and Ani—a plane where Ani's lethality wouldn't hurt Devlin and his High Court restraint could be loosened.

Chapter 25

Ani dreamed she was on a beach. Behind her were sandstone cliffs with thick forest atop them. The tide was coming in, and the water lapped against her feet. The bottoms of her jeans were wet and collecting sand.

Devlin stood in front of her. He looked around as if expecting to see someone else too. "What if this isn't just a dream, Ani?"

"It is," she insisted.

"Do you dream of me, then?" He smiled, freer than he was in the waking world.

"Maybe." She blushed, but she didn't let her attention waver. Her gaze took in the details, the foreboding posture and inhuman eyes, the more-than-faery strength and not–High Court violence that were just barely hidden. "You're easy to look at."

"As are you." He reached out and caressed her face. With a serious expression, he traced the edge of her jaw with his thumb. "You're beautiful, Ani. In all of eternity, there's never been another faery who could make me want to forget everything and everyone else."

"Because you like the way I look?" She rolled her eyes. "Apparently, my dream mind is shallow."

"No, not the exterior. *You* . . . the tempers and follies and passion . . . even the way you care for that infuriating steed." Devlin gazed at her like she was precious. "Even knowing you could be fatal, I would've said yes."

Her chest hurt like she had held her breath too long as she asked, "To?"

"Whatever you wanted." He didn't reach out and pull her into his embrace. Instead, he took one step forward, leaned down, and kissed her.

When his mouth opened against hers, she didn't drink down his energy. It was just a kiss. Admittedly, it was a forget-your-name kiss, but it was not deadly.

Nor was it lust.

Nor was it anonymous.

Kissing Devlin was unlike every other touch she'd known.

She leaned back and stared at him. "I don't ever want to hurt you."

"You won't. Not here." Devlin was so close that she felt the words on her lips. "We're safe here."

The wolves that appeared so often in her dreams were stretched on the sand, peering out from caves in the base of the cliffs, waiting in the trees far above the beach. They all watched with unusual contentment.

"Stay with me," Devlin whispered, drawing her gaze back to him. "Just a little longer. We can deal with the rest when we wake."

She wasn't sure though if his words were a question or a statement. She ran her hands over his bare chest. Like most faeries in her court, his body was one of faint scars and tight muscles. Faeries healed most everything. To have that many scars meant that he saw plenty of violence. "In the room, I tried not to do this."

He didn't move away. "Do what?"

"Feel your scars. I'm sorry I don't have many to share." She felt a growl in the back of her throat. "Gabriel won't let me fight."

"I like the way you fight."

She grinned. "Mmmm. What else would the dream version say to me? Would you tell me what you really think of me?"

"I would."

"Would I want to know?"

"I'm not sure." He kissed her again, briefly this time, and added, "Why don't you ask me when you are awake, Ani?"

At his tone, Ani wondered if this *was* a dream. She stepped back and looked at him. He stood topless and barefoot on the beach with her. The sea beyond them was motionless, but for the splashes of curious beasts that occasionally broke the surface. It felt like neither dream nor not-dream.

"Am I dreaming?" she whispered.

"We both are."

"If this is a dream, why can't I make clothes vanish?" Ani spoke to herself as much as to him. She reached out to his jeans. "Buttons. Zippers. It's silly to have these in a dream."

He didn't resist. "It is. They're a nuisance in the waking world too."

Ani gasped as he slid his hand under the edge of her shirt. "I'm dreaming."

"Yes, but this"—his fingers curled around her side—"is"—he tugged her closer—"*real* too."

Then he kissed her, emotions raw and available. When he pulled back, he told her, "You were the one who stopped, Ani. Not me."

"For your own good," she reminded.

"You underestimate me." He wasn't walking away, nor was he weakened by the energy she was drowning in. "Don't walk away this time."

For a beautiful moment, she was reminded of the first instant when she'd seen him, shadowed and looking like trouble. She'd thought him like Irial then, but as she pulled him to the sand with her, she admitted that Devlin had replaced Irial as her fantasy that very day.

She unbuttoned his jeans and gave herself over to the kisses she'd craved.

Ani jolted awake still in Devlin's arms, but they were in the motel—not on the beach. For a moment, there were more emotions washing over her than she'd thought she could swallow. She closed her eyes and let the skin contact and emotional deluge fill her up, but touching could be enough to weaken him if he was letting his emotions free simultaneously. It wasn't as bad as kissing, but it was still dangerous.

"Stop . . . something," she whispered.

Rather than stop holding her, he walled his feeling up. He ran his fingers through her hair, tugging gently as the sleep snarls caught on his fingers.

Ani felt better than she had since she discovered her dual appetites. "I'm . . . sated."

"You sound surprised." His hand continued down her shoulder and onto her arm.

"It's the first time." She kissed him quickly, lips closed, and then rolled over and stretched. *"Ever."*

"Good." He didn't move at all or have any inflection in his voice.

The lack of emotion was so different from the version of him in her dream that she felt a foolish surge of sadness. In her dream, Devlin had no barriers, no hesitation, no impenetrable wall. He'd reached for her hand. He hadn't needed to hide his feelings.

But that wasn't real.

In the real world, Devlin couldn't kiss her with his emotions laid bare: she'd drain the life from him.

"Do you want to shower before we leave?" She sat cross-legged beside him.

He still hadn't moved. His brow was furrowed, and his emotions were locked down. "We should talk."

"About?" Her heart began to race, pounding like a drum.

Not all faeries had the same sensitivities, but she'd begun to realize that Devlin was attuned to Hunt-like qualities. Her thrumming pulse was as clear to him as a thundering bass would be to most faeries.

"I received a message—"

"Wait." She put her hands on the mattress on either side of his still bare chest, bracing herself as she leaned over him. She kissed him for just a moment, lost herself in the touch of his lips against hers, his breath tangled with hers, his skin against hers.

His hands were on her hips, not pulling her closer or pushing her away, just keeping her steady. It wasn't like the dream, but it wasn't all restraint either. He stared up at her curiously for a moment. Her heart raced just as loud, but now it was the right sort of reason.

She leaned back and sat atop his legs. "Okay."

To his credit, he didn't question her actions. He resumed his sentence: "I received a message that requires a change to our plans."

"When?"

"In my dream." He stared at her. "Before our dreams . . ."

"That was real? What we . . . you and me . . . and . . ." She leaned closer until she was once more braced over him, and placed a hand on either shoulder.

"I told you it was real." He reached up and threaded his fingers through her hair. "Do you regret it?" He let none of his emotions leak through, but she didn't need to taste his emotions to know he was afraid of her answer.

"Awake or asleep, I want you," she assured. "The only reason I'd say no in the waking world is because I *like* you, but if it's safe there—and it is, right?"

"Yes. It's safe there." He smiled, but there was also tension in his expression.

"How? How did we do that? Share a dream, I mean."

"There are those who can walk in dreams," he murmured.

"And *we* did? You knew, and we—" She broke off and kissed him until she was breathless. "Are you tired enough to sleep more?"

"I would rather stay here with you, fall asleep or stay awake, just be with you, but I need to go." He paused, frowned, and then said, "Faerie is coming unmade. I need to retrieve Seth and deliver him to Sorcha."

"Say that again." She stared at him, trying to process the enormity of what he'd announced so casually. The revelation about what they'd done—*and that it was real!*—shook her world, but the second announcement wasn't the good kind. "What you just said. Repeat it."

Devlin propped himself up on his elbows. "I need to collect Seth before we can resume . . . anything."

Ani realized that she was watching him like she was transfixed. "Give me a sec here, Dev." She slid farther back from him and tried to focus. "Faerie is coming apart . . . what does that even *mean*?"

"Within Faerie, reality is a reflection of the queen's will. Once there were two courts there, and the world was the combined visions of the two monarchs. With the Dark Court gone from Faerie, there is only Sorcha, and she appears to be ill from mourning her s—*Seth's* absence. If Faerie vanishes, we all die with it." Devlin sat up and wrapped a black leather tie around the hair he'd gathered at the nape of his neck. His movements were unhurried; his tone was calm.

And the world is ending.

It wasn't like Ani thought often about Faerie, but it was their *homeland*. In some primal part of herself, of every faery, there was a chord that was struck at the thought of Faerie. For her, Faerie was forbidden, but somewhere inside she'd still known that it was *there*.

"I will take him to her and return quickly." Devlin stood and retrieved his shirt. As he spoke, he put on his shirt and shoes. "I'm certain we will resolve it. I'm not sure the seasonal courts need to be made aware, but the Dark Kings need to be informed. Perhaps if I cannot wake her, they can . . . come home."

"What do you need me to do?" she asked.

"Tell your steed that invisibility and optimum speed are required. Blending in with the mortals aids us in hiding you, but I fear that the time to retrieve Seth for the High

Queen is limited." Devlin's words and manner were becoming increasingly aloof.

"Devlin?" Ani put a hand on his arm.

He paused.

"Is she going to be okay? Your sister?" Regardless of what Ani thought of the High Queen, Sorcha was Devlin's sister. If Tish were sick, Ani would be lost.

"The High Queen has never been ill," he said. "I will do what must be done, but I cannot say that I am without worry . . . or frustration. Her behavior is—" He stopped himself. "The High Queen should not mourn. She should not grow ill over emotion. Something else has happened, but Rae didn't tell—"

"Rae?"

"She delivered the message from Faerie."

"You know Rae," Ani said slowly. "Rae from the dreams?"

"Yes." Devlin gave her an unreadable look. His emotions were so tamped down that she had no idea what he felt.

She didn't know what to say.

And when she didn't respond, he asked, "What do you need to do before we depart?"

"Give me fifteen minutes." She walked past him to the bathroom.

Rae is real. Ani had just learned that her dream with Devlin was real, but hearing Devlin mention Rae so casually startled her. *Who is she to him? What is she?*

Ani absently went through the motions of washing up and brushing her teeth as she replayed every detail she knew about Rae. There were more questions than Ani could fully process, but in light of what Devlin had told her, asking about Rae seemed unnecessarily selfish.

CHAPTER 26

Devlin held Ani's discarded shirt in his hands. He'd kissed Ani, shared a dream with her, and for a few brief moments, his life had been his own. After an eternity of existing as an object in an endless conflict between his sisters, the possibility of living on his own terms was intoxicating—and interrupted already.

Sorcha's maudlin emotion over Seth was forcing Devlin to choose between staying at Ani's side to keep her safe from his mad sister or abandoning her because of the solipsism of his other sister. Being near Ani had made him realize he wanted a life that he knew he couldn't have as the High Queen's Bloodied Hands. He was made to exist as the fulcrum between Order and Discord; he only had value because he served the will of the Unchanging Queen and reminded War not to kill them all by killing Order.

I want to determine my own path.

Ani returned to the main room. "I have questions. You're

keeping things from me, but they'll wait. I'll wait."

"You'll wait for what?"

"Answers. You. Time. Whatever this is"—she came over and took his hands—"it's not going to go away. I don't really buy the whole fate thing. I know the Eolas claim to know the future, and so do . . . your sisters, but it's not always as set as all that. Some things, though, feel like they're *right*. You and me? It's one of those things. I don't know what they see or why things are such a mess, but in the middle of it all, I do know that being around you is really the best thing that's happened to me in, well, *ever*."

Her words only made him surer that he needed to keep her safe.

"My sisters cannot see your threads." He looked down at their hands and then back at her as he added, "They cannot see those whose threads are tangled into their own futures . . . or, they say, into mine."

She held tight to him and asked, "So I'm in their future or yours? Can *you* see future threads?"

"I can." He pulled his hands free and paced to the window of the tiny room. This wasn't a topic he enjoyed discussing.

"Can you see mine?"

"I tried, but . . . no." He didn't look at her or speak of the fact that this meant that their lives were entangled as far as her future stretched. "The only way for *them* to see you is through ordinary channels—a faery who carries word to them, or your presence where they can see you."

"You can't see my future at all," she prompted.

He wasn't hiding his emotions away, not now. Instead, he let Ani feel his worry and his hopes. "I haven't been able to see your future since you were not-killed . . . since I didn't . . . It's not that you've lacked an existence but because you . . . we . . ."

"Because your life and mine are entangled," she finished.

"In some way." He looked out at the parking lot. "Maybe you should stay here in the room, maybe—"

"No." She was right behind him when she said it.

He looked over his shoulder at her. "Either of my sisters would kill you without compunction. I can't lose you."

"I know." She put a hand on his arm and tugged so he was facing her. "You aren't using *any* sort of logic, Devlin. Hounds can't stay trapped, and even if I could, wouldn't it at least be safer to have someone with me?"

He growled, a sound that was very not–High Court, but nothing inside of him felt High Court anymore. "I don't know whether you're safer in the mortal world or in Faerie. Perhaps stay *here*, and Irial—"

Ani reached up and pulled him down for a kiss. "No."

"Call Irial. See if he'd come here." Devlin hated the idea of Ani trapped in a room with the embodiment of temptation, but he hated the idea of Ani being killed even more.

All of these emotions are . . . too much.

She felt them all, knew every emotion he was trying to make sense of, allowed him to express them even if his centuries of hiding them kept them from being visible.

"What do you want?" she asked.

"You with me and safe." He knew it wasn't logical, but he didn't want to be apart from Ani.

"One problem solved then." She picked up the shirt he'd been holding earlier. After she shoved it and the rest of her belongings into the bag, she zipped it. "That's what I want too. I'm going with you at least as far as Huntsdale. We'll figure out the rest after we talk to Iri."

"And Niall. We will consult the Dark King," he said.

She lifted her bag. "And Gabriel. He's likely to be difficult. There's this whole no-dating-the-Gabriel's-daughter thing. . . ."

Devlin shrugged, but he let her feel the excitement that filled him. "We are, though."

"We are," Ani repeated in a soft voice. She stared up at him. "I would fight him for you . . . well, if he *would* fight me, but he's afraid I'm going to get broken."

For a moment, Devlin stared at her, not wanting to tell her that she was far more likely to break others than to be broken. He was willing to sacrifice everything he'd ever been for her. He brushed his lips over hers. "Gabriel is a fool. You are not invincible, Ani, but you are not mortal-weak. You are a worthy fighting partner." Devlin reached through a false pocket on the side of his trousers and slid a knife from a thigh sheath. He held it out. "Here. I know you have yours, but . . . I would give you . . . if you . . ."

She took it. "A girl can never have too many weapons."

He lifted her bag from her shoulder. "You need to wake the steed."

"Dev?" She gave him a very serious look and put her hand on his chest. "I'll do my best to be careful with everything you are giving me."

He didn't have the words to answer that, so he merely nodded.

She reached out to turn the doorknob, but before she opened it, he put a hand on hers: there were faeries who wanted her dead.

"May I go first?" he asked.

"Today, but not always." She smiled at him. "You *know* that if there's any chance to fight, I won't sit on the sidelines like some silly High Court faery."

"You're the daughter of Gabriel. I wouldn't expect anything less." Devlin repressed the surge of happiness he felt at having someone want to fight alongside him.

The Queen's Assassin was to be alone. He lived and fought alone. Sorcha had always made that detail explicitly clear. She'd given him soldiers and guards to train; she'd allowed him almost complete power in such matters. There were only two rules: unlike in the other courts, no High Court soldiers were to be female, and his own prowess was to be held as an example. His ability to kill efficiently was proof of his other sister's parentage. The bloodthirstiness Sorcha abhorred in Bananach, she exploited in Devlin.

Ani, without meaning to, challenged every limitation he'd lived by for eternity. He hadn't truly known what he lacked until Ani's vibrancy had illuminated the emptiness in his life. He had a fleeting image of training Ani. If they were able to leave Sorcha and live as solitaries, they'd need to be stronger than any other faery they met. Her heritage certainly predisposed her to be so: Gabriel had been the left hand of the Dark Court, the dispenser of Irial's punishments, for centuries. Other Gabriels had preceded him, and Ani was very much like them. Devlin suspected that expectations of mortality were all that had kept Gabriel from training her to lead her own pack. Devlin knew better: when the last of her mortal blood was consumed by her faery blood, she would be able to stand against most any faery.

He thought of the wolves that attended Ani in her dreams. They were harbingers of the Hunt, but they weren't feral things pacing near her. They looked to her for guidance.

Was that what you saw, Sorcha? That she would be strong? Or was it merely that she would be mine?

Once the High Queen was retrieved from her dream, Devlin had questions he wanted answered before he left her side.

CHAPTER 27

Rae returned to the room where Sorcha slept. Outside the window, the sky appeared to have dimmed, not into darkness but into a chalky palate as if the color was being leeched away. Neither day nor night existed, only perpetual dusk. It meant Rae was free to roam, but that freedom was of little consolation when the world was vanishing.

"Could you go to the other world?" Rae asked the queen's attendants. "The mortal world—"

"No." One of veiled mortals turned to face Rae. "We stay with our queen. If she dies, we die."

"Why?" Rae stared at them.

"There is nothing for us there. Our queen brought us here, and here is where we stay." The mortal paused, and longing crept into her voice as she added, "The lives we had there are gone; the people we knew are dead; the rules . . . it's not *our* world now, not with the way time passes."

The muted light that fell through the window threw gray

shadows over the glass-encased bed. The bed had shrunk and now had a more funereal shape. Rae wasn't sure if the casketlike appearance was a reflection of the shrinking of the queen's world or something more; regardless of the reason, it was unnerving.

With nothing else to do but await dissolution of the world, Rae entered the queen's dreams once again.

The leonine guards hissed at her.

"I don't want to see you," Sorcha said. Her gaze did not leave the mirror.

"Devlin is bringing Seth to you, but he says that Faerie must be as it should be so Seth can reach you."

Sorcha gestured at the image in the mirror: Seth was walking down a street. "I can see him. He is *not* in Faerie."

"He will be," Rae insisted. "Maybe you should wake to ready yourself."

At that, Sorcha did pull her gaze from the mirror. The look she gave Rae was withering. "I need a heartbeat to ready myself, child. I am the High Queen, not some mortal who must work at attempting to achieve perfection. When he comes, I'll wake, but not before. Go and do not disturb me until he is here."

There were no more words. One of the winged creatures licked its maw and gave Rae an approximation of a smile. The High Queen's dreaming guards were extensions of her will, and her will was that she not be disturbed.

Rae shuddered and stepped back into the darkened room in Faerie.

Hours later, the stillness was broken by a scream—and another, and then several more. Through a tall glass window on the far side of the cavernous room, Rae could see an unfamiliar faery striding down the street. As she walked, she slashed out with a battle-ax and flung knives at fleeing faeries. All the while she smiled.

I know you. Rae wasn't sure how, but the new faery felt familiar. The faery had thick feathered wings, dark tresses that were a combination of hair and feathers, and patterns drawn on her face. Her gaze was darting around assessingly.

She paused across the street and looked at Rae. The smile she gave Rae was familiar, an unpleasant match to Devlin's. *Devlin's other sister. Bananach.*

"There you are, girl."

Rae heard the words; through wall and glass they flew as if they were physical things sent crashing toward her. She stepped backward, putting herself between Sorcha and the faery who must be Bananach, the High Queen's mad twin. It wasn't that Rae could stop Bananach: the insubstantial couldn't impede the physical. It wasn't even that she cared to protect Sorcha: the High Queen had done nothing to earn Rae's loyalty. Rae's action was the instinctual movement to keep safe the entity that created the world around them. Sorcha created; Bananach destroyed. That simple fact was enough to align Rae's loyalty for the moment.

Bananach grabbed a sleeping faery and tossed him through the window. Shards of glass crashed on the stone floor in a dangerous shower. The faery she'd thrown lay unaware and bleeding. The queen's two mortals didn't react at all. They stayed beside their queen's casket.

"Run. Now," Rae said to them. She didn't turn to see if they obeyed.

The destructive faery looked to her left and right, reached down and uprooted a small sapling, and used it to knock out the remaining glass in the window frame. Shards hit the stone floor like a glittering rain shower.

Rae didn't move, couldn't move, as Bananach stared at her.

Bits of glass crunched under Bananach's boots as she stepped through the window frame into the room.

"You belong to my brother," Bananach said by way of greeting.

The raven-faery leaned close enough to Rae that for a breath it felt like she was going to walk into Rae. Rae moved to the side.

Bananach sniffed, circling Rae as she did so, and then paused. She tilted her head so close to her own shoulder that it looked as if her neck muscles had been severed. "You smell like him. He's not here."

"He's not," Rae agreed.

Beyond Bananach, Rae could see a few still-awake faeries who stood in the street. They watched the raven-faery as she stalked and circled Rae. They didn't move, not to help or to flee. They stared with very un–High Court looks of horror on their faces.

"You have worn his skin"—Bananach sniffed again—"more than a few times. He let you inside of his body."

"Devlin is my friend," Rae said.

Bananach cackled. "He has no friends. He wasn't made for such things."

Rae straightened her shoulders and stared at the faery. "I am whatever he wants me to be."

The faery stared at Rae as if she could see things, and Rae suspected she *was* seeing things, looking at the threads of Rae's future. The sensation of being studied thusly was disquieting. Bananach was weighing and measuring her, and if the results weren't to her liking, there was no reason to believe she'd ignore Rae.

Can she kill me?

But whatever Bananach saw as she peered into Rae's future apparently wasn't cause to try to strike her. *Does she see anything?* The expressions on the faery's face were unreadable. She merely nodded and stepped around Rae.

"And there *you* are, sister mine." Bananach reached out as if to touch the glass casket. Her talon-tipped hand hovered in the air over the blue glass. "Do you hear me?"

Rae had an unpleasant moment in which she wanted very badly not to respond, not to draw the raven-faery's attention back to her. It was a normal response: prey rarely wanted to summon the predator's gaze. It was also not the acceptable response. If Bananach could injure Sorcha, could further disrupt the High Queen's grasp on reality, the consequences were too large to fathom.

"She can *not* hear you," Rae said.

Bananach's head swiveled at an inhuman angle. "But she hears you, doesn't she?"

Rae shrugged. "Sometimes."

"And what does she dream, the mad queen?" Bananach's hand lowered to the glass even as she stared at Rae. Absently, she scraped her talon-nails over the glass, making a screeching sound.

"Ask Devlin."

Bananach's wings flexed, opening so that the shadows blocked the scant light from the window. "He's not here, child."

"He will be."

"Aaaah, he will be . . . do you suppose he and the Hound received my message then?" Bananach asked. "I left them a gift."

"A gift?"

"Bloodied, but no longer screaming." Bananach looked crestfallen for a moment. "If I could have saved the screams, I would've, but they died with the body."

Rae didn't know what to say or do.

Bananach shook her head. "I have faeries to kill before I speak to my brother, Dreamwalker, but I'll be back soon."

Even as she spoke, she brought both fists down on the glass. A large clang echoed throughout the hall, the sound loud enough that Rae winced and covered her ears. The walls seemed to shudder—but the glass was unbroken.

"Alas." Bananach laid her cheek on the glass over

Sorcha's face. "I'll slaughter them all while you rest. Well, not all"—she stroked the glass—"today. I needed a bit of discord to soothe me, to help me make ready to destroy the betrayer."

She left as calmly as she had come, stepping through the window frame. As Rae stood helplessly, Bananach departed, resuming her slaughter as she went down the street—stabbing abdomens, twisting necks, and flinging bodies. She did not distinguish between the sleeping and the alert. The world of Faerie shifted around War. Fires for the dead flamed into existence; screams echoed long past the ends of lives; and a charnel scent rose in the air in a sickening cloud.

Come soon, Dev.

Chapter 28

Ani didn't steer; at the speeds they traveled back to Huntsdale, it would be impossible for her to try to direct her steed. Barry was currently in the form of a GT by Citroën; one beauty of being able to shift form at will was that the steed could be a car that wasn't even in production. She knew that Barry had plucked the image from her mind to make her smile, but even the joy of rocketing across the country in a matte-black version of the gorgeous concept car didn't cheer her.

The weight of the situation felt like it had settled atop Ani's lungs, making breathing more difficult than it should be. Faerie was dissolving, and Devlin could be caught in that. Ani wasn't sure if she could go to Faerie. Sorcha had ordered Ani's death; Devlin had disobeyed her. *Would she kill me if I went there? Would it be worse for him?* Ani couldn't figure out whether she would be a help or hindrance if she went.

Being in Huntsdale where Bananach was didn't sound particularly appealing either. She'd fled to avoid War's attention, but the only faeries she knew who were strong enough to stand against Bananach were in Huntsdale.

If I'm going to die either way, I'd rather stay with him. She was pretty certain *that* wasn't a line of argument that would be useful in discussion with anyone. She glanced at Devlin. His eyes were closed, and his face was expressionless, but she felt his fear and anger. He wasn't hiding his feelings.

"Why does Seth matter to Sorcha?" Ani asked. "I get that she made him a faery and all, but . . . what's the big deal about him?"

"That's a question I intend to ask the High Queen." He reached out and laid his hand atop hers, entwining their fingers. "What I know right now is only what Rae told me."

"And you're not telling me everything, are you?"

"No. I'm not," he admitted. Devlin pulled his hand away rather than hide his emotions. "The queen's secrets aren't mine to share, but . . . I can say that I need to bring Seth to her."

"There are secrets about the queen and Seth?" she asked.

"Yes."

They traveled in silence for a few moments until Devlin finally said, "She has Seth. Perhaps she will not oppose my being solitary."

Ani stilled. "Could you do that?"

"Many faeries do so." That wasn't a real answer though: Devlin wasn't most faeries.

Neither am I.

The idea of Sorcha letting him walk away seemed ludicrous. He was hers as much as Gabriel belonged to the Dark King.

Could I convince her to let me come and go in Faerie?

What happened next was dependent on so many things beyond their control and so many answers they didn't know.

Like why she wanted me dead.

She reached out and took Devlin's hand again.

He turned his head and opened his eyes. "I'm sorry I can't set this aside, but after—"

"Duty isn't something to apologize for." She held his gaze. "I'm glad you aren't afraid of me. I'm glad you found me, and"—she smiled—"didn't kill me."

His emotions vanished as he asked, "Which time?"

"Any of them."

"And I am glad you didn't kill me"—his emotional guard slipped only long enough for her to glimpse how worried he was—"and that you kissed me."

She brushed her lips over his. "Which time?"

"All of them."

They went back to silence as the landscape blurred around them.

With her free hand, Ani dialed Tish—and was dumped into voice mail instantly.

"Call me," she said.

She was about to call Pins and Needles when the phone rang. HOME was on the caller ID. "Hey."

It wasn't Tish or Rabbit. Irial was calling from the shop number. "I need to you to come home," he said.

Her hand tightened on her cell at his emotionless tone. "On the way already."

"With Devlin?" Irial prompted.

"Yeah." She glanced at Devlin. "He's here. Did you need to talk to him?"

"Not yet," Irial said. "Stay with him until you get here. Promise."

"What's going on? Iri?" Ani felt her hands start to sweat. "Talk to me."

"I will. I'll meet you *here* . . . at the studio." His voice was gentle, but there was no doubt as to his lack of malleability. "Come home, Ani."

"Is everything okay? Where are Tish and Rabbit? Are they with you?"

Irial's pause was almost too long. "Rabbit's here, and Tish is at my house."

She disconnected and told her steed, *Barry, I need you to go faster. Can you?*

Maybe a little. Barry had already covered almost all of the distance they'd crossed, but holding two passengers and traveling at its fastest pace wasn't easy.

Nothing in this world can move as fast as you, she told the steed.

In this world or in Faerie, Ani, Barry added. *I would be even faster there.*

If I go—

If we *go,* Barry corrected. *I am your steed, Ani. We will always be together . . . even though it means putting up with him.*

After Barry's voice faded away, Ani was left with nothing to do but break the silence with music or conversation. Strangely for her, loud music seemed unappealing, and conversation felt futile. Everything felt tenuous.

Devlin reached out for her hand again, and they sat in the dark of the car, silent and holding on to each other for several hours.

At some point, she fell asleep, and the next thing she heard was Devlin saying, "Wake up, Ani."

Good idea, Barry said. *We are here.*

She blinked her eyes and tried to focus on the road in front of them. Now that they were in city limits, Barry had slowed to a normal speed and resumed his default appearance of a Barracuda.

I am exhausted, Ani.

"Rest," she murmured. Gently, she stroked her hand over the dashboard. "No one has a better steed."

"Agreed," Devlin said.

They pulled around the back of the shop. Before the engine was off, Irial was standing at her door. He opened it and took her hand. "Come inside."

Still sleepy, Ani let him pull her close to his side, but it felt odd to be so near anyone but Devlin.

"What's going on?" she asked.

"Inside first." Irial looked over at Devlin, who'd immediately come to stand on the opposite side of her.

Ani stepped inside the studio. "You're scaring me."

The lights were all off, and the CLOSED sign was in the window. Through the glass, Ani could see several Hounds standing guard at both ends of the block. Devlin entered the studio, but positioned himself between her and the door, so anyone who managed to get past the Hounds outside would have to confront him. As nervous as she was, she didn't object to being protected instead of standing beside him. He glanced at her, and then returned his attention to scanning the street, the shop, anywhere threats could lurk.

"Iri?" she asked.

"Sit down." Irial tried to pull her over to a chair. "We can talk out here. Rabbit's finally sleeping."

"Rabbit's *sleeping*?" She looked around, listened to the pervasive stillness in the studio, and felt her fears rise up. "Where's Tish? Why is she at your house?"

"I'm sorry." Irial had hold of her arm, keeping her still, trying to direct her to the chair.

"What's going on?" She tugged her arm away. "Are they hurt? Who's h—"

"I'm so sorry. I thought they were safe; I thought she . . ." Irial had tears in his eyes.

Ani felt panic rising. "Take me to Tish."

She looked over at Devlin. He stepped closer to her.

Irial started, "Ani—"

"No! Where is she?" She pulled away from Irial and went toward the door that led from the shop into the living space of her home.

"Ani. She's gone." Irial pulled her hand away from the door, peeling each finger from the knob. "Bananach killed Tish. Tish is d—"

"No!" Ani shoved him. "She's . . . *no.* Tish didn't do anything. She didn't have anything to do with Bananach. She's . . ."

The floor seemed to come up to meet her as she slid down the wall. The world felt wrong. Her stomach twisted as everything that made sense in the world was suddenly gone.

"Tish is dead? My Tish gone?" Ani looked up at him. "When?"

"Last night." Irial crouched down in front of her.

"How?" She pushed away every emotion, not by choice, but by necessity. Her feelings threatened to drown her. She shook from the intensity of the rage snarling inside her. Rage made sense, chased away the tears. Her skin stung like crawling things were all over her. It hurt too much to even let the anger well up.

Focus.

She took several breaths, caught Irial's gaze, and asked, "How did she . . . did it happen?"

"It was quick," Irial hedged. "Can we leave it at that for now?"

Ani stared at him. Her once-king, her protector all of

these years, was undoubtedly devastated too—and guilt-stricken.

"For the moment," she whispered. There were tears inside, but letting them fall meant Tish was really gone.

She can't be.

Ani stood. "I should go to Rabbit."

"He's fine. Your house is the safest place in the city tonight. I *promise.*" Irial reached out and brushed her hair back. "I'm sorry, Ani. We thought we had enough guards, and she hadn't tried anything. There were Hounds here, and if Tish hadn't . . ."

"Hadn't what?"

"She slipped out." Irial scowled; at himself or at Tish, Ani wasn't sure. "You'd think they could keep track of her, and . . . I don't know why she did it."

"She didn't like to be caged. She did better than I do, but after a few days, she was still Gabriel's daughter, and . . ." Ani shuddered at the thought of telling her father. "Does he know?"

"He does. The Hunt all know." Irial looked lost, like he wanted to say something that would make everything right, but there was nothing. "Ani . . ."

She looked at him, not wanting to comfort him, not wanting to hear his words, not wanting the conversation to continue.

"Go check on Rabbit, please? I need . . . I need . . ." Ani's words faltered. She looked past Irial to Devlin.

He crossed the room to her side.

She folded her arms over her chest, but it didn't stop the trembling.

"Bananach would have to kill me in order to touch Ani." Devlin said the words evenly. "Anyone killing me is very unlikely."

Irial looked from one to the other, and then he left.

The quiet in the room was so much worse than before. It was empty. Tish wouldn't ever come running into the studio again. She wouldn't be there arguing over the music they played. She wouldn't scold Ani. She wouldn't *anything.*

Bananach had killed her.

Ani's heart felt like it would stop, and for a moment she wished it would. *It should've been me.* Tish was gone, and Ani was left without her.

Ani looked at Devlin. "I want her dead for this."

Chapter 29

Devlin had no words for Ani as she stood there silently. He knew this was when comfort was to be offered. Logic insisted there should be something he could say. There really wasn't. His sister had killed her sister.

Ani didn't weep. She stared at him with dry eyes. "Help me? I need to fix . . . this."

"It isn't something you can fix." Devlin wished there was more he could say, some word, some promise. He couldn't. War destroyed lives, families, hope. If they didn't find a way to nullify Bananach, this would be just the first member of Ani's family to die.

Words weren't of any use, so Devlin pulled her into his arms.

The tears she'd been refusing to let fall started to race down her cheeks. "I'd undo it all if I could. If you could've killed me, then Tish and Jillian would be okay and—"

"No. Neither of them would've wanted that." Devlin

kissed her forehead and held her.

He wasn't sure how long they stayed that way. Ani wept almost silently, her tears soaking his shirt and her cries muffled against his chest. Devlin knew it wasn't even the edge of her grief, but her brother slept on the other side of the door. She wouldn't wail now, not when it could upset Rabbit.

Devlin listened for the sounds of movement outside in the street or in the house, but heard only Ani and those who were there to care for her. Irial made a number of calls; the timbre of the former Dark King's voice revealed none of the fury that Devlin knew lurked not far below the surface. Irial's family had been stricken, and of all the courts, it was the Dark Court that held family as almost sacred.

Unlike the High Court . . .

Somehow, in the grief that was weighing on all of the house's inhabitants, he needed to broach the reason for their return.

Irial opened the door. "He's awake."

Ani stretched up and brushed a kiss over Devlin's lips. She didn't speak as she went inside.

Irial and Devlin stood together for a moment. There was no way to ease into the discussion, and no way to postpone it. Seth needed to be taken to Sorcha. The timing was unpleasant, but the reality was what it was. Crises didn't abide by schedules.

"We need to talk. Sorcha is unwell," Devlin began.

Irial held up a hand. "Let me start the coffee first? I haven't slept yet."

Devlin nodded and followed the former Dark King into Ani's home. Being there was disquieting. These tiny rooms attached to the tattooist's studio were where she had healed from the consequences of what his sister had ordered, and now it was where she wept for the consequences of his other sister's cruelty.

His sisters were the source of her pain. He walled his emotions up more tightly. He'd do what needed to be done, and he'd try to find a way to give her a better future. *Maybe I can return Jillian to her.*

Ani stood in the hallway between the kitchen and what appeared to be the bedrooms. "Rab?"

"Ani." Rabbit's voice was raw with mourning. He stepped into the hall and grabbed Ani. "You're safe. Gods, I was . . . You have to listen. You will do whatever it takes to stay safe from her. Tell me that. Tell me. . . . Promise."

"Shhhh." Ani wrapped her arms around her brother, holding him against the torrents of tears streaming down his cheeks. "I'm home. I'm sorry I wasn't here. It's my fault—"

"No," Rabbit and Irial both answered.

Ani looked at them. "Yes."

"No. Mortals are breakable," Devlin said. "Even if you were here, she would've—"

Ani shoved past him back into the studio and then outside. The slam of the second door was accompanied by the clatter of the bell that hung there—and Ani's angry scream.

"Stay." Irial put a hand Rabbit's arm when the tattooist started to follow. He looked at Devlin pointedly.

As if I needed encouragement to follow her . . .

Seeing Ani like this was so outside his realm of experience. His own emotions were as locked up as they'd ever been, but it still ripped him apart inside. Ani was hurt.

Devlin went into the studio and paused. There were Hounds out there, and she stood just on the other side of the large front windows of the shop. *I could go through the window if she were in immediate danger.* The threat was too much. *I need to be beside her if there is an attack.* He took a deep breath before pushing the door open.

She refused to look in his direction. Instead, she stared resolutely at nothing.

He leaned against the wall beside her. "It wasn't your fault. You must know that."

Tears slid over her face, but she didn't brush them away. They fell down her chin and cheeks, coursed down her neck, and dripped onto her shirt. Ani glanced sideways at him. "I don't know anything right now."

He sighed and tried again. "What do you need?"

"Rabbit made safe, and then your sister made dead." Ani bared her teeth. "Breath for breath. She took my sister."

"You can't kill her."

"Really?" Ani pushed off the building and spun so she

was standing facing him. Her feet were spread in a fighter's stance. Her eyes were shimmering with the same sulfurous glow as the eyes of the Hounds' steeds. "Tell me why."

He'd told no one his sisters' secrets. For eternity, he'd lived for them, but Faerie was coming unmade, and the mortal world would be devastated if Bananach brought about a true faery war. The time for protecting the twins' secrets had ended.

"Come inside." He held out his hand to Ani. It shook. The thought of her refusing him mattered more than anything should. He'd still be there if she grew cold to him, but it would ache the way few things ever could.

She looked at him with the monstrous green gaze of the Hunt. "Irial is inside. He won't let me go after her."

He nodded. "I know."

"I am the Hunt. Tish is—*was*—my sister. She was a part of me, my best friend. *I cannot just accept this.*" Ani's tears had stopped; rage hummed in her words and body. "No one kills the Hunt without vengeance. Gabriel might not have called her Pack, but *I do.*"

"Come inside with me." He kept his hand outstretched and added, "Please?"

She took his hand in hers. "I want her blood, Devlin. I want her death. I want her to ache."

He opened the door to the studio and motioned for her to precede him. "I understand."

And he did. If anyone hurt Ani, he'd feel the same

way, but that didn't change the impossibility of killing Bananach.

There is no return from this. He wasn't sure that a return had been possible for some time.

"I go where you go, Ani," Devlin told her. "We need to talk first. I need to tell you and Irial"—he paused and considered the consequences of the trusts he was breaking—"truths that are not to be shared."

She held his gaze. "I want her to hurt."

He didn't flinch. "I know, but I need you to listen."

Mutely, she nodded.

He kept his fingers laced with hers as they went back to the kitchen.

"Rabbit's . . . he'll be back out in a minute." Irial glanced at the doorway. "He'll be better now that you're here."

Ani sat at the table, still holding Devlin's hand in hers.

Devlin took the chair next to her. There was no delicate way to share what he had to say, nor was this the time for prevarications. He simply said, "If you kill Bananach, Sorcha will die. If Sorcha dies, we all die. The twins are balanced halves, the two energies that came first. Before them and after them, there is nothing. If you kill either of them, every faery will die. Maybe some of the halflings will live, but the rest . . . we all expire if she dies. Sorcha is essential. She is the source of all our magicks, our longevity, everything. If not, don't you think Bananach would've killed her by now?"

Irial lowered himself to a chair.

Ani sat speechless for a moment, but then began trying to find the hole in his logic. She was irrepressible when she wanted something, and she very badly wanted Bananach's blood. "How do you know? Maybe they just—"

"I know. They *made* me, Ani. I call them sisters, but before me, there were only two. The opposition, the balance. It's what our whole people are based upon. Each court has its opposite. Too much imbalance will cause disaster. Sorcha . . . she adjusts what she must to assure stasis."

Irial looked up, and Devlin caught his gaze.

"She will arrange against her wishes to assure the greater balance"—he did not look away from Irial as he made the admission—"even for that court which is her opposition, even as her counterbalance has abandoned Faerie to live among mortals. The Dark Court balances the High Court, but Sorcha requires *more*: since the start of forever her true counterbalance has been Bananach."

"Well that just sucks, doesn't it?" Ani leaned back, but she didn't pull her hand away from his. "Bananach wants me to kill Seth and Niall—and oh yeah, she wants to kill me . . . and there's not a damn thing we can do without killing *everyone*."

No one spoke for several heartbeats: there was nothing to say.

Silently, Ani released his hand and left the room.

After Ani walked back down the hallway, Irial started, "Would Sorcha hide Ani?"

Devlin shook his head. "Sorcha ordered me to kill Ani years ago."

Irial asked, "Because she saw that Ani would . . . what?"

"I was not privy to that information." Devlin glanced at the hallway. "I can't let Ani kill my sisters or let them kill her."

Irial sighed and lowered his head again. "So we try to keep Ani, Rabbit, Seth, and Niall alive and hope War finds another amusement."

Devlin felt a strange guilt at adding to the already complex situation. He weighed his words carefully and settled on, "I believe it would be . . . catastrophic should Seth be killed. In truth, it might be catastrophic if Seth doesn't return to Faerie soon. Sorcha is asleep, mourning Seth's absence apparently."

"Well, that's . . . not very orderly, is it?" Irial said.

"Something is wrong with my sister." Devlin watched Irial pour several cups of coffee. To one cup, he added the cream and solitary sugar cube that Ani favored.

"We'll figure something out." Irial gave Devlin a knowing look that reminded him that he'd forgotten to cloak any of his feelings.

"I . . ." Devlin started. There weren't words though, not ones he could speak. His envy over the way Irial knew Ani, his worry over her, his futile emotions—none were of the High Court. For a heartbeat, Devlin just stared at Irial, waiting for the mockery or chastisement or reminder that he wasn't worthy of Ani.

Irial held out Ani's coffee. "She needs you right now. Go."

Devlin stood and took the cup—and paused at the roll of terror that told him that Gabriel had arrived.

Chapter 30

Ani had heard and felt everything Devlin shared with Irial. It didn't mute her grief or rage, but it was comforting to know that she wasn't alone. Devlin wouldn't kill Bananach but he wasn't going to abandon her, and she needed every strong faery they could rouse. She couldn't lose Rabbit.

Or Irial.

Or Gabriel.

Or Devlin.

She heard the arrival of Gabriel—and with him Niall and Seth. She didn't want to see them all at once though, so she stepped into Rabbit's room and waited for Gabriel.

Rabbit sat on the edge of his bed, looking lost. He'd undoubtedly heard the earlier conversation in the kitchen, and he knew as well as she did that their situation was growing increasingly bleak. They didn't speak. Instead, they waited—and listened.

Irial's and Niall's voices were low, but they were *here.*

Knowing the current and former Dark Kings were now both in her home was comforting; so too was the sound of Gabriel's boots as he came down the hallway.

"I'm sorry," was all Gabriel said when he came into the room.

"You failed." Rabbit looked at Gabriel with a ferocity that was matched on their father's face.

Gabriel didn't look away from the challenge in Rabbit's voice. "The Hunt will keep her—and you—as safe as we can."

Ani shook her head. "Well, since killing War isn't an option, I don't really see how that's possible."

None of them spoke.

Ani went over, took her brother's hand in hers, and tugged him to his feet. Reluctantly, he followed to stand in front of Gabriel.

Once Gabriel and Rabbit were face-to-face, Ani said, "Neither of you is to blame. I *get* the whole blame thing. She killed Tish because of me." She let go of Rabbit's hand and stepped back. "I couldn't give Bananach what she demanded, not my blood or the king's or Seth's."

She saw Seth and Devlin in the hallway behind Gabriel. She caught and held Seth's gaze as she told him, "I considered killing you, but Irial and Niall wouldn't like it. There'd be too many other consequences that would please Bananach. But if I'd thought I had to kill you to save Tish . . . maybe. Probably."

"We need a plan," Devlin started.

Seth looked over his shoulder to Devlin for a moment. "I know what I want: Bananach dead."

Ani smiled. "Seth, I think this the first time I might actually see why people like you."

Devlin frowned. "We cannot kill her."

"I know." Ani looked at him. "So what do we do?"

"The High Court's *assassin* doesn't make the decisions around here," Gabriel growled.

"No, I don't, but neither do you." Devlin didn't raise his voice or react to Gabriel's menace. "Do you have any idea what your daughter is?"

"Dark Court." Gabriel stepped into the hallway. "Unlike you."

"Devlin!" Ani started toward them, but Rabbit put a hand on her shoulder.

"Wait," Rabbit murmured.

Seth came into the room, giving Gabriel and Devlin space to sort things out. He reached out to Rabbit and clasped his forearm. "Sorry, man."

Rabbit nodded. "I'm glad you're here."

Ani didn't want to talk about grief, not now, not ever. She wanted to plan.

She raised her voice, though, and called out, "Irial?"

"Shush, love," Irial called back. "It's just territory stuff they need to square away before we can get to business. Let them talk."

Gabriel and Devlin were glaring at each other.

"That's *not* going to end with talking." Ani sat down

beside Rabbit and watched the confrontation.

Her brother put his arm around her. "Gabriel needs to deal with his grief."

"By beating my . . ." Her words faded as she tried to figure out what term finished that sentence.

"Your what?" Gabriel growled. He shoved Devlin. "Her *what*?"

"Stop." Ani jumped up, crossed the threshold, and stepped in front of her father. "He kept me safe."

"He's the High Queen's thug—"

"Yeah, and you're the Dark King's." She rolled her eyes. "So what?"

Gabriel reached out like he'd move her aside, and without thinking, Ani caught his hand in hers—and stopped it.

His eyes widened, and he grinned. Before she could react, he pulled back his other arm like he was going to punch her.

"I don't think so." She ducked and swung, and—for the first time in her life—saw her father actually moved by her punch.

Reflexively, he punched back—not the insulting love taps he'd thrown before, but a true punch from a Hound striking out at an equal.

"You tried to hit me," she murmured. "You actually tried to *hit* me!"

"I did"—he touched his face—"and you *did* hit me."

She leaned against him. "Finally."

Gabriel was staring at her with pride. "You got me one worthy of Che. *How?*"

"She's barely—if at all—mortal." Devlin's voice was even, sounding falsely calm. "Her mortal blood has been consumed by yours, Gabriel. It's part of why she is so unusual, and—I suspect—because Jillian had an ancestor who wasn't fully mortal."

"Huh." Gabriel scooped her up in a hug. "Still my pup, though. Still not going to hare off on your own again without telling us. Right?"

"I was trying to make sure you all were safe." Ani feigned a snarl, but she wasn't angry with him for being protective. It was a Dark Court trait *and* a Hound trait. "And Devlin and Barry were with me. I wasn't alone."

Gabriel lowered her back to the ground. "Barry?"

"I named my steed," she said.

Gabriel squeezed her shoulder, and Ani felt better.

With a flash of realization, she understood that Devlin had known that a bit of violence would soothe her. He mightn't have the right words, but he understood her. She looked at him and smiled.

The relief in his expression made her heart tighten. She reached out for his hand. "So, now what?"

Devlin nodded and turned to Gabriel. "If the fighting has calmed you, perhaps we can proceed to the planning?"

"This doesn't mean I like you any better than I ever did." Gabriel flashed his teeth at Devlin. "You fail her, and I'll beat you until you're begging—"

"If I fail her, a beating will be the least of my pain." Devlin pulled Ani close to him.

Gabriel paused, nodded at them, and walked to the living area, where Irial and Niall were waiting.

Devlin leaned back into the sofa and watched the others argue. They alternated between sitting on the worn leather sofa and chairs, pacing, and snarling at one another.

Too many kings at the helm.

Irial listened, but he was as forceful as he'd been as king. These were his people, his family. Niall, Rabbit, and Ani were precious to the former Dark King. The current Dark King was just as bad: Seth was as a brother to him.

And I must keep Seth safe as well. For Sorcha.

And Niall. Irial would be dangerous if Niall were to die.

And . . . all of them. For Ani.

And Ani. Devlin glanced at her. *Most of all. Ani must be safe.*

The thought of Bananach killing Ani was unacceptable. He understood then, on a very core level, that this was the danger of emotions. If she were killed, he would be willing to damn them all.

"Ani should stay with us," Irial repeated.

"Think for a minute." Gabriel shook his head. "You put all the targets in one building . . . Bananach isn't a fool. She'll come at us with everything if we make it that easy."

"Do you have a better plan?" Irial's voice didn't get louder, but everyone in the room flinched.

Niall put a hand on Irial's forearm. Irial pulled his gaze from the Hound who'd been his advisor for centuries and looked at his king.

"Gabriel's right, and you know it," Niall said. "You're not thinking clearly. Let me handle this?"

For a moment, Irial looked down at Niall's hand. "I cannot lose anyone else."

"I know." Niall did not look away, did not remove his hand. "We all want the same things. Your grief is in the way of your planning. Let your . . . king look after the court. Trust me?"

"Always," Irial assured him. Then he left the room and went into the kitchen.

After he was gone, Niall spoke as if there were no doubt. "Ani and Rabbit need to stay together, but Seth cannot stay with them. I can take Seth to Faerie if he is willing to go." Niall looked at Seth with a gentleness that seemed at odds with the illusion those in Faerie held of the Dark Court. "I won't insist on your return to Sorcha, but if Devlin is right . . ."

"It's cool. I can do more good there, but"—Seth pointedly looked at each of them—"once she is well, I'll be back *here*. If there's fighting with Bananach, I'll be a part of it."

Devlin said, "I'm not sure you, Niall, should be away from your court. Things in Faerie are untenable. They are used to seeing me as her voice and hands . . . if she is as unwell as I fear, I need to go."

The Dark King looked at Seth, who nodded.

"So Ani and Rabbit come to the house with Irial and me." Niall's gaze flicked toward the doorway through which Irial had vanished. "Devlin can deliver Seth to Faerie."

Ani had stayed quiet far longer than Devlin would have expected. He'd watched her expressions as her life was being decided. He knew that their plan wasn't going to please her, but he wasn't going to step in and give voice to Ani's objections. That wasn't his place.

She looked at them all. "And then what? We wait? I live in seclusion, under watch forever?"

Irial returned to the doorway between the living room and the kitchen. "Is our company so awful, pup? Niall isn't always glum."

She went over to Irial. "You know the Hunt doesn't do well in a cage," she murmured. Then she turned to Gabriel. "Could you live caged?"

Gabriel growled. "'S different."

Rabbit spoke finally. "It's not."

Ani flashed a grateful smile at her brother.

Devlin suggested, "You could remain here while I take Seth to Faerie. I'll return as soon as I'm able, and we'll keep roaming. . . . Or come with me now."

She looked over at her father and then at Devlin.

"Come with me," Devlin said.

She didn't speak, and he hated that in the wake of Tish's death she was having to deal with the consequences of Sorcha's mawkish behavior. He hated that she had to deal with *any* of the losses in her life that his sisters had caused.

Irial's voice interrupted the strained silence. "You are a child of the Dark Court, beloved by the last Dark King and"—he glanced at Niall, who nodded—"under the protection of the current Dark King."

"And mine," Devlin added. He walked over to stand in front of her. "Whatever punishment the High Queen would offer, whatever anger she has for either of us, is only on my skin, not yours. She will not ever harm you as long as I draw breath."

For a heartbeat, no one in the room moved. A vow of such extremity was rare, but to have a High Court faery offer it was unheard-of. His life, his safety, all were secondary to Ani's now.

Ani immediately said, "*No*. I release you from—"

"Yes," Devlin interrupted. He took her hand in his. "My vow, Ani: whatever punishment she might mete out is mine to accept, not yours. I am not asking for anything in return. You are not bound to me or beholden, but you *are* mine to keep safe. Neither my queen nor my other sister will harm you while I live. My life for yours. That is the answer we have. Should they need blood or death, it is my body that will absorb the strike."

Suddenly, Gabriel growled. "Move."

A gust of wind battered the building, and the howls of the Hunt rose up.

Gabriel shoved to the front so that he stood facing the door to the studio. "Behind me."

From inside the studio, glass shattered.

He tilted his head, listening. "She's here. Ly Ergs."

"Back door?" Niall took command. "Devlin, get Seth and Ani to Faerie as soon as you can get passed them."

Gabriel and Irial stayed facing the studio; Devlin and Niall turned toward the kitchen door. That left Ani, Seth, and Rabbit in the middle, protected on both sides.

Bananach came through the doorway to the studio in a blur of bloody feathers. "What a lovely little vow you've offered the pup, Brother . . . but I don't see why I need to strike only *one* of you. The more bodies, the better."

Chapter 31

Bananach's face was painted in patterns drawn in wet ashes and woad. Her wings were charred at the tips, and the blood on her arms was still fresh. "Your Hounds fought well, Gabriel."

He growled, but didn't go to check on them. "They're not done yet."

"Yet here I am." Bananach spread her hands wide.

Ani felt the Hunt. Her mortality was gone. For the first time, she could feel a connection to the Hunt. Those not here already fighting would come, would knock down the walls, would bring blood and death into her home. *But not soon enough.* Gabriel knew it too.

A full score of Ly Ergs filed into the house. Other faeries, some Ani did not recognize, followed.

Devlin stepped forward. "Do not do this."

None of Bananach's faeries attacked, but they had spread out so that the exits were blocked. They waited—for

Bananach to act or speak. Her faeries weren't strong enough to overcome all of the fighters in the room, but they were numerous enough that there would be injuries.

Silently, Ani slid out a *sgian dubh* and handed it to her brother. Beside her, Seth had a short sword and several of his own knives. She pulled out one of the holy irons; her other *sgian dubh* was in her ankle holster.

As Bananach advanced into the house, Irial continued to move so that Ani was directly behind him; Niall did the same with Seth. Gabriel positioned himself so he was behind Devlin, but still in front of both Niall and Irial.

Devlin took another step forward, away from them, closer to War. "Talk to me. We can talk, can't we?"

She lifted a bone knife and slashed open his arm dispassionately—muscles severed and flesh ravaged. "You were nothing more than an idea *Reason* had, but without my pulse . . . without me, you were lifeless."

He grabbed her wrist with his other hand.

Bananach reached out and pressed her fingers into the wound. "I think I want that pulse, that blood, *my* blood, back now."

"If you give your word that Ani will be untouched, I will give it to you freely." Devlin was motionless as she ripped open his skin. "Sister, please, spare Ani."

"Stop," Bananach screeched. Her hand was still dug into his bleeding arm. "I must do as I must. Seth was never meant to live. The Hound didn't do as she was told, but there are choices. There are always choices, Brother."

She turned her gaze to Ani. "Come to me, little Hound, and I'll spare them. Two lives I will give you. Your choice." Bananach's wings opened wide, and the shadows in the room shivered at the sight. "Would you save your king? Your lover? Your father? Two lives if you give me yours."

Ani stepped up between her former king and her father. Her blade was unsheathed, but no one there—including Bananach—thought that a Hound with a blade was strong enough to be a threat to War.

"Spare all of their lives," Ani said. "I'll give you—"

"You can have my life," Devlin interrupted. He put himself back in front of Bananach. "You can have my allegiance if you stop this."

"*You.* You betrayed me. You took her, hid her. Why?" Bananach looked devastated. "You were my own. Our child . . ." She lunged at Ani with two bone knives—one in each hand now—as she spoke.

Irial shoved Ani to the side, and Bananach drove both knives hilt-deep into his stomach. Instead of falling, though, he stayed upright between Ani and Bananach, keeping his body as a barrier to reaching Ani.

"Iri!" Ani screamed. She wanted to go around him, to launch herself at the raven-faery, but to do so belittled the sacrifice Irial had made. He'd taken the wound that was to be hers, and she wasn't about to ignore that in order to satisfy her own rage.

Not now *at least.*

Devlin grabbed Bananach and pulled her away from Irial

and Ani. She didn't resist as he held her to him. Instead, she released the knives, sliding her hands over the white bone and letting Irial's blood coat it.

Only then did Irial move. Now that Bananach was contained, he stepped backward. Niall caught him and lowered him to the ground at Ani's side. Irial's characteristic grace was absent; instead, he moved with almost mortal clumsiness as he tried not to jar the blades that pierced his abdomen.

The abyss-guardians that clung to both the former Dark King and the current one suddenly stood like warriors in the room. Ani had never seen so many of the shadowy figures. The entire room seemed populated with them. Steady flames of darkness formed an impenetrable wall of shadows encircling the Dark Kings—and Ani.

War smiled at them from the other side of the black wall, and behind her, Devlin, Seth, and Gabriel fought the Ly Ergs.

Inside their shadow fortress, Niall knelt beside Irial and pulled back the shredded shirt that covered Irial's wounds. "Iri . . ." He looked like he was in as much pain as Irial.

"Hush." Irial reached down and yanked out the first knife. Blood spurted from the wound, and Irial let out a small grunt of pain.

"Hold on for—" Niall started, but Irial had already taken hold of the second one and pulled it free as well.

In Irial's hand was a bloodied hilt: the blade itself was missing.

"Left hand for poison. Not solid now." Irial turned his head and smiled at Ani. "Not your fault, pup."

"Iri . . ." She dropped to the floor. "We need . . . you can't . . ."

"Devlin's what you need. Go with him." Irial looked away from her then. His gaze was only for Niall. "Trust yourself. I . . ." His words faded as a spasm of pain shook him.

Niall pulled off his own shirt and pressed it to the bleeding gashes. "You'll be fine. Just—"

"No. Listen." Irial wrapped his hand around Niall's wrist. They seemed to forget that there were others in the room, that War was there, that a battle waited outside their shadowy barrier.

Irial kept his hand on Niall's wrist and whispered, "Wish I hadn't been king when we met."

"Iri—"

"Get them gone. Safe. Not *here*." Irial let go of Niall and pulled himself away. "You too. Get out of here. Now."

The expressions that crossed Niall's face were ones Ani didn't dare name, but she tasted everything. Irial wasn't the only one wishing things had been different. *Hoping they still could be.* The Dark King stood. Niall's softness was only for Irial—and Irial had asked him to repress that tenderness. The shadows in the room shuddered as Niall crossed the barrier that they'd formed.

Ani started to stand, but Irial took her hand in his. "Not yet."

Niall was every bit the King of Nightmares in that moment. The rage that played under the edge of his emotions welled up like black tar. Ani thought she would choke on it—the loss, the fury, the vengeance. Here was the true Dark King.

"Twice now you've struck what is *mine*." Niall bit the words off as he stalked toward Bananach. "The girl Tish was mine to keep safe. Irial is mine."

"Was," Bananach pronounced. "He'll not survive the fortnight. He knows it."

A roar filled the room as Niall gave voice to the rage and grief that they'd all felt. He punched Bananach, shoved spikes of dark light into her skin. "You do not hurt what is mine."

She stayed motionless, said nothing.

Niall didn't look away from her as he spoke. "Leave here. Leave Ani alone. You are banished."

Bananach tilted her head, looking inhuman, but her words were calm. "War cannot be banished. You know that, *Gancanagh*. You aren't going to win. One by one, you lose. I grow strong as you fall."

Niall didn't take his attention from Bananach. "You gave me a vow of fealty. I could kill you for—"

"No, you couldn't," Bananach crowed. "My betrayer told you. Sorcha will die, and then all of you will die. Kill me, and I still win. Is the little Hound worth it? Is your anger over Irial reason enough?"

Then Gabriel's voice whispered inside Ani's mind: *Go to Faerie.*

Ani looked up and saw her father in the doorway to the kitchen with Rabbit and Seth. They were opening a path for her exit.

Ani, Gabriel snarled inside her. *Get them out of here.*

She felt it then: the Hunt was here. The Hounds filled the too-small house.

Now, Gabriel added.

Seth, Devlin, and Rabbit weren't making much progress against the Ly Ergs, but they were keeping the tide from reaching her and Irial.

"Please, pup?" Irial said. "The Hunt won't fight as well with you and Rab here."

"Come with—" she started.

"No." He had pulled himself to a sitting position with the aid of several abyss-guardians. "I stay with Niall. . . . Can't really run right now anyhow."

Gabriel and Niall were in a blur of violence with Bananach. In the hallway, Ly Ergs and other faeries Ani didn't know were already fighting with Hounds. One Hound toppled a shelf onto a cluster of Ly Ergs. The red-handed faeries were scurrying everywhere like vermin. Several thistle-fey accompanied them. One female Hound grabbed the fire poker and speared it into the leg of a thistle-fey, pinning him to the floor with the brass shaft.

Ani made her way toward the kitchen, where Devlin was launching knives from the kitchen block. His aim was still precise one-handed, and despite the blood running down his other arm, the look in his eyes told her that he'd rather fight.

If they didn't get Seth to Faerie, there soon wouldn't *be* a Faerie. If they stayed, they wouldn't all survive. This wasn't a fight they could win.

But it still took every once of control, more than Ani thought she possessed, to say, "Let's go."

Chapter 32

As they made their way through the fracas, Ani kept Rabbit behind her. Seth brought up the rear, and she and Devlin cleared a path. Even with blood streaming down his slashed arm, Devlin was fierce. His movements were clinical, though; there was a precision to the strikes. Hounds aided them, keeping their route open.

Once their small group was away from the studio, they maintained a triangle formation, but with Ani joining Seth at the back. Without speaking, they each scanned their respective sides of the street. He didn't try to watch her area—or fail to monitor his own.

For a nonpack faery, he's not bad.

As they proceeded farther from the fight, Seth's uneasy glances at Devlin seemed to match her own. *Why?* Seth's watch over Rabbit made sense: they were friends of a sort. The attention he paid to Devlin was equal to his regard for Rabbit.

"Let me help." Seth spoke quietly. "Devlin?"

"No." Devlin didn't even look at Seth. "Be silent."

The terse way Devlin spoke made her think that the unspoken topic wasn't about protecting them. They passed a number of mortals, and Ani was grateful that everyone other than Rabbit had the ability to don a glamour to hide their bloodied and bruised state. Rabbit, who walked in the middle, was spared attention by his position.

The few faeries who saw them passed either gaped at them or scurried away quickly. Seeing bloodied Dark Court faeries was not unusual, but seeing the Summer Queen's beloved in matching condition was noteworthy—as was seeing the High Court's assassin in the company of Hounds. If not for the worry and fear, she would find the fleeing faeries' reactions amusing.

Silently, she followed Devlin and waited for word from her father. Even at this distance, she could feel her link to the Hunt. She didn't speak to Gabriel, but she listened, knowing he'd warn her if any of Bananach's faeries escaped the Hunt.

Devlin and Seth both stopped. They had reached a graveyard at the edge of Huntsdale where Ani had attended more than a few parties.

Seth shot another worried look at Devlin's arm. The bleeding hadn't stopped, but it had slowed.

"Let me help," Seth offered again. "You need blood."

"Not here." Devlin had a thin sheen of sweat on his face. "I can wait."

"Let—"

"No," Devlin snarled. A shadow flashed out from his eyes. "Do not offer a third time. You will not manipulate me thusly."

Ani stepped up beside Devlin, not to get between them but to be nearer Devlin. "You want to clue me in?"

"That's what he *doesn't* want," Seth muttered. "He's lost too much blood, but my brother is being uncommonly stupid."

"Your *who*? What?" Ani looked between them. "Less clarity by the minute, guys."

Devlin swallowed with effort. "Can we not do this yet?"

"If you bleed out, what good are you?" Seth spoke gently to Devlin, but his attention was still on their surroundings.

"Once we reach Faerie, *Brother,*" Devlin said.

Rabbit and Ani exchanged a look. Rabbit shrugged and then asked, "So we're here? At the gate to Faerie?"

"One of them." Devlin stretched his bleeding arm into the air in front of him to grasp something that Ani couldn't see. His blood sizzled as if something in the air burned him. He closed his eyes briefly, not enough that his pain was obvious, but enough that he dropped the shield around his emotions—and Ani almost stumbled in the flood of pain and fear that washed over her.

A veil appeared as if out of empty air. *A gate.* To some degree, she'd always assumed that she would see the doorways to Faerie if she passed near them.

"Dev?"

He glanced at her—and then he toppled forward into a silver veil that stretched like moonlight between the earth and sky. Waves ripped through the surface when he fell; the shimmering silver light was displaced by his form. Just as quickly, though, it stilled. It looked like liquid, but the weighty fall of it was that of thick drapes.

Ani dove after Devlin, slipping from the mortal world into Faerie without the fear or hesitation she had expected. Seth and Rabbit came after her, and the veil fell in place behind them. The glimmer of light lingered for a moment, and then was gone as if there'd never been a door there.

"Seth?" Ani looked up at him. "I've never been here and . . . help?"

"Give me a minute." Seth shuddered, looking as pained as Devlin had.

As she watched, he became different. *Mortal.* Suddenly, Ani was crouched on the ground in Faerie with no one strong enough to fight beside her. Rabbit was more mortal than not in his strength, and while he could fight, it wasn't his greatest skill. Devlin appeared comatose, and Seth was a mortal.

"Well, this is going beautifully so far," Ani muttered.

"It's going to get worse if we don't wake his ass up." Seth sat down beside Ani. He was still shivering and sweating, but he looked less like he might vomit. "You trust me?"

Do I? He wasn't Dark Court, but Rabbit trusted him. The Dark King trusted him. *He's not Pack.* The Dark Kings' mortal beloved, Ani—and Tish's—friend Leslie, trusted him. *He might not be ours, but he fought with the Hunt. And he wants to kill Bananach.* Devlin trusted him.

"For now," she said.

"Good enough. We probably only have a few minutes till she comes." He reached out for her *sgian dubh*. "Can I take that?"

"Borrow."

He flicked his tongue at his lip ring. "Fair correction. *Borrow*."

She extended the blade, hilt first.

"He needs blood, Ani. That's the part he didn't want you to know."

"Blood?" She'd watched the Ly Ergs absorb blood through their palms, seen her own family blend it into ink and wear art in their skin with it. The Gabriel always carried his king's—or queen's—blood in the living oghams on his forearm.

Blood feeds the magick. The words whispered in the air. *Blood binds, and blood promises.*

"Devlin requires blood to live," Seth confirmed. "He has always required the blood of both who made him."

Ani let her gaze roam over their surroundings, assuring that no one attacked without their noticing, verifying where her brother was, but she listened to Seth's words.

"I see the future, Ani." Seth stared up at her. "I see things that . . . are secret."

Ani froze. Seth's eyes held unspoken knowledge. He knew things he shouldn't, things he hadn't told her.

"Your blood is different." Seth glanced at Devlin, who was motionless, and then continued, "It's what they fight over. It's what Irial tests. . . . And it's unusual enough to nourish Devlin."

"If I . . . What does it mean if I give him my blood?" She felt as much as saw the world shifting.

"You'd be bound to him," Seth said. "It's . . . your choice, but if you do this, he's bound to *you*, not them."

Behind him, the world was changing. A dead landscape was bursting into spring all around them. Trees were blossoming in a riot of scents. The grass under them was growing, brightening into a vibrant green. It was a world waking from dormancy.

Faerie will survive now that Seth has returned to Sorcha.

Seth didn't look at any of that, though. "It's the oldest magick, and the future will shift if you do this."

"For the better?" she asked.

"I see threads, not answers." Seth tugged his lip ring into his mouth. "I'm new to this world, Ani. Still guessing and hoping."

She heard the things he wasn't saying, the words he didn't offer to her. "You think it'll be for the better, though."

"For the people I care about? Yes," he admitted.

She glanced at her brother, who stood silently gazing on the peculiar landscape around them. "That includes Devlin? And Rabbit?"

"Yes. And others you don't care for." Seth gave her a very serious look. "And *not better* for Bananach."

"Okay." Ani took the *sgian dubh* and slashed open her forearm. She knelt on the soil beside Devlin and clasped his hand in hers, so that their arms were resting bloody sides together.

Seth told her the words and she repeated, "Blood to blood, I am yours. Bone to bone. Breath to breath. My hungers yours to feed, and yours mine to feed."

The world shifted to shades of gray all around her as her blood flowed into Devlin's wounded arm. Her wolves, the feral things she'd dreamed so often, lay alongside them in the grass. Their eyes were no longer green but red. *No longer of the mortal world.* The part of the Hunt that she carried was different here. *Ours.*

From the earth beside them, a hazel tree burst forth. It stretched to the sky, shading them with twisted boughs from which flowers hung. As she watched, a copse of smaller hazel trees surrounded them.

"And I am yours," Devlin said.

She looked at him.

He had opened his eyes and was staring at her with the same eyes as their wolves. "Blood to blood. Bone to bone. Breath to breath. My hungers yours to feed, and yours mine to feed."

He kissed her, swallowing her energy as she'd taken his, but it did not drain her—or him.

The growling of wolves pulled her attention. The creatures she'd dreamt of weren't merely dream now: they were alive and snarling at the silver-eyed faery who approached.

Sorcha.

Her dress was that of some long-gone era; everything about her bespoke a more formal time. She was corseted and coiffed, and as she walked, veiled attendants accompanied her. *This is the faery I've feared?* She was utterly unlike the mad raven-faery.

Seth stood, placing himself between them and the High Queen. "Mother."

For a moment, it felt that the world held its breath. Sorcha extended her hand to Seth.

He quirked a brow at her, before taking her hand and pulling her in for a hug. "I missed you."

She pursed her lips as if she was debating chastising him. "Seth. That is not how one greets a queen."

He laughed and kissed her cheek. His voice was low as he murmured, "It's *okay* to hug your son."

The High Queen nodded, but her gaze drifted over him like the most overprotective of parents seeking minute scratches or bruises. "Who injured you? I couldn't *see* you the past few hours."

"I'm fine."

"It was Bananach, wasn't it? Or"—she turned her gaze to Devlin—"you? Did you harm him?"

"No." Seth stayed between them, drawing her gaze back to him. "My brother and I stood together against her."

Sorcha opened and closed her mouth as she looked from Devlin to Seth and back to Devlin. Holding Devlin's gaze, she said only, "I have one son."

Devlin sat up. "I know that, Sister."

Gingerly he came to his feet; as he did so, he kept Ani's hand in his.

The High Queen took in the change in her world. Her expression was not one of pleasure as she looked at the copse of trees. "*These* are not of my will. Why are they not vanishing?"

No one spoke. Ani didn't know the answer, and if anyone else did, they weren't speaking.

The High Queen stepped toward Rabbit. "You, halfling—"

The wolves growled. Rabbit was leaning against one of the trees, clearly under the watch of wolves.

"You are welcome here," she continued. "You may stay and heal. There is now a cottage for you in the artists' section. It will have what you require. Be welcome in Faerie."

Rabbit bowed his head.

"But *you*"—Sorcha glared at Ani—"are supposed to be dead, yet you appear not to be. Why is that?"

"Sister, my Queen—" Devlin started.

Ani cut him off. "Because Devlin isn't as much of a bastard as you want him to be?"

The wolves' growling vibrated under her skin. Their eyes gleamed with the red she'd seen when she lay on the earth beside Devlin. His eyes were the same red, and she suspected her own were as well.

Sorcha stared only at Devlin. "Will you kill her? Set this right."

"No." Devlin clutched Ani's hand tighter, whether to assure her or keep her still she didn't know. "I would give any life before hers."

"*Any* life?" Sorcha echoed. "Would you sacrifice my life for hers?"

"I would rather you were both well," he said.

Sorcha opened her mouth as if to speak, but Seth touched her arm. The High Queen looked at him and was silent.

"I would stay here in Faerie with Ani, Sister." Devlin started to kneel, but Ani refused to let go of his hand; he rose back up and looked at Sorcha.

Sorcha shook her head. "And who will feed you? Do you think to cast me off and still come to my table?"

The look Seth gave Ani was intense enough that she felt like he was trying to will words into her head. *What did he say earlier?* Ani replayed the things Seth had told her.

"I will," Ani blurted. "I'll give him whatever he needs . . . or find it or whatever."

The High Queen scowled, but Seth smiled approvingly.

"So mote it be," Sorcha whispered before turning.

And then she walked away with Seth.

Chapter 33

Devlin watched his sister, his queen, leave. There were so many questions he needed to ask, so many answers he required, but before that, he had to make sense of what Ani had done. Not only had she shared her blood with him, she'd also offered to nourish him. She had stood at his side against the High Queen. They were bound in ways he had never fathomed possible.

Perhaps we always were.

The Hound, his partner unto eternity now, held his hand in her own. All around them wolves waited.

"We made those trees." Ani looked up at him. Her words were a question, a demand for verification. "Together."

"And wolves," he added. "They are flesh now."

"Sort of." She looked at the wolves and said, "Come."

In a chaotic blur, the wolves began to leap into her body, vanishing inside her skin one after another. Muzzles and tails, blood and bone, fur and muscles, all and each vanished into the skin of the Hound holding his hand.

"It feels different than in dreams," was all she said when the last one of them had entered her.

"It looks different too." Devlin could see red-eyed wolves shifting under her skin.

"Oh," Ani whispered. She looked down at her arms in awe. "They're *here*."

Rabbit pushed away from the tree and came over to stand in front of his sister. "Look at you, all painted up without my help."

Ani reached out to him. "They left room for your art too, Rab. When you're ready . . ."

"Someday." Rabbit brushed her hair away from her face and gave her a look of pure adoration.

Then he glanced at Devlin. "Sorcha says I'm welcome . . . but the shop . . ." His words faded away. "The shop's gone too. Our home . . ."

Devlin gestured for Rabbit to walk. "There are other artists here. *Many* artists. Halflings and mortals."

"There's nothing left for me over there." Rabbit still sounded weary, but not as much as he had when Devlin first saw him at the studio.

"Stay here," Ani urged, "at least until we figure out what to do. Please, Rab?"

Rabbit nodded.

Without any further discussion, Devlin took Rabbit to the artists' cottages.

After they had delivered Rabbit to a pristine cottage filled with various art supplies and tattoo equipment, Devlin led Ani to his own home.

When they reached his quarters within the queen's palace, he found Rae in his previously unused sitting room. A smile played on his lips at the sight of her. No longer hidden away in a cave, she was dressed for court and awaiting him.

"She's awake," he told her.

Rae smiled. "And Faerie is intact once more. Such a simple thing, isn't it? You bring Sorcha's son home, and the world wakes."

"Indeed." Devlin wished he could embrace her. He couldn't, but he could tell her what he felt. "You saved Faerie. Without you, I wouldn't have known—"

"Without me, she wouldn't have been lost in her dreams," Rae corrected. "Do not forget how she was able to see Seth in the first place."

"You can do all sorts of things in dreams, can't you?" Ani's voice was soft, but there was a fear in it.

"I didn't create any illusions, Ani." Rae stayed as still as any prey. She didn't straighten her arms or legs. "I simply stitched your dreams together."

"Why?"

Rae shrugged. "You needed each other."

And in that instant, Devlin understood something he'd not admitted. "You knew."

The world stilled for Rae. "Knew what?"

Devlin, the center of her world, crossed the room to her. His voice was soft. "All these years, you knew Ani was meant to be in my life. Did you know that when you asked me not to kill her?"

"Oh, Devlin, don't ask me too many more questions." She lifted her hand as if she would touch his shoulder. "I knew things I shouldn't have . . . or maybe things I was supposed to. Who can predict what threads are the ones that were meant to be?"

"Threads?" He frowned as he tried to piece together some clarity from the clues she'd given him. "What all did you know?"

"I cannot answer that," Rae whispered. "I wish I could."

Ani sat on a high-backed chair with one foot tucked under her. The wolves in her skin shifted restlessly, but Rae couldn't tell if that was in response to Ani's worry or Devlin's discomfort. The wolves were a part of the New Hunt, the one that belonged in Faerie, and they'd respond to both Devlin and Ani.

Will this Hunt protect me as well?

Rae waited as Devlin puzzled out the things he was learning. If Rae had her way, she'd tell him that he and Ani were meant to be in Faerie, that the whole order of Faerie was awaiting his understanding of what he could make real. If she had her way, she'd have told him everything years ago, but the Eolas' injunctions were binding.

"Please, Devlin," she said. "Think on what you know,

but don't ask me questions I am forbidden to answer."

A knock at the door of the outer chamber made them pause.

"Stay here." Devlin walked away to answer it.

Once he was gone, Ani looked at her. "You love him a lot."

Rae sighed. "Your bluntness is not always charming, Ani."

The Hound grinned. "I believe you've mentioned that before."

As Devlin returned, the look on his face was dire. "She's summoned me to the hall."

Devlin entered Sorcha's main hall. The insult of being summoned in front of all and any who cared to watch pricked his temper. He tried to suppress it as he had done for eternity, but he was failing. He'd been advisor, assassin, *family* to her for eternity, yet she beckoned him into her hall in front of the masses.

The High Queen sat on the throne looking emotionless. Behind her, Seth stood with one hand on the back of the queen's throne. Like Sorcha, his emotions were hidden. Devlin, for a change, did not endeavor to disguise his feelings: he was furious. Sorcha had come near to unmaking Faerie, but she acted as if she were unfazed by her folly.

Devlin crossed the crowded room to the dais. He stopped in front of her, but he did not bow. For the first time, he did not bend his knee to the High Queen.

No one in the room spoke. *But they watch—and she knows.* He had not spent eternity simply killing for his queen; he knew how to wield unspoken as well as physical threat.

"How much have you hidden? That is the question I am forced to ponder now, Devlin." Sorcha sounded calm, but there was an edge that was new. There, in front of the denizens of the High Court, she spoke to him like he was nothing.

He crossed a line then that he'd never crossed: he stepped up and grabbed his sister's arm. "We will not discuss this here."

"Cease!" she demanded. She tried to pull away, but he tightened his grip.

"You embarrass us both by doing this here," he whispered.

Seth stepped forward, but in Faerie, he was mortal, and mortal movement was not fast enough. By the time Seth had moved, Sorcha and Devlin were well away from the dais.

Devlin glanced back and said, "The High Queen is not in physical danger."

The assurance was primarily for Seth, but the rest of the assembled faeries heard the words as well.

Seth nodded.

Sorcha continued to resist. She shoved ineffectually against Devlin's chest and hissed, "Release me."

"Sister, you will come gracefully, or we will discuss *everything* in front of them."

The High Queen pursed her lips, but she stopped resisting.

Then he dragged his sister-mother-queen across the room and shoved open the door to her garden.

She stepped in front of him, and for the first time in the millennia they'd stood alone together in her private garden, he saw ire shimmering in her eyes. The silver veins in her skin glittered like moonlight storming beneath the surface.

"How was Seth made faery?"

"I don't see that—"

"How?"

"You know the answer or you wouldn't be acting like this. I gave him of my own essence to remake him. I did not expect the consequences or *emotion*, but I don't regret it." She crossed her arms over her chest. "I wanted a child of my own. I wanted a son, and he needed a m—"

"You *had* a son, if you weren't too cruel to admit it. . . ." He pulled his gaze away from her.

"No, I have a brother. You are my brother, made by order and violence. I wanted someone who was just *mine.*" She grew agitated, not orderly, not in control of her emotions as the High Queen should be. After an eternity of balance with her twin, she was unsettled—because she had made herself so. The High Queen, the Unchanging Queen, had changed.

"It was the right choice," she insisted. "I needed him. He needed me."

"Could we sit?" Shakily, Devlin gestured to the space between them.

Sorcha made a table and two chairs appear. He sat and stared at her. After more millennia than either of them likely could recall, Sorcha had changed everything. Devlin wasn't sure what that would mean for Faerie or the mortal world, but the consequences thus far—Sorcha's mourning and Faerie's almost ending—weren't particularly encouraging.

Carefully, Devlin touched her hand. "What have you done, Sister?"

"Freed myself from her. We're *different* from one another now. I have taken a mortal's taint into myself, given him part of me. Don't you see? Bananach and I are no longer perfectly opposite." Sorcha smiled, and the moon glowed brighter overhead. The air tasted purer as her happiness grew. "It was not my intention, but it has . . . oh, it has given me so much more than I realized I could have. I have a son, a child of my own, emotions I did not understand, and I can see my twin-no-more without feeling unwell. I may even be able to kill—"

"You *cannot.*" Devlin gripped his sister-queen's hands. "Think. If you're wrong, if you're still bound like that . . . would you kill us all?"

"If she hurts Seth, I would." Sorcha yanked free of his grasp. "Maybe it's time that she's not the only one to go back and forth to the mortal world. Maybe things need to change."

"You're the *Unchanging Queen*." Devlin forced his voice to even, despite the growing panic he felt. "You cannot go over there for more than a few moments. Reality will—"

"Adjust. Yes, but is that so awful?" She had the look of a zealot. "Faerie bends to my will, and look how good it is here."

Devlin felt alarmed by the sensation of a sudden unraveling around him. He closed his eyes, and he saw them, threads tangling and weaving together, lives altered and possibilities ended, deaths they couldn't overcome. As long as the veil between worlds was open to the twins, but their balance was missing, Sorcha was in danger—and all of Faerie was in danger.

He went to his knees in the garden. "I'm sorry I failed you."

"I wanted you to be my son," she whispered, "but I couldn't have *her* child as *my* child. You're still my brother. Family."

"I know." He kept his worries hidden from her. If she learned that Bananach was trying to find a way to kill her son, if she learned that her twin-no-more had asked Ani to kill Seth, the queen of Faerie would be enraged, and an omnipotent angry queen pursuing War in the mortal world was not in the best interests of either realm.

Separating from Bananach meant that Sorcha was feeling emotions she'd never known. It meant that the one faery who held perfect clarity had lost her balance. Until balance was returned, there was little chance of stability.

So how do I rebalance her? He was the only other strong faery in Faerie, and he didn't have an answer. The answers he needed weren't going to be found by waiting in Faerie either. He needed to return to the world of mortals.

Chapter 34

Devlin stood in his rooms with Ani and Rae. After he explained what he'd learned, he added, "I don't plan to be gone long, but I need to talk to Niall."

"No." Ani gestured with the blade of the knife she'd been cleaning. "Did you forget the fight we left over there? It's not safe for you, and . . . you aren't going anywhere without me, Devlin. Just *no.*"

"Bananach came here when the queen slept, Devlin. *Here* is not safe either." Rae sat stiffly in one of the uncomfortable chairs as if she had physical form. She didn't shudder, but there was horror in her expression. "War was awful. The bodies . . . She will come here."

"We shouldn't be apart," Ani snarled. She continued cleaning her already spotless knives. According to Rae, in his absence Ani had begun cleaning every weapon in the chamber. Her own knives were laid out on a table with several of his. The sight made him smile. Ani's scowl, however, did not. She furiously polished one of the short blades he'd had on a low table alongside the settee. "I can't believe you think I'm going to sit here while you go face *Bananach*."

"Ani," he started.

"I waited here while you talked to Sorcha, who, by the way, is crazy. Now you are off to the mortal world where the crazi*er* one is?" She crossed her arms. "I was there, Devlin. Bananach could've *killed* you, and really? We've been bound together for like five minutes and you're suddenly darting off into danger without me. I don't think so."

"She has valid points," Rae murmured.

"See?" Ani shoved one *sgian dubh* into its sheath. "What happened to logic?"

"And taking you back there is logical?" Devlin's voice was calm, but the emotions he felt weren't. The image of Bananach launching herself at Ani was still too fresh in his mind. "One trip, and then everything will be better."

"No." Ani glared at him. "If you fight, I fight. Not negotiable."

"You don't need to go there in person." Rae did not rise from the seat where she appeared to be resting. She stayed, hands folded demurely in her lap, and said, "Not everything is a fight."

Ani and Devlin both paused.

Rae looked at Ani. "You have a close bond with one of the kings, correct?"

"Irial, but it's not a *bond* like we"—Ani shot a look at Devlin—"have."

Slowly, Rae stood, keeping the illusion of solidity. "I can find Irial through you. Devlin can come into the dream too because I've already tied your dreams together. Let me in, and then we'll all curl up to nap."

The Hound frowned at them both. "Let you in *where*?"

Devlin stilled. He hadn't quite explained the possession detail to Ani yet. "Rae is incorporeal. Outside of dreams, she only has a body if someone—"

"Just Devlin so far," Rae interjected.

"If *I* let her animate my body." Devlin added, "It's a not-unpleasant experience."

"Not unpleasant?" Rae laughed. "He has a fabulous time, Ani, but he doesn't like admitting how much he enjoys the freedom of sensation without responsibility."

For a moment Ani looked at them both. "Huh. Here I thought the High Court was boring. Who knew?"

The tension that Devlin had felt building evaporated at the smiles on both Rae's and Ani's lips.

Then Rae was standing directly in front of Devlin. Her pupils were dilated with the usual excitement she felt at blending together into one body. "So let's see if the Dark Court is resting."

He looked at her, the spectral mortal who animated his body, and then at the Hound whose dreams he was tied to. "I'm not sure . . . it's . . . I can go to the mortal world quickly, Ani."

She took his hand and then looked at Rae. "Well? Possess one of us already."

Rae laughed. "I think I'm going to like having you around, Ani."

Ani's answering smile was wicked.

And for a brief, nerve-racking moment, Devlin felt more than a bit frightened. He just wasn't sure of whom. With as mild a gesture as he could, he motioned to his bed. "Let us dream of the Dark Court then."

It was an odd sensation, though, to feel Rae within his body—yet still feel Ani's presence. He'd gone from solitude, to hiding them, to coexisting with them. *And I'm not sure which was most difficult.* All he did know was that he couldn't imagine life without either of them.

They followed the path created by Ani's connection to Irial. In the dream, Devlin suddenly stood with his hand outstretched to the gargoyle on the former Dark King's door. Ani was beside him, and somehow it was also her hand the gargoyle bit.

Inside a now empty white landscape, Irial stood. "Ani, love?"

"We need to talk to you and Niall," she told him. "Can we . . . entwine your dream with his?"

The look on Irial's face was one Devlin would prefer not to see near Ani, but it wasn't directed *at* Ani.

"You have someone I don't know with you," Irial said, looking around as if he would find Rae. "Not faery."

"A dreamwalker," Ani admitted. "We really *are* here. You get that, right?"

"I do, pup." Irial walked away. "I've not dealt with emotions this long to miss the taste of the jealousy your"—he glanced at Devlin—"partner is trying to hide."

A semifamiliar room appeared out of the white landscape. A wallpaper of raised fleurs-de-lis covered the walls; flickering candles crowded the room in freestanding candelabras and in wall sconces. It reminded Devlin of a more decadent home of the former Dark King's, back when Niall and Irial hosted feasts of debauchery.

Ani sat down beside Irial. "Are you well?"

"Well enough," he muttered.

She lifted the bottom of his shirt. The skin was an angry red, with black bruises all around the remaining wound. It looked like it was only a moment or two healed. For a faery as strong as Irial, the injury should be almost gone—as the other one was.

"Why is *this* one unhealed?" she asked. "Iri?"

"Stop." He took her hand and gently set it back in her lap.

The former Dark King leaned back then, as if he were uninjured. "So . . . can your dreamweaver leave a path so I can slip into Niall's dreams later too?"

Niall walked into the room. "Perhaps you should ask me what I think of that idea first?"

"Aaah, there you are." Irial greeted his king with shadows dancing in his eyes. "I wasn't sure if you were finally asleep, Gancanagh. You're fretting too much over things that are beyond your control."

Niall stopped in the middle of the room and glared at Irial. "I do not accept that answer."

Then, without another word to him, Niall approached the obsidian throne that appeared in the room, and Devlin idly wondered who was crafting the images in the dreamscape.

I am. From their various imaginings. Rae sounded fascinated.

He heard her laughter.

I am *fascinated, Dev, I've never been able to do this. I wonder if—*

Not an experiment, Rae, he reminded.

With more effort than he liked, Devlin walked toward the throne where Niall sat. Something in him rebelled at standing in front of that throne as if he were a supplicant. He wasn't even sure what court he served. He wasn't Sorcha's advisor in his heart anymore, but he didn't want to swear fealty to the Dark Court either. In truth, he served Faerie itself. Perhaps he always had.

Devlin stood respectfully in front of Niall, but he didn't bow or offer any gesture of submission. "You need to return the Dark Court to Faerie."

"No."

Devlin pushed back his emotion as he'd done for most of eternity and added, "Sorcha is unbalanced. She wants to come *here*. Do you have any idea of what that would do to the mortal world?"

Niall—once an almost-friend to Devlin, once an

almost-favorite of the High Queen, cherished of several courts—stilled. "Are you telling me what to do with *my* court, Devlin?"

Across the room, Irial tensed. He didn't move, didn't respond in any way that would draw attention, but Devlin saw the change. He knew the hope that led to such a movement. Niall had been a reluctant monarch. Centuries after Irial had first offered the court to him, Niall was finally the Dark King.

"I do not take direction from anyone, nor am I seeking your advice. I still have an advisor." Niall's attention flickered to Irial briefly. "Sorcha's recent ailment is not my priority."

"Would you sacrifice this world?" Devlin asked.

The look Niall gave him was disdainful. "Sorcha took my friend, made him her subject—"

"Her *heir*. Seth is far more than a subject." Devlin still didn't let his own anger into the words, but it was there all the same. Despite his eternity of loyalty, his mother-sister-queen had chosen a virtual stranger to be her heir.

"I've been heir to a court. It's not writ in stone." Niall gestured at Irial. "*He* kept his court for more than nine centuries after declaring me his heir."

"You refused," Irial reminded. He came to his feet and took a position of support behind Niall. "If you recall, Niall, you refused being my heir."

"Yet look at where I sit." Niall didn't deign to glance back at Irial as he spoke.

"Seth is her heir. He is the consort of the Summer Queen, friend of the Winter Queen, and brother to the Dark King. He's not in danger because of Sorcha's action. She *saved* him from mortality, gave him the strength of a king, and other gifts that are not mine to reveal." In the moment, Devlin wasn't sure who he resented more.

"She claimed him as a pawn," Niall said.

Devlin didn't argue, *couldn't* argue. Sorcha undoubtedly had considered the ramifications of her choice when she made the mortal a faery. What she hadn't considered was the way it would change her. The High Queen had made an error in judgment, and the cost was one to be paid on both sides of the veil.

"Come to Faerie," he repeated.

"No."

"She needs a court to balance hers. She must be kept in Faerie." Devlin's anger was no longer hidden. His voice was filled with it.

"The Dark Court belongs in this world. I know my court, Devlin. I know what's best for them. Each and every one of them is connected to me. I *feel* them, but"—Niall glanced back at Irial—"a king's duty is to consider the well-being of his court first. Personal desires come second. Old friendships and worry for others are not how the Dark King governs."

"You'd sacrifice mortals and faeries? If she comes to your world, that's what will happen."

"If she comes here, the discord will not injure my court.

Taking them to Faerie would." Niall lifted his gaze to Devlin's face. "The Dark Court will remain here."

Niall's words made all of the shadows in the room shiver.

"Faerie needs the Dark Court." Devlin's anger slipped further out. "Sorcha needs a court to balance her."

"Devlin?" Ani approached.

With a strange expression, Ani looked first at him, and then at Niall and Irial. "It *does* need that, doesn't it?"

"Yes, that's why we're here . . . but your king"—Devlin looked at Niall—"isn't cooperating."

Ani stepped between Devlin and Niall. She reached out to Irial and squeezed his hand. He smiled at her, but didn't speak.

"Once upon a time," she began, "Faerie had two courts. The Dark Court left Faerie, and as the centuries passed, new courts were born of the strongest solitaries to fill the needs of the faeries who lived in the mortal world. If the Dark Court won't return, there is need for a new court in Faerie. Someone who is strong enough to stand up to the High Queen needs to form that court . . . and such a court would need a Gabriel . . . or *Gabrielle*."

"It's not that easy," Devlin objected. "There already is a Dark King."

Niall shook his head. "I'm not going to Faerie. That leaves you."

"Or Irial," Devlin said.

"You don't *seriously* think I'm up for the job?" Irial

drawled. He lowered a hand onto Niall's shoulder. "I am where I belong."

"Order needs Discord, Devlin." Ani spoke softly. "I know you. Tell me it's not the solution we need. Save your sister. Remake Faerie so it's *our* world too, not just hers."

"I can't be k—" he started, but the words weren't ones he could speak. They were a lie. "You ask me to stand in opposition to my sister?"

"No," she said. "I ask that *we* do."

The wolves that were Ani's Hunt came into the room, crouching and pacing throughout the spaces between the elegant furnishings. They watched her eagerly. Red eyes reflected the glow of the smoldering embers in the fireplace.

"I'm already bound to you. Blood to blood, Devlin. We're in this together." Ani stared up at him. "Trust me. Trust *us*."

Their wolves pressed against them both like they would urge them to movement.

"I do." Devlin looked at Niall. "The veil to Faerie will be sealed. One sister will be locked on either side."

Ani squeezed his hand and added, "Call out to us, and we will answer if we are able."

"And Rabbit?" Irial asked.

Ani looked up at Devlin, and he nodded.

"He's safe with us. . . . Tell Gabe . . . Dad . . . that we are all well?"

"I will." Irial came over and pulled her into his embrace,

whispering something in her ear.

She approached the Dark King's throne. "Take care of Gabriel and Irial?"

"In exchange," Niall said.

"For?"

"Your dreamweaver doing as Irial asked," Niall murmured. He didn't look at Irial as he said it.

"Weaving the two of your dream selves together?" Ani clarified.

The Dark King's nod was curt.

Ani looked at Rae, who nodded.

"Done," Ani said.

And then she turned to Devlin and the pack of wolves crowding the room. "Let's go home."

CHAPTER 35

Devlin opened his eyes to find Rae and Ani both staring back at him from Ani's body. He was holding them against his chest. The sensation of holding Ani was still new enough to be breathtaking; to realize that he also held Rae was a heartbeat too near perfection.

They are my life.

With them, he would rebalance Faerie.

And become enemy to both my sister-mothers.

Gently, he cupped Ani-Rae's face in his hand. "You were right."

"About?" Rae asked.

"Saving Ani. Pushing me."

"And?" Ani prompted.

"That I am king." He didn't kiss them as he'd kissed Ani before. In truth, he didn't know if Rae would mind his kissing them, so he was careful as he pressed his lips to theirs.

Either Ani or Rae—he wasn't sure which—had no such hesitation. The gentle kiss he'd offered became something as fierce as the kisses he'd shared with Ani when she was draining his energy from him. Then Ani-Rae pulled back and grinned.

"I've been waiting for that kiss for decades," Rae whispered.

"Welcome to the New Dark Court," Ani said.

The wicked laughter that spilled from Ani's—*or Rae's?*—lips made Devlin shake his head. "Shadows. The Court of Shadows," he corrected. "We're not a replica, but something new. We don't use an old name."

Rae and Ani separated. They exchanged a look.

"I like it," they both said.

In a breath, he removed the wall between them and the outside. The wolves leaped from Ani's skin. Darkness fell in front of the Shadow Court, allowing Rae to walk alongside them. With Rae on his right and Ani on his left, Devlin stepped out of the High Queen's palace, and together they walked to the moonlight veil, the first but not the only gate in and out of Faerie.

Just inside the gate, Barry stood. The steed was currently in the form of an actual horse. He was shadows made solid. *Leaving without me was bad form.*

The steed spoke in Devlin's mind, but before he could answer, he realized that it was speaking to Ani.

I'm sorry, she answered. Her words to the steed were inside Devlin's mind as well.

Other steeds waited in the shelter of the hazel trees.

I have called the Unclaimed for our New Hunt, Barry said.

We are here, Ani and Ani's Partner. The steeds watched their approach, but none advanced.

Devlin answered aloud, "Welcome, *Ani's Steed* and all."

Barry laughed. *I may grow to tolerate you. Get on with it,* Devlin. *They need to claim their riders.*

Faeries had begun to gather, as if they had responded to a summons. Curiously, they watched the steeds, Devlin, Ani.

You will make a wonderful queen, Barry assured Ani. *Worthy of being my rider. Worthy of beginning the Hunt that was lacking.*

Ani's words, to Barry and to Devlin, were confident. *I just needed to find my pack.*

"And we needed to find you," Rae added with a smile, and Devlin realized that they all three could hear the mental conversation with the steed.

"Let's do this." Ani held out the *sgian dubh* she had used to cut her arm earlier. "Blood and breath."

Devlin took the black-handled blade from Ani's hand.

"With the hands that they made"—he cut a diagonal stripe in his right palm—"and the blood of Faerie . . ."

A chiming noise began to echo through Faerie.

Rae slipped into Ani's body, so the breath they shed was hers as well.

"With the breath"—Rae and Ani took the blade—"of mortal and faery . . ."

"We close the veils between the worlds," they all said.

"Closing this veil is as all veils," Devlin whispered into the air. "So mote it be."

For a moment, the world was still. Behind them, more faeries had gathered. The cries and murmurings swirled together in an emotional cocktail of fear and hope and wonder. He could feel them, not all of them, but those faeries that were meant to be a part of his court, the new court.

This is right. He felt a calm that he'd never known before. The world was in order. He had found the place he belonged.

He turned to Ani and saw a look of fury on her face. "Ani?"

She was looking past him though—at the faery who now held a knife to his throat.

Ani had raised her own blade in reply.

"What have you done?" Sorcha asked from behind him.

Ani snarled, "You do not threaten my king."

The wolves around her growled in agreement, as did Barry.

"Your *what*?" Sorcha asked.

Devlin turned to face the High Queen. Her knife pressed against his throat as he moved, leaving a trailing cut there.

"Our king." Rae moved so she stood to his right. Her hand, though not solid, appeared to rest on Devlin's forearm.

"The King of Shadows." His gaze was only on Sorcha, but Devlin spoke loudly enough that the assembled faeries could all hear. "The king to balance the High Queen in Faerie. Faerie was never meant to be ruled by only one court. *Our faeries* were not meant to have only one choice."

"You cannot." Sorcha stared at him. She lowered her knife. "Brother . . . Devlin . . ."

Seth came behind her and put a supporting arm around her. He did not speak, but the expression on his face was not one of surprise. He'd known what was coming long before Devlin had.

"I am neither son nor brother to you, Sorcha. I am that which stands as your opposite within Faerie. I am that which balances your court." Devlin spoke softly, wishing he could say the words to his queen-no-more in private, but she had removed that option by appearing here with her knife to his throat. He clung to the hope that she would see the rightness of his actions. "Bananach cannot come here. She cannot touch you, your son, or the faeries of your court or mine."

Sorcha stared at him. Her expression shifted to a familiar one of objective observation as she felt the change within Faerie, as she became more herself again. Devlin hoped that she understood: what he did, he did to balance her; what he did, he did to keep his sisters from killing each other; what he did was the right answer for all of them.

This was the inevitable next step for them all. Every emotion he'd repressed for all of the long millennia behind him felt like it was rising up inside of him. His would be a court of passions, of emotions, of the very things that he'd fought to hide.

As such, he didn't hide his relief or his sorrow as he told the faeries, "To prevent Bananach from coming here, our worlds are divided. None among you can cross the veil to the mortal world without the aid of *both* the Shadow Court and the High Court."

Sorcha's spine was stiff; the emotional instability she'd been falling prey to of late was no longer present in her visage or her posture. She nodded at him, and then turned away.

"Those of you who belong *not* to me, who would choose the . . . Shadow Court, know that I understand your actions. They are—as this was—inevitable," she told them.

Then with a regal air that had been missing since the day Seth had left Sorcha to return to the mortal world, the High Queen turned her gaze to her son. "My advisor and heir, my *son*, your prince, will be liaison to the Shadow Court."

With not another word, Sorcha left, attendants and many faeries in tow.

But not all.

In front of Devlin, Ani, and Rae were faeries, several score, who looked to them expectantly.

This is ours. Our world.

A twinge of grief washed over him that he'd lost both of his mother-sisters. To keep them safe from one another—to keep everyone safe from the conflict between the twins—he'd betrayed both of his mother-sisters.

"This has always been the next step," Rae whispered.

"It's the right choice," Ani agreed. "You know that."

Devlin nodded, and together they crossed the expanse of Faerie.

As they walked, new vistas sprang into existence, filling in voids that were meant to be something more but hadn't had the chance.

Until now.

EPILOGUE

Devlin stared through the veil. He raised one hand to touch the tenuous fabric that divided the two worlds, that divided the twins.

"Have you thought about the consequences?" Seth asked.

Devlin turned to face his brother, his replacement in the High Court.

"For *them*"—Seth gestured to the other side of the gate—"now that Faerie is closed?"

"They are not my concern." Devlin let his hand drop, putting his *sgian dubh* in easy reach. "The good of Faerie is my concern."

"I'm not here to fight you, Brother." Seth held his hands up disarmingly. "I will fight Bananach though."

"And if Bananach's death still kills your *mother*? Why should I let you cross over there, knowing that it could bring disaster on us?"

Seth looked away, almost quickly enough to hide the

fear in his gaze, but it was only a flash. He smiled then. "You cannot keep me here. The terms of her remaking me were that I can return to the mortal world. Even you cannot negate her vow."

"If they came home, if the other courts returned here . . ." Devlin had thought of it, all of Faerie returned home once more, away from the mortal world, no longer divided into factions and seasonal courts.

Seth laughed. "Do you think that Keenan would give up the Summer Court? That Donia would give up her court? That Niall would become a subject to you or to our mother? Pipe dreams, man."

"They would be safe here now that Bananach cannot enter."

Seth shrugged. "Some things are worth more than safety."

"I cannot speak of what would happen to our . . . to *your* queen if you died." Devlin stared through the veil, wishing that he had the ability to see the future in the mortal world. "I would come with you, but protecting Faerie comes first. I cannot risk Faerie for the mortal world."

"And I can't abandon Ash or Niall."

Devlin paused. "Tell me what you see."

"Nothing. Over here, I'm mortal. I see nothing until I go back. . . ." Seth bit his lip ring, rolling the ball of it into his mouth as he weighed his thoughts. "I don't *see* anything, but I'm worried. . . . Ash is dealing with her court alone. Sorcha was to balance Niall, but now *you* balance her. What will that mean for him? Irial was stabbed. Gabe was outnumbered. Bananach is murderous and only getting stronger. . . . Nothing there makes me think everything is going to be all right."

They stood silently staring through the veil. "When you are ready . . ."

Seth stared at him for a moment. "If . . . you know . . . I *die*, she'll need you. She doesn't like admitting it, but she will."

Devlin put his hand on the veil; Seth did the same. Together, they pushed their fingers through the fabric and parted it.

Devlin put a hand on Seth's forearm. "It will not open for you to return unless you call to me to be here also."

"I know." Seth stepped into the mortal world, leaving Faerie.

Devlin thought about their recent reentry to Faerie, about fleeing while he was injured, about the danger of Faerie being locked to the other regents and to Seth. He looked through the veil at Seth's departing figure and said, "Try not to die, Brother."